ONE NIGHT SCANDAL

Christie Kelley

ZEBRA BOOKS
KENSINGTON PUBLISHING CORP.
http://www.kensingtonbooks.com

ZEBRA BOOKS are published by

Kensington Publishing Corp.
119 West 40th Street
New York, NY 10018

All Kensington titles, imprints, and distributed lines are available at special quantity discounts for bulk purchases for sales promotion, premiums, fund-raising, educational, or institutional use.

Special book excerpts or customized printings can also be created to fit specific needs. For details, write or phone the office of the Kensington Special Sales Manager: Attn. Special Sales Department. Kensington Publishing Corp., 119 West 40th Street, New York, NY 10018. Phone: 1-800-221-2647.

Zebra and the Z logo Reg. U.S. Pat. & TM Off.

ISBN-13: 978-1-4201-0878-1
ISBN-10: 1-4201-0878-6

First Printing: June 2011
10 9 8 7 6 5 4 3 2 1

Printed in the United States of America

SHE SMELLED LIKE LAVENDER
AND TASTED LIKE SIN . . .

"Are you nervous?" he asked.

She spun around with a forced laugh. "Of course not!"

"I have wanted to strip that beautiful dress off you since you walked into my study."

Sophie swallowed and watched as he walked to the cheval-glass mirror and turned it toward the bed. "What are you doing?"

The smile he sent her almost buckled her knees. She had heard of many peculiar things men liked in bed from her mother, but Sophie never imagined her body reacting so intensely to the idea of watching Nicholas make love to her. Her pulse thrummed and her folds dampened with desire.

"Come here," he whispered, holding out his hand to her.

She walked over by the bed where he stood. He turned her to face the bedpost and then kissed her neck again. Sophie shivered as his fingers went to the buttons on the back of her dress and slowly slid them through their holes. From the angle of the mirror, she could see his mouth follow the path of the buttons down her back.

He slipped the silk off her shoulders. The dress looked like a glittering pond with the light of the fire dancing upon it. His hands moved to her stays and quickly unlaced them. In only a moment, she was standing naked by the bedpost with the rest of her undergarments strewn across the floor.

She held onto the bedpost for support as he trailed hot kisses down her back to her derrière. He slowly turned her so she faced him again.

"Why am I naked and you are not?" she asked, reaching for his coat.

"That is a problem most easily solved."

Books by Christie Kelley

EVERY NIGHT I'M YOURS

EVERY TIME WE KISS

SOMETHING SCANDALOUS

SCANDAL OF THE SEASON

ONE NIGHT SCANDAL

Published by Kensington Publishing Corporation

Chapter 1

Venice, 1818

Sophie Reynard stood on one of the many small bridges that spanned the multitude of canals in Venice. She didn't know if this one had a name but doubted it was anything special. Wrapping her shawl around her tighter to keep out the cool February wind, she glanced down the dark waterway. Music sounded from one of the grander homes slowly sinking into the canal. For some odd reason the music comforted her and reminded her of home.

London.

She planned to depart Venice in three days to return home after a two-month absence. A part of her missed London while another part of her would love to stay in Venice a few more weeks. It wasn't as if her friends would have missed her much. Now that they all had their husbands and children, her friends were constantly busy. Of course, most of their happiness was her doing.

Sophie had matched all her friends with her skills

as a medium. Even her half brother, Anthony, was now married to one of her dearest friends.

While Sophie had no one.

After matching Anthony and Victoria, Sophie had scurried away from London. Afraid that she had lost her friends, afraid that she would never find a love of her own. But more than anything, frightened of spending the rest of her life alone like most of her life had been thus far. Something had told her to come to Venice.

There must be a reason why.

After almost a month under sail and then a month in Venice, she had no indication of a man entering her life. Nothing that had happened so far made her believe this trip had been anything but a lovely holiday. Perhaps that's all it was supposed to be.

Leaning far over the balustrade, she stared down at the cold, murky water, looking for some sign that she should stay here longer. Another disheartening thought crossed her mind, perhaps she wasn't meant to find love.

But she wanted love.

All her life she'd wanted someone to love her, not just care for her because her father paid their salary. She supposed in her own way, her mother loved her. But lovers always took precedence over a daughter. Even tonight. While Sophie was outside alone, her mother had gone to a party in hopes of enticing a new man. Nothing much had changed in twenty-six years.

Sophie continued to stare at the water, concentrating completely, hoping to see a clue of what she should do with her life. Nothing came to her but frustration. What had caused that sensation two months ago, prompting her to leave her home and friends for a trip she could ill afford?

There had to be a reason. But as she gazed down,

trying to let her mind free itself of inhibitions, the only thing she saw was water. Focusing all her energies on the water, she scarcely heard the sound of children's voices getting louder, coming closer. She ignored their noise, preferring to envisage what she hoped would be a sign of her future. She felt a quick jolt.

Suddenly the water she'd been staring at was getting closer.

And closer!

Oh, dear God!

She was falling into the canal!

No wonder she couldn't see anyone in her future. She didn't have one! Releasing a loud shriek, she fell and hit her head on something before the water and darkness swallowed her.

"What the bloody hell?" Nicholas looked up as a figure plummeted from the bridge, hit his gondola, and slipped into the water.

"I no swim, *signore*," his gondolier said as the small boat rocked from the wake.

Nicholas tore off his jacket and jumped in the water, wondering how a man who made his life on the water couldn't swim. The frigid dark water made finding her difficult but luckily her skirts had caught on something, holding her in place.

He ripped her skirt and then grabbed onto her waist. Pulling her up through the cold water almost took his breath away. But he continued, determined not to die in some stinking canal in Venice where no one would ever find him and Emma would never know what happened to him.

As Nicholas broke the surface, Vincenzo heaved the wet woman into the boat. Nicholas thrust himself over the side of the rocking gondola. He turned his attention on the unconscious woman lying on the bottom of the boat.

"Vincenzo, take me home quickly," he ordered in Italian, and then sank to his knees.

Nicholas remembered what his father had taught him about drowning and pressed all his weight on that spot just below where her ribs came together. After pressing down three times, she coughed up the water.

Vincenzo docked the boat as the woman continued to bring up more water and gasp for air. A servant opened the door. Nicholas gently picked her up and brought her inside the warm house. Several servants swarmed around them.

"Get a hot bath and put her in my bedroom. I will bathe in another bedroom." He walked toward the steps and then looked back. "I want a fire in my bedroom, too."

He didn't wait for a reply but carried her up to the third floor where his bedchamber was located. He placed her in the chair by the fireplace and hoped her teeth would soon stop chattering.

She blinked her eyes open but her dark brows furrowed.

"Shh," he whispered. Speaking in Italian, he said, "I ordered a bath for you."

"*Grazie*," she said softly. "Where am I?"

"I brought you to my friend's home. You can bathe to get clean and warm. The servants will find you something to wear. Then I shall escort you home."

The minutes passed in silence as they waited for the water to heat. She kept her eyes closed much of the time either trying to ignore him or to keep the pain of her accident away.

Finally, a knock sounded at the door and then the servants entered with a large tub and steaming buckets of water. They placed the tub by the fireplace as he requested.

She blinked her eyes open and watched the bustling activity in the room with a frown. She rubbed her head and winced.

"Are you all right?" he asked slowly. "Does your head hurt?"

She stared at him a moment then nodded. "My head hurts but I believe I shall live."

Hearing her resigned tone, a horrible thought crossed his mind. "Was it your intention to die?"

Her soft laugh danced in the air around him. "No, *signore*! I did not try to kill myself. It was an . . ." she paused a long moment. "An accident."

The pause made him wonder if she spoke the truth. "Shall I call for a physician?"

"No, I am all right. *Grazie*."

"I will have a maid assist you," he said, and then left the room. Walking to the second bedchamber, he wondered about the woman who bathed in his room. With her black hair, gray eyes, and oval face, she was one of the most beautiful women he had seen since arriving in Venice. Though she wasn't as olive toned in complexion as most of the women he'd seen here.

He tugged at his wet cravat, which only seemed to tighten the knot at his neck. He pulled a knife out of his ruined boots and cut the offending garment off. After stripping out of his soaked clothes, he slipped into the warm clean water of the tub.

His mind wandered back to the beautiful woman in his room. As he thought about her, naked in the tub across the hall, his cock hardened with desire. He hadn't had that swift of a reaction to a woman in ages. He was tired of the artifices of women. Most of them wanted the one thing he wasn't willing to give yet: marriage. The others wanted the gossiping rights to say they slept with a future duke.

The only woman he knew not like that was now married and had a son. And she had never considered him anything but a friend, or worse, like a brother to her. Then again, he never had the nerve to discover if anything more was possible. Perhaps she might have been amenable to a different relationship. Not that it mattered now, he had wasted his chance.

But the woman in the tub had no idea who he was, and he intended to keep it that way. If she discovered his identity then she would be as shameless as all the rest of the women he had met. Not that any of it mattered. He would return her to her home and never see her again. For all he knew, she was married. And he avoided married women.

He finished washing the stench of the canal off him and stepped out of the tub. Standing by the fire, he dried himself and then poured a splash of brandy in a snifter. As he glanced about the room, he noticed his valet had not delivered dry clothes to him yet.

He pulled the bell and waited for a servant. Now dry and warmed by a fire and the brandy, he wanted to dress and find out more about the lady in his bedchamber. If only his friend Dominic was still here. He might know of the woman. But Dom had urgent business in Milan and left Nicholas to enjoy his Venetian home.

"*Si, signore?*" the servant asked as he entered the bedroom.

"*Per favore*, send Lane in with my clothes." He sipped the last drop of brandy and placed the glass on the table.

"Signore," the servant started and then paused.

"Si?"

"The lady in your bedchamber locked the door and won't open it."

He chuckled softly. "She must want her privacy. Ask Signora Costa to knock on the bedroom door and explain the situation."

"Si, signore."

Nicholas sat back in the chair, wearing only his towel, and waited. Closing his eyes, he listened to the sound of footsteps and then rapping of knuckles on the door across the hall.

"Signore?"

"Si," he replied without opening his eyes.

"The *signorina* does not reply."

He blinked his eyes and frowned. Could something have happened to her? She had hit her head on the gondola before she dropped into the water. Not willing to let an injured woman die in his friend's home, he strode from the room.

Mrs. Costa stood before the door with an armful of clothes and shrugged. "She no answer, *signore,*" she said in her broken English.

"Open the door and check on her."

Mrs. Costa shrugged again. She took the ring of keys from her pocket and opened the door. The servant walked into the room and glanced around. After returning to the hall, she said, "The *signorina* sleeps."

"Grazie. I will get my things."

Mrs. Costa handed him the clothing for her. Nicholas walked into the bedchamber. Slowly, he walked into the bedroom and stopped at the threshold. The woman lay on his bed with her eyes shuttered tight, her breathing even.

Nicholas shook his head. He needed to get his

clothes and leave her alone. The poor woman had been through enough this evening. He walked farther into the bedroom and stopped again.

Drawn to her by the force of desire, he stepped closer to the bed. He sat on the edge and stared at her. Her black hair curled around her face and appeared still slightly damp. He reached out to sweep a few dark tendrils off her cheek. She shifted and turned away from him, baring an ivory shoulder to his lecherous gaze. Discovering that she lay naked under the coverlet only increased his yearning.

Leaning over her, he gently kissed her soft shoulder. She smelled like lavender and tasted like sin. He was being completely foolish, wanting a woman whose name he didn't even know. His unruly cock hardened again. What was it about this particular woman that made him desire her so badly? He couldn't remember ever wanting a woman with this much force.

She moved again, this time so she rested on her back. Her eyes blinked and a pair of the most beautiful gray eyes he had ever seen looked up at him. Her eyes rounded with surprise but a slow smile lifted her full red lips.

Sophie's smile turned into a frown. Even after napping for a few minutes, she felt dazed by the accident. Who was this man staring down at her?

The pain in her head had lessened slightly but the confusion in her mind remained. She stared at the bare chested man and trembled. Hard muscle shaped his strong chest and fine brown hair formed a line that traced a path downward. Her gaze followed that path until she realized it went under the towel that covered him.

A towel. He only wore a towel!

No gentleman would appear in front of a woman in a towel. Could things be that different in Venice? She highly doubted it but wondered why he would be here dressed as such. If anyone saw them together like this she would be ruined. Not that anyone knew her here.

She moved her gaze to his face, assuming that would be a safer place to look. She was dreadfully wrong. His chestnut hair was a tad long for the conventional English gentleman. Perhaps she had not noticed that the Italian men wore their hair longer. He had warm brown eyes that crinkled as he smiled back at her and a nose that while larger than some, seemed to fit perfectly on his face.

Was he the reason she'd felt propelled to Venice? She had to know.

She closed her eyes for a long moment and focused on love just as she had for the past few months. *Her love.* A hazy image of a man came to her. Finally! She could see an image of the man she was supposed to love. He looked like . . . she blinked her eyes open.

"You," she whispered in Italian. The man in her vision was *him*. He was the reason she traveled here. Her intuition hadn't steered her wrong as she'd wondered. She had to find out more about him before he sent her on her way back to her rented rooms.

"Me?" he asked in reply.

"The man from the gondola," she said, trying to make up an excuse. "I'm sorry. I fell asleep in your bed."

"I truly do not mind." His smile widened revealing two deep dimples.

Her heart fluttered. This was the man she was supposed to fall in love with, she was certain of it. She had absolute trust in her visions. "I was dreadfully cold even after the bath and the maid hadn't returned with any dry clothes."

"I never mind having a beautiful woman in my bed."

Heat crossed her cheeks with his implied meaning. She seemed unable to look away from the handsome man. "Thank you," she said quietly.

"For what?"

"Saving my life."

He smiled down at her. "You practically fell onto my lap."

"Still, you didn't have to jump into the canal to save me." But she was so grateful he had. Was it just gratitude warming her insides? She really didn't think so. She had met many handsome men in London and yet, not one of them ever set her heart beating as swiftly as this man had.

"I couldn't let you drown," he replied. "It would have been ungentlemanly of me."

She'd been waiting for years for a man to fire her passion. The ladies she had matched with husbands had told her how they knew the man was the right one with just a single kiss. She desperately wanted him to kiss her, touch her . . . make love to her.

Make love? Could she really want to do such a thing with him? She'd only just met him.

Her gaze slid down from his eyes to his lips. Experiencing passion with this handsome man would be a lovely end to a long trip. She couldn't take her gaze off his lips. Full and beautifully molded lips. She had to kiss him.

"What is your name?" she finally asked.

His dark brow furrowed, and he paused a bit before answering, "Nico. And you?"

Instinctively, she knew he was lying. But why? What was he trying to hide from her? Could he be married? A libertine? Glancing around the room, she doubted either was the case. The high ceiling was painted with cherubs and angels, a large crystal chandelier dominated the ceiling. But the rest of the room was remarkably stark and functional. Not the sort of room a wife would like, also not the sort to impress a woman as a libertine might prefer.

She reached out and clasped his hand in hers. Closing her eyes, she attempted to read something from him. He was difficult to read. She'd had other people who were hard to read, but he was the most challenging. The only thing she felt was he wasn't a rake. He loved and respected women.

With a small smile, she opened her eyes to see him staring down at her with a look of confusion. "Your name?" he asked again.

"My name is Sophia," she said, giving the Italian version of her name.

"Sophia," he whispered.

Watching his lips move as he said her name brought her mind back to kissing him. But would he want more than a kiss? Could she give him more? The more she stared at him, the warmer her body felt. If this man was important in her life, and he must be in some way, then giving herself to him would be either a wonderful thing or the biggest mistake ever.

She didn't think he could be a blunder. Taking him to bed might be the thing that would break her free, allowing her to see her own future clearly for once instead of the strange hazy image she had received tonight. Once she'd been with him, maybe her personal insight would be stronger.

"Sophia, are you married?" he asked softly, breaking the silence that had enveloped them.

"No. Are you?"

He smiled down at her. "No."

She wondered why he hadn't commented on her Italian. Her grasp of the language was excellent but still, he should have noticed her accent. Yet, he never asked her about it, or from where she originated.

She wondered what would happen if she let him seduce her tonight. Would he discover that she was the woman for him? Would he prevent her from leaving Venice in three days as she'd planned?

She rather thought he would.

If he was the man for her, as she believed, then making love with him was perfectly acceptable. All of her friends had been with their husbands before marriage. None of them would condemn her for making the same decision.

She skimmed her finger up his strong arm. He tensed under her whispered touch, but she sensed his desire. One thing was for certain, if and when she returned to England, she would not be a virgin.

His eyes widened as she trailed her fingers up to his neck and slowly brought him closer. As he leaned over, she said, "I am still quite cold. Do you think you could warm me?"

Chapter 2

Nicholas stared at her for a long moment. He had no idea what made him pause. Here was a beautiful woman who wanted him to make love to her, and he hesitated. What the bloody hell was wrong with him?

Perhaps Sophia would be the woman to break the spell the other woman he loved had on him. He wasn't looking for love with Sophia, just the ability to forget for a while. His erection throbbed, wanting him to make the right choice. With his mouth only inches from her full lips, he made his decision.

"I believe I can warm you thoroughly."

He leaned forward and gently kissed her lips. Desire rushed through him as she responded to him. He deepened the kiss, slipping his tongue into her mouth. Hearing her soft moan of pleasure sent him over the edge. He had to have her tonight. Nothing would stop him now.

He shifted his weight until he lay on top of her. Her soft body molded to his, her breasts pressed against his chest. As her tongue played with his, he could think of nothing but spreading her legs and plunging into her depths.

He trailed his lips to her ear. Gently bringing her earlobe into his mouth, he smiled as she moaned again. Her hips instinctively rose up against his hard cock. God, she was so sweet.

Nicholas burned a path down her neck. Sliding the coverlet as he went, he finally found his target. He stared down at her erect pink nipple. Watching her reaction, he gently rolled her taut nipple between his thumb and finger.

"Oh," she whispered, as her eyes grew large with desire.

"Do you like that?"

"Yes," she mumbled.

He slipped it into his mouth, suckling her until she squirmed under him. Passion thrummed through him, urging him on as he attempted to slow down and thoroughly enjoy her glorious body.

He couldn't remember the last time he felt such driving passion as he did with Sophia. After being with too many women, the excitement had waned in the last year. He had become bored with women and life. It was part of what had made him decide to travel. But he felt no boredom with Sophia. Her moans of pleasure were driving him mad with desire.

Skimming his hand downward through her downy hair, he split her folds and gently rubbed her sweet little nub. He smiled against her breast as she bucked under his hand.

"Oh, my," she whispered.

"Sophia, I want you so desperately," he said, moving his attention to her other breast.

"Yes, Nico."

He didn't need to hear more. He slid his finger lower until he reached her moist depths. His control slipped further as he stroked her. Feeling her tightness, he gently brought another finger inside her.

"Nico," she moaned.

Hearing her moan his name sent him over the edge. He shifted until his erection waited at her opening. Slowly, he entered her. His body screamed at him to plunge in deeper but she was small and tight and needed time to adjust to his size.

Finally, he tried to go further but couldn't. His eyes widened when he realized the cause.

"Sophia?"

"Don't stop, Nico," she whispered. "I want you."

With desire ripping his restraint, her words only made things worse. She suddenly brought her legs around his hips and pressed him fully into her. Nicholas closed his eyes against the passion overwhelming him. Knowing this was her first time changed everything. He had to wait until she was ready to continue.

If he had only known before, he could have made this so much better for her.

Sophie gasped as he broke through her maidenhead. Having him deep inside her stung, and part of her wanted to push him away. She'd known it would hurt but no one had told her how strange it would feel to have him inside her.

As he showered her neck with kisses, she started to adjust to having him in her. Her breathing settled and the sensations of his kisses on her neck sent shivers down her back. He moved his lips to her breast and teased her nipple until he finally brought it into his warm mouth.

Skimming his hand down her belly, he slipped it between them until he found her clitoris. He rubbed his thumb there, making her forget the stinging sensation he had caused. Moisture pooled in her, surrounding his cock and she realized the pain had lessened. She moved her hips slightly and released a sigh. The minor movement felt odd but in a very interesting manner.

Feeling his smile against her breast, she lifted her legs higher on his hips. This time they moaned in unison.

"Are you ready to proceed?" he whispered.

"Yes."

He lifted off her until he could stare down at her. Sophie couldn't take her gaze off his warm brown eyes. He moved slowly out of her and she groaned in disappointment. Her mother had explained everything that happened between a man and a woman. This couldn't be all there was to it.

Just before he slipped out of her completely, he slid himself back inside. She moaned from the fullness of him. She had never felt anything as incredible as Nico deep inside of her. He quickly increased the tempo. He moved her hips with each thrust of his hard cock. She met his lunges and found the ancient rhythm. Her passion increased, higher she went until she thought she could go no farther. His thumb returned to her nub, rubbing harder this time. Closing her eyes, she felt as if she was breaking into a million pieces.

"Sophia," he muttered as he thrust in her two more times before stilling his body over her and groaning.

She smiled as she watched the absolute pleasure on his face. She had done that to him. Her body had brought him such satisfaction. Closing her eyes, she relished the moment.

He rested on top of her, breathing hard. As his breathing slowed, he nipped her shoulder with his teeth. She smiled at the sensation of his teeth on her skin. While enjoying the time with him, she knew if he were like most gentlemen, she must account for her actions.

"Sophia," he said, then kissed her neck again.

"Hmm?"

"Why?"

"I wanted you, Nico."

He lifted his head and stared down at her. "We only just met this evening."

She smiled at him slowly, seductively. "And you have never wanted a woman you just met?"

"That is completely different."

"Why? Because you are a man?" She arched a brow at him. "Women can't feel the same desire a man does?"

He rolled off her and lay back on the bed. "It is different for a woman. Especially a virgin."

"Is it? And you would know this how?"

"Women want emotions involved in the act. Not just a quick rutting like a man."

She laughed softly and rolled on her side. "Then why after just looking at you, did I want you? I certainly do not love you. Nonetheless, I still wanted you tonight."

He turned on his side so they were face to face. "Can you honestly tell me that this meant nothing to you?"

"Of course, it did." She skimmed her hand down his strong jaw. "You were my first, Nico."

Grabbing her hand, he brought her palm to his lips. Little shivers raced down her arms at the contact.

"What if I want more?" he asked.

She stilled and slowly smiled. She had made the right choice. He was supposed to be her perfect match. "We would need to discuss that."

"What are you hiding, Sophia?" His brown eyes gazed at her.

"Nothing," she lied. She couldn't tell him much of anything about her yet. First she needed to see how things proceeded.

He released a resigned sigh. "Can you stay the night?"

"No, but I can stay a few more hours," she replied, then caressed his cheek with her hand.

"Then we had better make the best use of our time together."

"Oh?"

"Oh, yes," he whispered and pulled her on top of him.

Nicholas breathed in deeply, attempting to gain some measure of control over his senses again. He had never experienced a woman like Sophia. He hadn't known such an exquisite creature existed. After making love with her twice, he wanted her again.

Pulling her close to him, she rested her head on his chest. He wrapped his arms around her. Perhaps he could change her mind about leaving. He tugged the coverlet back over their naked sated bodies.

There were so many questions he wanted to ask her, but he wondered if she would even answer them. For whatever reason, she'd wanted to experience a man. He supposed the fact that he saved her life might have played into the decision. But he hoped that wasn't the only reason.

She lifted her head and looked down at him. A slow smile lifted her lips upward. His heart increased its speed again.

"What time is it?" she asked softly.

He frowned believing she must be thinking about leaving him already. He didn't want her to leave just yet. Glancing over at the small clock on his night-stand, he answered, "A little before midnight."

Her smile fell. "I need to leave."

"Why?"

"My aunt was out for the evening but will return soon. I must be there when she arrives."

"Very well." He wrapped his arms around her again. "But first, how did you end up in the canal?"

She giggled softly. "I was staring at the water."

"Well, yes you were," he said with a deep chuckle. "But why and how did that cause you to end up in the water?"

"Some boys ran by and knocked into me. I was leaning over so far that I lost my balance and fell in."

He frowned. "But why were you staring at the water so far over the balustrade?"

"Sometimes staring at the water helps me focus."

"Focus on what?"

She sighed. "Me. My future."

"And what did you see for yourself?"

She went silent for a long moment. "Nothing," she finally answered quietly. "I saw nothing. There is noth-ing for me."

And that answer revealed more than she probably wanted him to discover. He wondered why such a vibrant woman would feel as if there was nothing in life for her. "So was that why you decided I was the man to lose your virginity with?"

"And if it was?" she whispered as her fingers splayed across his chest.

"Do you think it was the right reason?"

"I think you are too concerned with what I gave you."

"It should have been your husband's gift, not mine." He felt her eyelashes blink rapidly on his chest. A tear fell, damping him.

"I wonder if I shall ever marry," she said so quietly he almost did not hear.

"Why?"

"I am twenty-six, twenty-seven in a few months. Far too old for most men."

"Is that so?" He laughed. "I happen to know of three women who married about the age of twenty-six and one at twenty-eight. All married well."

"Not where I am from," she commented and then glanced away from him with a frown.

"And where would that be?" he asked softly, praying she would give him real information about herself.

"Nowhere important," she replied.

Unfortunately, she was right. Learning more about her would only drive him mad when he had to leave. The woman was Italian and probably Catholic. His father would have an apoplexy if he brought home a Catholic from his travels. Nicholas understood his father's expectation. As a marquess and future duke, the right wife was vital. She had to be someone in Society who would give him heirs and have her charity work to keep her busy while he attended Parliament.

Sophia was not that type of woman.

With Sophia, he would never want to leave their bed. Even after making love with her twice this evening, he desired her again. No woman had ever done that to him. He rolled her over onto her back and stared down at her gray eyes.

She smiled seductively at him. "Again?"

"Are you too sore?"

"There is only one way to find out." She wrapped her arms around his neck and brought him closer.

Sophie dozed for a while before she awoke. She had never felt so wicked in her life. Sleeping with a man she had just met, laying naked next to him and feeling no shame. Never had she imagined anything could be so wonderful.

But it was over now.

She glanced over at his clock. It was already after one and she had to arrive home before her mother returned from her assignation. Her mother, the actress who pretended to be Sophie's aunt to give her the slightest sense of respectability. Sophie had always prided herself on not being like her mother. Now, after bedding a man she'd just met, she wondered. Perhaps she was far more like her mother than she might want to admit.

Easing her body off the bed, she stood and stared down at the man who had been her first lover. She prayed her vision about him was correct. If so, he would find her tomorrow. He would court her until they knew each other a little better. Then they would marry. While she wished she didn't have to leave yet, prolonging her departure would only make this process harder.

As she looked down at the hard planes of his face, she wished she could draw him. Not that she had any talent. She left all ideas of painting and drawing to Jennette. Her friend would do an amazing job at capturing his strong features.

She blinked and realized it was time to leave. Two candles lit the room, allowing her just enough light to find the clothes Mrs. Costa had left for her. After slipping into the serviceable brown wool gown, she walked to the desk in the corner.

She could not depart without at least leaving a note good-bye and telling him where to call on her. Finding paper on the desk, she pulled out a quill and dipped it into the inkwell. She thought about what she needed to say and translated it into Italian. Hopefully, she had made no mistakes.

Staring down at the note, she hesitated. What if she had been nothing but a quick tumble to him? She shook the nonsense from her mind. Her vision had shown her that all would be well. She folded the note and wrote his name on the front of the paper.

The stack of papers on the desk intrigued her. She might be able to find out a little more about the man who was her first lover. Glancing back to the bed, she noticed he slept deeply now. Her gaze returned to the papers and she bit her lip. She reached for a well-worn paper. The note looked as if it had been lovingly read over the years.

As soon as she touched the paper, she felt the hum of emotional residue on it. Whoever wrote this note meant something to Nico. Obviously written by a woman, Sophie realized that he loved this woman a great deal. She closed her eyes and focused on the emotions running through the letter. The woman loved him in return but in a different way.

Sophie opened her eyes and stared down at the note. She should put it back on the desk and walk away. But something drew her to it. Some force propelled her to unfold the letter carefully.

It was in English!

Here she had been speaking and then struggling to write in Italian when the man could read English. Reading the salutation her hands started to tremble. It did not read *Dear Nico,* but *My Dearest Nicholas* and was dated three years ago.

The note was a warm letter regarding the social scene of London.

London!

She glanced back over to the bed. He could not possibly be English. She would have sensed it! If he were English then what happened tonight would be a mistake indeed. He would know or could learn who she really was—the bastard daughter of an earl and an actress.

God help her if he was truly English.

Biting down on her lip, she continued to read the letter but stopped when the woman mentioned the name Banning. It had to be a coincidence. Banning was Jennette's brother and married to Sophie's dearest friend Avis.

Unable to contain her curiosity, she scanned to the bottom of the letter for the signature. The paper dropped out of her hands, fluttering to the desk.

Sophie couldn't move. She sat staring at the paper for at least a minute. The signature taunted her.

Jennette.

How did Jennette know this man? Sophie scanned a

few of the papers on the desk until she found another letter written to Nico . . . Nicholas.

Only this letter was written to Lord Ancroft.

Lord Ancroft.

Sophie clutched the desk as her world began to spin around her. She could not have just spent the night with an English lord. An English marquess!

A man who'd paid his mistress to leave London and their daughter behind for him to raise. While not one of the biggest rakes in town, he'd had more than his share of mistresses and widows.

Her entire body shook. This was going to get even worse if her memory served her correctly. Not only was Lord Ancroft a friend of Jennette and Banning's, he was Elizabeth's cousin.

There was no hope for a loving relationship with Nicholas. She was a nobody while he was a marquess and future duke.

Oh, dear Lord! She crumpled the note she'd written for him and tossed it into the glowing embers of the fireplace. Perhaps he would think she meant this to be just for tonight. She prayed he would not attempt to find her. Sophie backed out of the room, watching the sleeping man as she went. This was the worst mistake she'd ever made.

She had slept with her best friend's cousin.

Chapter 3

"What is wrong, Sophie?" Victoria asked.

Sophie glanced up from her tea to find all her friends staring at her with looks of concern on their faces. After returning to London three weeks ago, she still hadn't talked to them about what happened. It was odd because all of them had confided in her about their men. It had taken her this long just to face them again. During the past few weeks, she had created several excuses for avoiding them, but today she knew she had to see them again.

Even now, as she sat in Avis's parlor, Sophie's nerves tingled every time she heard footsteps. She had no idea if Nicholas had returned to London, but knew it wouldn't be odd for him to show up at Lord Selby's home. The fact that they hadn't met before was strictly providence. Before Avis and Jennette married their husbands, the only chance Sophie would have had for an introduction to Nicholas was at Elizabeth's home. And the friends had rarely met there because of Elizabeth's cantankerous aunt.

Nicholas had never called on his cousin while Sophie

was there. But now, he might visit Avis's husband Banning. Or call on Jennette and her husband. Or even Victoria's husband Somerton. It appeared Sophie would at some point be introduced to Nicholas. Hopefully, her intuition would let her know before he arrived at the door. Not that she had one idea of what she would do. Nor did she trust her intuition at this point.

"Sophie, you have been exceedingly quiet since your return," Avis said. "Won't you tell us about your trip?"

"Yes, tell us about the trip," Elizabeth added.

Of the four of them, there wasn't one to whom she could confide. Victoria had married Sophie's half brother in December, and Anthony had known Nicholas since childhood. Elizabeth was Nicholas's cousin. And Jennette was the woman Nicholas loved. Even Avis, was the wife of one of Nicholas's friends.

They all knew him and would believe he should offer for her after what happened in Venice. But Sophie knew he was not the man for her. In addition to being in love with Jennette, he was a marquess. As such, he would never marry the bastard child of an earl she couldn't even name. And worse, since she'd left his room in the middle of the night, she had never been able to "see" him again when concentrating on her future. All she'd seen was the blackness again. Clearly, her addled brain had given her a vision of what she wanted at that moment. Not her true love or match. Her cheeks burned as she thought about just how much she'd wanted him that night.

"Sophie!" Avis scolded. "You are not paying the least bit of attention this afternoon."

"There is not much to tell," Sophie finally said.

"Venice was lovely. The weather a bit cold but nowhere near as frigid as London in January."

Avis laughed softly. "So after being in Venice for four weeks, all you can tell us is it was lovely and the weather fair. We all know you better than that, Sophie. Did you meet someone?"

She couldn't stop the heat from crossing her cheeks. "I cannot talk about this, Avis."

All four women giggled.

"If not us, then who?" Elizabeth asked. "We have all told you about our men. Even our experiences before marriage."

Sophie looked over at Elizabeth. With her red hair, freckles, and green eyes, Elizabeth looked nothing like her cousin. Sophie closed her eyes and remembered his light brown eyes. She could have drowned in his eyes.

"Sophie, I have never seen you like this," Victoria added. "Please let us help you."

For once, the only woman in the group not urging her was Jennette. Sophie stared at her dark-haired friend, wondering why she looked so pale and out of sorts.

"Sophie!" Elizabeth exclaimed.

Sophie knew if she didn't tell them something, they would likely continue to badger her. "All right. I did meet a man there. But it was three days before I was to leave. So nothing came of it."

"Oh," Avis said quietly. "But you wish something had happened, don't you?"

Sophie knew she had no choice but to lie. There was no chance of anything happening between them again and her friends would never discover the man was Nicholas. "Yes. He was a lovely man."

"I'm sorry, Sophie," Victoria said, staring down at her skirts. "You matched all of us and you deserve a wonderful man, too."

Sophie pressed her lips together and blinked furiously. "Thank you, Victoria. I'm just thrilled for you all."

And she truly was happy for her friends. Jennette and Avis had young children now, and Elizabeth would be delivered of her first child in October. As Sophie gazed at Victoria, she smiled seeing the glow of an unannounced pregnancy on her sister-in-law's face. That meant Sophie would be an aunt. All her matches had worked out perfectly.

Sophie started at the sound of boots stomping down the hall. Avis's husband stopped at the threshold and leaned against the doorframe with a warm smile.

"I really do need to come up with a new name for you all," he said with a laugh. "The Spinster Club just isn't right now."

As much as she liked Selby, his remark cut to the quick. How she wished she understood what was wrong with her lately. Every little thing seemed to make her want to cry.

"Banning, that was dreadfully unkind to Sophie," Avis reprimanded her husband.

"I apologize, Miss Reynard." He nodded in her direction and then glanced over at Elizabeth. "Your Grace, I have found your errant cousin."

"Nicholas!" Elizabeth exclaimed.

Oh, God, please don't let him be here, Sophie prayed. While meeting him was bound to happen, she could not deal with the explanations required today. She had been friends with these ladies for seven years and had never met him before. Perhaps her luck would continue to hold because the only other option would be to give up her friends. And she truly did not want it to come to that.

"Yes, he was at White's this afternoon. He will be joining us for dinner tonight. In fact, why don't you and your husbands join us?"

Avis smiled. "What a wonderful idea, Banning! I shall tell cook that we shall be ten for dinner."

Sophie's heart started to beat so fast she thought she might faint. "I am sorry, Avis, but I am meeting a client tonight."

"Tonight?"

"Yes. Had I known sooner I might have been able to change my plans."

"Very well," Avis said, standing. "I shall tell cook to plan on nine."

Sophie released a long held breath. Now, she had to leave in case he arrived early.

Selby inclined his head and said, "Good afternoon, ladies."

Most of them murmured some reply but Sophie could not move. She held her hands tightly together so no one would see her trembling.

"I did not realize you hadn't seen Nicholas yet," Jennette said to Elizabeth. "He called on us almost a fortnight ago."

Elizabeth shrugged. "He and Will haven't become the friends I'd hoped for yet."

Nicholas had seen Jennette already. Sophie shook her head. What a fool she'd been to think she might mean something to him. He was still in love with Jennette.

"So who is your client?" Victoria asked Sophie.

"Lady Cantwell." Sophie stood. "It was lovely seeing you all but I must leave now."

"So does anyone want to guess what that was all about?" Avis said after walking back into the parlor.

Elizabeth shook her head. "I would have to say Sophie fell in love while in Venice. I have never seen her act so oddly."

"Damn," Jennette muttered. "How are we supposed to introduce her to Nicholas if she won't stay for dinner?"

"We don't," Victoria said with a smirk. "Anthony told me that Ancroft said he would start his search for a wife when he returned. And he might even pay a visit to a certain matchmaker in town to find his true love."

Avis smiled fully. They had all decided over the winter that Sophie and Nicholas would be perfect for each other. Now that they had both returned from their travels, it was time for an introduction. Since Sophie had matched all of them, they had determined it was their turn to find her love.

"Then all we need to do is push him in that direction during dinner," Avis commented. And everything would work out as planned.

Nicholas handed his greatcoat to the Selby's footman and then followed the butler to the salon. He smiled hearing the sounds of laughter coming from the room. While it felt good to be back home, that feeling of something missing had been with him since he awoke to find Sophia gone from his room.

He had asked around but no one seemed to know of her. With nothing more to go on, he had given up his search for her and decided to return home. Still, he needed to know who she was. He'd stupidly forgotten to withdraw from her during intercourse. He knew better. That was how he ended up with his darling ten-year-old daughter.

"Lord Ancroft, my lord," the Selby butler announced.

"Nicholas!" Elizabeth cried and then came running into his arms. "I have missed you so much these past few months."

The rest of the occupants of the room all murmured his name and said some endearing remark. But the only one he heard was Jennette. She smiled at him as she sat next to her husband, Lord Blackburn.

"It's so good to see you again, Nicholas," Jennette said with a genuine smile.

"And you, Jennette."

"Sit down, Ancroft," Selby said, pointing at a chair far too close to Jennette's seat.

Instead, Nicholas moved to the chair closer to Somerton. "Evening, Somerton."

"Nicholas," Somerton replied. "How was your trip?"

"Yes, Nicholas," Elizabeth said. "Tell us all about your trip. Was Florence as beautiful as everyone says?"

Nicholas told them all about his trip to Florence. The museums that he saw, the operas he attended and the churches he visited.

"And Venice?" Victoria added. "I have always wanted to see Venice."

"And so you shall, my dear," Somerton said, leaning closer to his bride.

Victoria blushed as she smiled back at her husband. It warmed Nicholas's heart to see them so happy. He doubted he would ever have a love like any of the people in the room. His father's patience had run out with regards to marriage. Nicholas knew he had to start searching for a wife.

"Venice was lovely," Nicholas finally responded. "It is a beautiful city with the water surrounding you. A bit warmer than London in winter. Though people say, the city can become very odorous during the warmer months."

He noticed the women all glancing at each other with a strange look of confusion on their faces.

Finally, Jennette spoke up, "It seems rather odd that one of the most beautiful cities in the world gets described more by its weather than its splendor."

"What do you mean?"

"Nothing at all," Jennette murmured with a shake of her head.

A footman entered the room and announced dinner. Thankfully, there were no name cards so Nicholas chose to sit near Somerton and Victoria. Nicholas felt far more comfortable with the married couple than the woman who only considered him a friend.

"Nicholas," Jennette said before sipping her lemonade. "I heard a rumor that you planned to seek the assistance of Miss Reynard to find you a wife."

Nicholas tensed and slid a glance to Somerton who only shrugged. "Perhaps. I have not thought about it much since leaving town."

"But now that you have returned, you really must see her," Avis commented. "She is the best in London at finding people their perfect husband or wife."

"I just haven't decided if now is the right time," he bit out, trying to constrain his growing frustration.

The last thing he needed was his friends' wives attempting to marry him off. That was his father's job.

"Oh," Elizabeth said with a smile. "She won't match you unless the timing is exactly right. So there really is no reason not to pay a call on her."

"I will think upon it, Elizabeth," Nicholas said.

"Don't be angry with us, Lord Ancroft," Victoria finally said. "You are a dear friend and we want to see you happy, that is all this is about."

Nicholas breathed in deeply. After meeting Sophia in Venice no other woman had crossed his mind. Not once. And the idea of visiting a matchmaker held no appeal. "I realize that. As I said, I will consider paying a call on Miss Reynard."

Somerton and Selby started to chuckle while Blackburn and Kendal stared at the women in amazement.

As dinner finished, the men stayed behind to have a glass of brandy. The conversation went from staid politics to questions about the women in Italy.

"Are they as beautiful as everyone claims?" Selby asked with a laugh.

"I did not get much chance for such activities," Nicholas responded.

All the men chuckled. He had no doubts that they all saw straight through him. While he would love to depart their company, he came here for one reason— a chance to speak with Somerton alone. After more questioning about the Italian women, the men finished their brandies.

When the men slowly rose to join their wives in the salon, Nicholas placed a hand on Somerton's arm. Somerton replied with an arched brow and a smirk.

"Go ahead," Somerton said to the others. "I need to speak with Nicholas about something in private."

"Thank you," Nicholas said, once the other three had left. "I know you can find things others are unable to find."

"Just tell me what you want, Nicholas," Somerton said impatiently.

Nicholas pulled a diamond earring out of his jacket pocket. "I need to discover to whom this belongs."

He snatched the earring out of Nicholas's hand. Somerton frowned as he examined it. Staring at the earring, he said, "So I believe your trip was far better than you had informed us."

"It was only one night in Venice. I don't even know her name. She told me her name but I doubt she spoke the truth."

"Why?"

"Because I didn't tell her my real name."

Somerton shrugged. "There are no identifying marks on the earring."

"Is there anything you can do?"

Somerton went silent for a moment as if in deep thought. With a grimace, he said, "Take it to Miss Reynard. She might be able to give you some information."

"Bloody hell! Not you too."

Somerton smirked and shook his head. "She is also a medium. She has assisted me numerous times when I worked for Ainsworth."

"You think she can tell me who owns this earring?" Nicholas held out his hand for the earring.

"Oh, I think she will know exactly who owns the earring." Somerton scraped back his chair and rose. "Excuse me."

Nicholas nodded. Instead of immediately joining the group, he stared at the earring wondering once more where Sophia was at that very moment.

* * *

Sophie heard Hendricks open the front door and she wondered who was here so early. None of her clients arrived before noon and it was only ten. Hearing the hard footfalls, she knew who was here and the idea of seeing her half brother lightened her mood tremendously.

But the closer he came to the small parlor where she sat, the more she felt his dark mood. Something was wrong.

He stopped at the threshold before walking into the room and slamming the door behind him. "Ancroft?"

Sophie's heart skipped a beat. He couldn't possibly know! "What are you talking about, Anthony?"

His fury came closer to her. "Ancroft! You slept with him in Venice."

"He knows?" she whispered. "He knows it was me?"

"No, he doesn't know it was you. He believes he slept with some Italian woman who wouldn't give him her real name." Somerton put his hands on the arms of her chair and leaned in closer. "How could you have slept with him?"

She knew his tactic was to frighten her, but that was the last thing she needed at this point. Fear of discovery had been biting on her heels since she left Venice.

"I did not know it was him," she mumbled. "I had no idea it was Ancroft until after . . ."

He growled and turned away from her. "You let him touch you when you didn't even know who he was?"

"And I suppose you have never done such a thing," Sophie said in a sarcastic tone.

"It's different for a man."

"Oh, so all those women you had sex with must have already known you then, isn't that right?"

He turned back and glared at her. "This is not about me. Besides, none of those ladies were my sister."

"Are you certain?" When she least expected it, the bitterness of their father's promiscuity returned. There was no telling how many other bastards of his were living in London.

"Anthony, Ancroft saved my life." She held up her hand to stop his interruption. "I did not sleep with him because of that. I thought he was the man for me."

"What do you mean, thought?"

She explained about seeing Nicholas when she thought about her future and love after falling into the canal. "But since I left Venice, I haven't been able to see him again for me. Maybe I was wrong. I honestly don't know."

"So you let him seduce you because you thought he was supposed to become your husband?"

She nodded. "When he came into the room and sat on the bed where I was laying . . . I could not look away. I wanted him to . . . kiss me. I have been around numerous charming men, Anthony, but I had never felt such a powerful attraction."

She blinked and looked away, knowing he would not understand. She scarcely believed it herself.

He finally sat down in the chair across from her and looked down at his hands. "I understand, Sophie. It was always like that with Victoria. No other woman, only her."

"Anthony, I thought I was giving myself to a man who would become my husband at some point. And I was comfortable with that. I had no idea it was Ancroft. If I had, I would have left before he touched me."

"Why?"

"He would find out about my past. Once he learned who I was he would never want to marry me." She laughed scornfully at her situation.

"How did you find out it was Ancroft?" he asked softly. "Or did you just *know*?"

"No, I didn't know it was him. I found him very difficult to read. I wrote him a note, thanking him for saving my life and telling him where he could contact me." Her voice caught. "Then I noticed a worn letter on his desk. I picked it up and read it." She closed her eyes, remembering the strong emotions on that paper. "The letter was from Jennette."

"You understand that I have to confront him about it. Call him out if necessary."

Sophie laughed. "You do not have to do any such thing. The only people who know you are my brother are family members. How would it look to Ancroft if you're defending my honor?"

"It is not your choice to make, Sophie. If he doesn't propose to you, then I will call him out for ruining you."

"I am far from ruined, Anthony."

"Are you with child?"

"No," she answered honestly. She thanked God for that small blessing she'd received on the return trip. She knew how to prevent a pregnancy and had done nothing that night, assuming he would be the man to marry her.

"It changes nothing. Your honor has been tarnished. It is up to me to make certain Nicholas does the right thing."

"There is no right thing to do, Anthony. I'm a bastard. No one cares about my honor." Her anger rose with his good intentions.

"I do." He tilted his head and smirked. "I suppose I can always bring this situation to Father's attention."

"As if he would care what I do." Sophie shook her head. "As long as I don't mention his name to anyone, he pays me no notice."

Somerton leaned back against his seat. "But you are forgetting that Ancroft will be duke someday. Our father might be extremely interested in bragging rights that his daughter caught a duke."

"Don't you dare," she warned, pointing a finger at him. "Besides, we both know it would not matter. He could never claim me as his at this point. Think of the repercussions. Please, just stay out of my life."

"It's far too late for that, Sophie."

She closed her eyes and swallowed down the emotions choking her. There was only one way to stop him, but she wondered if he would believe her threat. "If you go to Father, I shall tell everyone about your mother."

No one in the *ton* knew that his mother ran the most fashionable brothel in Mayfair. Everyone believed she'd died years ago, which was what his father had told the world. If it ever came out, Anthony and his family would be disgraced. He stared at her until she opened her eyes and almost gasped at the fury on his face.

"Very well, then," he said.

But one thing bothered her about her brother's interference in her life. "Anthony, how did you find out?"

"It appears you forgot something in his bed."

Thinking back to that night, she remembered getting out of the tub and drying off. She was completely naked under the coverlet. "I do not think that is possible."

"An earring, perhaps? One that I bought for your birthday last year."

She covered her mouth. When she'd arrived back at the rooms she and her mother had leased, she removed one earring but assumed she must have lost the other in the canal. It never occurred to her that it might have fallen out in his bed.

"He has my earring," she mumbled.

"Yes."

Sophie bit down on her lip, wondering what to do. She loved those earrings, not because they were diamonds, but because her brother had given them to her. And now Nicholas had one. How could one night have caused so many problems?

"I heard your *aunt* decided to stay in Italy. Is that correct?"

Sophie closed her eyes against the sudden stab of pain. For several years, her mother had been acting as her aunt and chaperone when it suited her. "Mother decided a certain Italian count was too sweet to resist. She stayed behind to become his mistress. So I am without a chaperone for the moment."

Anthony muttered a curse. "Would you like me to hire a companion for you? Someone who can help keep your reputation safe."

"No. It's not the first time she has left. She will come running back home in a month or two when the count tires of her. And for now, I would prefer to be alone." She hated being alone but preferred the silent house to having a stranger with her.

"Very well. But I want you to hire a few additional footmen. I want at least two at the front door besides Hendricks. He is far too old for keeping out a determined man."

She knew he meant Nicholas, but Sophie doubted he would be that determined to see her again. She had been nothing but a brief affair amongst the many in his checkered past. Still, there was no point in arguing with Anthony on her safety, not when he did it out of love. "Yes, Anthony."

He started to stand and then sat back down. "Nicholas is an honorable man, Sophie. Once he finds you there is every likelihood he will offer for you."

She shook her head. "It does not matter, Anthony. I am not the right one for him. And he is not the right man for me."

He looked at her and shook his head. "Are you certain?"

"Yes."

"Very well," he said with a sigh. "But be warned he will be calling on you soon."

Sophie shot to her feet. "You told him!"

"No. Your friends were encouraging him to call on you to help him find a wife."

She laughed. "I get very few men as clients. Most believe I am nothing but a charlatan being paid by some ambitious mama."

Anthony smirked. "I don't think you have anything to worry about there. He wanted to know if I could find out anything about the owner of the earring. I told him that you could use your powers to help him." Anthony rose and walked toward the door. He paused at the threshold and turned to her with a smirk. "So, what you do is up to you."

Sophie watched her brother leave as sadness darkened her heart. There wasn't a thing she could do. Nicholas was a mistake, nothing more. And she would have to do her best to avoid him.

Chapter 4

Nicholas reached the top step of Miss Reynard's home for the third time this week. Each day he'd arrived, her butler told him that Miss Reynard would see him tomorrow. Well, not today. She would see him even if he had to force himself past her butler and footmen.

"Welcome back, Lord Ancroft," her butler said as he opened the door.

"And will she see me today, Mr. Hendricks?"

The butler attempted to hide his smile. "I shall see if she is at home."

Once again, Nicholas was shown to a small receiving parlor in the front of the house. Instead of sitting in the same pale green chair he'd sat the previous days, he paced the room. He stopped and noticed the oil painting of a small cottage that reminded him of Banning's cottage. Nicholas looked at the artist's signature and shook his head. He should have known one of Jennette's paintings would hang in her friend's home.

"My lord, Miss Reynard would be pleased to see you this evening at eight. Unless you have other plans."

"Eight?" He walked closer to the gray-haired butler. "Tell me, Mr. Hendricks, do you believe she will actually see me then?"

Hendricks nodded and handed him a note. "This is from her."

Nicholas scanned the letter. She apologized for putting him off but other clients had already been scheduled. She promised she would see him tonight.

"Very well, then," Nicholas said, pocketing the note. "Tell her if she does not allow me entrance this evening, I *will* see her anyway."

"I will give her your message." Hendricks walked to the front door and opened it for him. "We shall see you at eight, my lord."

Nicholas left the house and returned to his own home. He walked up to the nursery to find Emma and her governess reviewing history lessons. His daughter looked up at him and her brown eyes twinkled.

"Papa!" Without waiting for her governess to excuse her from the lesson, she raced to him with her arms open wide.

"Emma," he said with a smile as he hugged his little girl. "You act as if you haven't seen me in weeks."

"I didn't see you at breakfast," she said with a wide smile. "I always miss you when I don't see you."

Feeling the warmth of her embrace made him forget everything else in his life. More and more, he realized his daughter needed a mother. A good mother. One who would love Emma despite the fact that she'd been born on the wrong side of the blankets.

"Now," he said, breaking away from her. "What are you learning about today?" He walked toward the table where the governess stood. "Good afternoon, Mrs. Griffon."

She curtsied quickly. "Good afternoon, my lord."

"I hope I haven't disturbed you."

"No, sir. You are always welcome in the classroom."

"Has she been studying?" he asked.

"Yes, sir. She is quite intelligent."

"Very good." He looked down at the grammar paper on the table. "So if she is doing as well as you say it wouldn't harm her education too much if I stole her away for an ice at Gunter's."

Mrs. Griffon smiled over at Emma. "I believe it would be just indeed, my lord. She has been putting in much effort at learning Latin."

"Excellent." Nicholas hired Mrs. Griffon because she had no qualms with giving Emma a superior education. He wanted his intelligent daughter to have the best education possible. He held out his arm for his daughter. "Shall we?"

Her bright smile filled him with love. "Yes, Papa!"

By the time they arrived at Gunter's, carriages lined Berkeley Square. The waiter took their order as they sat in the phaeton enjoying the unusually warm April afternoon. Nicholas watched the people as they ate or waited for their ices. As he glanced over at two ladies seated in one carriage, he recognized Lady Somerton. But the other woman held his attention. She had dark hair and an oval face, and smiled back at something Lady Somerton had said.

Nicholas shook his head. It was not her. Sophia was in Italy not London. Still, he couldn't look away. The lady in question turned her head and stared directly at him. Even from the distance of several carriages, he could see the look of shock on her face. Before he could even move, their carriage rolled away.

He was not imagining things. It had been her. His

Sophia. If Emma hadn't been with him, he would have chased after the coach to discover where she resided. Instead, he must wait and then call on Lady Somerton to get his answers. He wondered if Sophia was visiting London to find him. Perhaps she'd found herself with child and needed to inform him.

But how would she know Lady Somerton?

As soon as Emma finished her lemon ice, he drove her home then circled around to Somerton's home on Duke Street. The butler left him in the parlor to wait for Lady Somerton.

"Lord Ancroft?"

He glanced up to see Victoria standing at the doorway with a look of confusion on her face. "Lady Somerton, you look lovely today."

"Thank you," she replied, taking a step into the room. "Did you wish to speak with me? Somerton is at White's."

"I did wish to talk to you for just a moment, if you please."

She walked to a chair and sat. "Would you like me to order tea?"

"No, this should not take more than a moment or two." He cleared his throat. "I was at Gunter's today and noticed you sitting a few carriages away."

"Yes, I was there with a friend."

He nodded. "Yes, I came to inquire on your friend. Why is she in London?"

She tilted her head. "She lives here, my lord."

Sophia lives in London. God, she must have left Italy because she found out she was with child. "Would you give me her address? It is imperative that I speak with her."

She smiled at him. "Oh, how wonderful that you

are taking our advice. Miss Reynard will find you just the right woman."

"Miss Reynard? What does this have to do with her?"

Victoria drew back. "That is whom I was with today, my lord. Sophie and I have been friends for years."

"Sophie?" Why didn't he know her name was Sophie? "Has Miss Reynard been traveling lately? She looks very much like a woman I saw, but did not have a chance to meet, in Venice."

"Why yes, she was in Venice only weeks ago."

"Thank you, Lady Somerton." He stood to leave.

"Don't you want her address?"

"I have it," he answered with a smile. And at eight this evening, he planned on meeting Sophia again.

Sophie breathed in deeply as she adjusted her turban. She added kohl to darken her eyelids and lend her a far more mysterious appearance. After a dash of rouge on her cheeks and lips, she glanced in the mirror and barely recognized herself. With all this and a very dimly lit room, he would never recognize her. Everything would work out perfectly.

After turning him away for days, she had to see him. If she was being truthful with herself, she wanted to see him. She just didn't want him to discover her. All she had to do was provide him with a reasonable explanation why the woman who owned the earring did not want to be found. She would see him and then he would leave her alone forever.

Forever.

It sounded like a very long time. She clenched her fists in frustration. What was wrong with her? Ever since meeting him she'd been morose. Making love with him in Venice meant nothing to him and should mean nothing to her, too.

If only that were true.

Even today when she noticed him at Gunter's, she had wanted to get closer to him. She assumed the young girl in the carriage had been his daughter. The sight of him had shocked her. He looked different, harder and more arrogant. And yet, she still wanted him. Closing her eyes, she could picture him without his clothing. She could feel the sensation of his hard hands gently caressing her body. Still taste the warmth of his kisses.

This lusting after him had to stop. Nothing good could come of it. Determined to put her amorous feelings out of her mind, she walked down the steps.

"Good evening, Hendricks," she said as she reached the last step. "Please bring Lord Ancroft into the study when he arrives. Do not make him wait."

"Yes, ma'am."

Strolling into her study, she extinguished all but three candles. With the fire in the fireplace burning down, the room was just dark enough that he would not be able to make out her features. The clock struck eight and a knot tightened in her belly. She had everything planned. If she did not get off course, this meeting would not take long and then he would leave her alone.

A loud knock on the front door started her heart beating rapidly. She could do this, she told herself. Hearing male voices speaking in low tones sent a tiny shiver down her back. He would not recognize her. She forced air into her lungs and blew a long breath out.

"Lord Ancroft, ma'am."

She looked over at him. With the light from the hall behind him, she could barely make out his handsome face. Not that she needed to remember what he looked like. His appearance was etched in her mind as clearly as the night she first saw him.

"Good evening, my lord," she replied unevenly as she rose from her seat. "I have been expecting you."

"I am sure you have," he said, strolling into the room.

Hendricks looked over at her, and she nodded at the unasked question. Leaving the room quietly, he closed the door.

"Please have a seat across from me at the table." Sophie returned to her chair.

"I was told you might be able to assist me in finding someone." Nicholas took the seat across from her.

"Perhaps," she answered vaguely. "What do you want from me?"

His full lips moved upward. "I have an earring and would like to locate its owner."

"My intuition is not always perfect, but many times I can read the emotions left on an item."

"I see."

"Why do you want to find this person?"

"I would like to know that she is all right. I would like to know more about her. When we met, she did not give me much information about herself."

Sophie looked down at her hands. "Sometimes people need to keep secrets, my lord. As such, I may not be able to read everything and give you the answers you are looking for."

"I'd heard you were the best," he commented.

Ignoring his comment, she said, "Let me see the item."

He held out her earring until she grabbed it from him. Somehow, she had to get him to leave the earring here with her.

"Do you see anything?" he pried.

Sophie closed her eyes and actually concentrated on the earring. Once again, she saw nothing. In her mind's eye, she should have seen all that occurred between them. But other than that one night in Venice, she'd never clearly seen or read anything regarding her future.

"Well?" he asked with a little impatience tracing through his voice.

She had to tell him something. "You met in Italy . . . I see water all around . . . Venice, I believe."

"Yes."

She wondered why she heard humor in his reply. "Yes, Venice. She was injured when wearing the earring . . . but you saved her." For a little dramatic effect, she added, "Oh, my."

"What is it?"

"You were lovers," she whispered.

"Yes, we were."

Sophie's muscles tensed at the seductive sound of his voice. Sitting across the table from him with her eyes shuttered, she remembered everything they had done that night. This had to stop before she blurted out the truth of her identity.

"She does not wish to be found."

"What?" he said roughly.

"She believes it was a mistake. Therefore, I cannot get any further information from the earring." She opened her eyes but avoided his piercing gaze. Handing him the earring, she softly said, "I am sorry."

"Are you?" he whispered as his eyes narrowed.

She frowned and looked down at the table to evade his prying stare. "I wish I could help you. But there is nothing left to say." She cleared her throat and looked longingly at the earring her brother had given her. "If you would like, I shall keep the earring and try again later when no one is around. Sometimes the uninterrupted silence helps me concentrate."

"Ah," he said, leaning back slightly in his chair. He snatched the earring from her open hand. "I do not think I can part with it yet. Sentimental value, you see."

"Oh." Disappointment washed over her until she realized his keeping the earring meant he must care . . . at least slightly. She tamped down the exciting idea. While it was a thrilling sentiment, it did not matter if he cared for her. She was too far below his station.

Perhaps Somerton could pilfer the earring from him. She so wanted her earring returned.

"You appear distraught that I won't give the earring to you. Now, why would that be?"

She blinked and finally looked him in the eye. "I am certainly not distraught or disheartened that you wish to retain your keepsake from an illicit liaison."

"Illicit?" His low husky laugh brought gooseflesh to her arms. "There was nothing illicit about it." He leaned closer to her and whispered, "Sensual. Passionate. Erotic. But not illicit."

Sophie swallowed, unable to move her gaze away from his warm brown eyes. She could lose herself in his eyes. Her lips parted slightly, and she wished he would lean just a little closer to kiss her. To feel the scintillating sensation of his lips on hers would be far too difficult to resist. A mere kiss would never be enough.

She jerked back against her chair. A smug smile lifted his lips as one brow arched at her. It was almost as if he knew what she'd been thinking! He couldn't possibly know.

He leaned back almost tipping his chair. "So tell me, Miss Reynard, have you ever been to Venice?"

"No," she lied and immediately regretted it. With their mutual friends, he could easily discover she had been in Venice only a few weeks ago.

"Never?"

She shook her head. Now that she'd started the lie, there was no going back. "No."

"You should travel." He scraped back his chair and walked closer to the fireplace. He held out his hands to the fire as if chilled.

"Lord Ancroft, I do not believe there is anything else I can tell you. Perhaps you should leave now."

He leaned against the mantel and smiled at her. "Do you really think I should leave already?"

"Yes," she whispered. A quick flash of fear shot through her. The man was dangerous on so many levels.

"But we have so much more to discuss."

"Do we?" Sophie's nerves tingled. "What exactly do we need to discuss?"

"Why a beautiful woman like you would lie to me." He slowly walked closer until he stood behind her chair.

"What have I lied to you about?" she demanded.

"So much." His fingers grazed the back of her neck then untied her turban.

"What are you doing?" She started to move from her chair but his hands clasped onto her shoulders forcing her to remain seated.

He loosened her hair, each pin tinkling against the wood floor.

"If you don't stop, I shall call my footman!"

He bent down and grazed his warm lips across her neck. She trembled from the sensation, remembering far too well exactly how sweet his kisses tasted. God, she wanted to taste him again.

She couldn't stop her head from leaning back and tilting, allowing him better access to her neck. His breath warmed her as his mouth closed over the sensitive area where her shoulder met her neck. She wanted to be closer to his mouth, to him. The hard grip he had on her shoulders lightened, and his thumbs gently caressed her.

What was it about this man that caused her to react so passionately? She wanted to turn around and fall into his arms for the rest of the night. His lips moved slowly up her neck. His tongue traced the outer shell of her ear until she quivered with yearning.

"I haven't heard you call for a footman yet," he whispered in her ear.

"Hendricks," she called halfheartedly.

"He will never hear that." He laughed softly. "You must try harder."

She needed to do just that. But his hot mouth returned to her neck and all thoughts of calling for assistance faded. His tongue swirled against her skin as his hands slid down her arms. Her body screamed for more than this gentle seduction, but he didn't seem to hear.

Slowly, his hands skimmed across her breasts, teasing her through her dress, chemise, and stays. One hand moved away as the other continued to rub against her breast. She closed her eyes and he moved away. His booted footfalls stopped. Opening her eyes, she could only stare at the look of betrayal on his face.

He knew.

"Tell Sophia that I do not like liars."

He turned to leave but she had to stop him. She had to explain why she'd told him she wanted him to leave her alone.

"Nicholas, wait."

Chapter 5

Nicholas had his hand on the door handle when her voice stopped him cold. Walking away from her when he was rock hard with desire nearly killed him. He'd told himself it was the only way to teach her a lesson. Yet, he felt as if he was the one being punished, not her.

"What do you want, Sophia? Or is it Sophie?"

"It is Sophie, but I think you already knew that, didn't you, *Nico?*"

He turned and stared at her. Seeing her disheveled and absolutely sensual appearance, his grip tightened on the door handle. *Walk away,* his brain told him. But he could not get his feet to move.

"Yes, I knew your name and that you were the woman from Venice. So why did you lie to me?"

She looked away from him. "I didn't lie about everything. I do wish to be left alone."

"Liar," he whispered. Loneliness poured from her soul. He knew the feeling all too well.

"I am not the one you are looking for."

"I am looking for the woman who fell into bed with

me in Venice. I want to know who she is, and why she can't be truthful with me. And why she left without even leaving me a note."

She stood quickly. "And what about you? Why didn't you tell me you were English? Why didn't you tell me you were Elizabeth's cousin? Why didn't you tell me you were in love with Jennette?" She clapped her hand over her mouth.

"What did you say?" he stalked her with a deep scowl. "How the bloody hell did you know I was in love with Jennette?"

He stopped only when he was directly in front of her. Her gray eyes widened. No one knew of his feelings for Jennette.

"How did you know?" he demanded again.

"I'm a medium," she retorted.

"Then why didn't you know I was English? If you're such an all-powerful medium, why did you continue speaking Italian to me? Why didn't you know I was Elizabeth's cousin?"

Her lower lip trembled slightly. "I read the letter on your desk from her," she finally admitted.

His brows furrowed deeper. He'd purposely kept that note on him so no one would believe there were any improper feelings toward Jennette. "There is nothing in that note that would give anyone an indication that I had feelings for her."

"You're right." She took a step backward. "So I must be mistaken."

"How did you know?" He moved closer.

"I had to pick up the note to read it," she answered as if that would make him understand her logic.

"And?"

"And I could read your emotions all over that letter.

You have read that note so many times I could not begin to count. You keep the letter with you in your pocket. Even now, when you come to me looking for a woman you slept with in Venice, the note is on you."

She turned away and almost tripped over her chair. He reached out to keep her from falling.

"Don't touch me," she cried, pounding her fist on the table.

"I can't seem to stop," he admitted. "I'm sorry if I hurt you."

She kept her back turned away from him. "Why did it have to be you?" she mumbled.

He spun her around to face him. He was certain he'd heard her correctly but wanted confirmation. "What did you say?"

"Nothing." She looked away from him.

He didn't quite believe all this medium nonsense. People couldn't read other's future or thoughts. It was a mad idea.

Staring down at her forlorn face, frustration grew inside of him. He wanted to hold her, kiss her, comfort her and make love to her. But he couldn't do any of those things. She knew the secret he'd been keeping from everyone. Nevertheless, his hands cupped her cheeks, his thumbs caressed her cheekbones, and with only a moment of hesitation, his lips touched hers.

What was wrong with him? He loved Jennette, and yet, he could not stop thinking about Sophie. Maybe she was the key to forgetting Jennette.

He felt her resistance and almost smiled. She seemed to be trying not to respond to his persuasion, but as her lips parted, she failed. He should walk away from her, leave before things went too far, but as her velvety tongue touched his, he was lost. Drowning in the passion that flared when she was near, he drew his hand down her back and cupped her derrière.

She moaned as he brought her roughly against his hard erection. He brought his fingers up the length of her back until he found the small buttons on her gown. Quickly unbuttoning her dress, he started to slide the silk down her body.

"What are you doing?" she whispered frantically. "What are *we* doing?"

Nicholas stared down at her trying to catch his breath. "Christ, what the hell is wrong with me?" he muttered, stepping away from her.

Sophie stared at his strong back, silhouetted by the fire. She shoved the sleeves of her silk dress back up. "It wasn't just you," she whispered.

"I realize that," he said. "But I started it."

"This time." Her heart still pounded in her chest. "I believe last time was all me."

"Well, Miss Matchmaker, what exactly does it mean when two people cannot seem to keep their hands off each other?" He moved to sit in the wingback chair by the fireplace.

"Lust," she whispered with a little shrug. "My mother was an actress and a mistress to several men. She told me all about lust and how both dangerous and powerful it can be."

"Powerful?" he said with a laugh.

"You don't believe me?" She strolled toward him intent on teaching him the power of lust. Placing her arms on his chair, she leaned over until her dress gaped. His gaze went to her breasts. His eyes darkened as he stared at her.

"Perhaps I was wrong," he said softly.

"Oh?"

His lips lifted in a large smile revealing deep dimples. "I would give just about anything to make love with you again."

"Would you?"

"I would. But tell me," he said, skimming a finger across the top of her breasts, "does this power work in both directions?"

"What do you mean?" She attempted to ignore the shiver of desire that went directly toward her belly.

He glided his hands lower until he cupped her breasts. His thumbs gently caressing them until they ached to be touched with his bare hands or better yet, his mouth. "Would I possess such power over you?"

She should tell him that he would not, but as his hands slid behind her and brought her down to straddle his lap, she could only nod.

His smile widened again. "So we appear to be exactly where we were five minutes ago."

Feeling his hard erection through her drawers made her moist and warm and unable to think about anything but him. She closed her eyes and swallowed, trying to draw some strength from a deep recess in her. But as she opened her eyes again, her weakness for his kisses overcame her again. She didn't want to be strong. She wanted to feel his hands on her bare skin, feel his strength as he entered her, and watch his face as he succumbed to the pleasure they would both experience.

She leaned in closer and brought her lips to his mouth. Instantly, his hand cupped her neck, bringing her tighter to him. His mouth opened to her and his tongue played with hers. With her desire rippling through her, she tugged at his cravat eager to feel his skin under her fingers.

His hands moved to her gown and finally lowered the bodice to her waist. Their kisses became frantic as passion overtook them. She wanted him now, deep inside her, stroking her, sending her higher.

With a groan, she broke away from his mouth and attacked the buttons on his waistcoat. As her fingers fumbled with the buttons, he pushed them aside and ripped at his clothing until he was bare chested with only his trousers in the way.

"Sophie," he groaned and pulled her closer again. "This is insane."

"I know," she mumbled against his lips.

As he kissed her again, he loosened her stays and finally unlaced them and tossed them to the floor. He brought her close and moved her chemise down to her waist, allowing unfettered access to her breasts. Suckling her deeply, his fingers slowly bunched up her skirts. He fumbled with the buttons on his trousers and shifted them both.

His hard cock rubbed against her bare skin, sliding against her wet nub until she moaned. He moved her hips upward and then down on the full length of him. Sophie gasped as he filled her. There was no stinging, no pain, only a sensual feeling of fullness that made her quiver.

"Oh, Nicholas," she whispered.

"Better than last time?" he mumbled against her neck.

"Yes."

He placed his hands on her hips and showed her how to move up and down the length of him. Each movement brought tremors of pleasure through her.

As she increased the speed, tremors turned to full quaking. Knowing she was not about to control the climax rushing through her, she closed her eyes and shook with passion.

In the midst of such pleasure, she felt him bring her hips down on him one last time. He groaned her name as she watched his handsome face filled with satisfaction.

But as she stared down at him, she realized one horrible thing. She had done it again. She had let her passion override her sensibilities, and her knowledge of preventing a child. Now she would have another few weeks of waiting and praying she hadn't gotten herself in trouble.

Nicholas leaned his head back against the chair as his heart thundered in his chest. What the bloody hell was wrong with him? He'd always been able to control his reaction to a woman. But with Sophie, everything was different. Her kisses tasted sweeter and her body softer than any other woman's.

She rested her head on his shoulder, and he wondered at her thoughts. Most likely, she wanted marriage, he realized. But as he had that niggling notion, dreadful thoughts came to mind. Could she have known who he was in Venice? Was it possible that she had followed him in order to get him into bed? Women had been trying to trap him into marriage since he was eighteen.

A sad sounding sigh escaped from her. She lifted her head and stared down at him. "No," she whispered.

"Pardon?"

"I said, no." She kissed his lips softly. "I did not follow you to Venice. And we both know marriage is not a possibility."

His muscles tensed. "How did you know what I was thinking?"

Her eyes twinkled in the dim light of the candles. "We are connected." She shook her head as he looked down to where they were joined. "I meant emotionally. Whatever is between us allows me to sometimes read your thoughts, especially when we are this . . . intimate."

He grimaced. "I am not certain I like that idea."

"You should not worry overmuch about it. You are very difficult to read. Otherwise, I would have known you were English when we were in Venice." She smiled at him seductively.

"I'm still not sure I like the idea of you reading my thoughts."

"Why is that? Do you have secrets to keep?"

He tilted his head and stared into her gray eyes. "Don't we all?"

She looked away and pressed her lips into a tight line. "Perhaps we do."

He wanted to learn her secrets. Why she seemed so lonely when he knew she had several good friends. Who was her father? Nicholas had heard he was an earl who would not recognize her as his daughter. He cupped her cheeks and brought her lips to his. After savoring her sweetness once more, he said, "Will you ever tell me your secrets?"

"I think you had best leave now," she said, then scrambled off him. Quickly, she grabbed her clothing and held them in front of her.

"Sophie?"

"Please, Nicholas."

"Very well, I shall go." He stood and dressed, watching her the entire time. If only he could read her mind as she had with him. He tied his cravat and then pulled on his jacket.

For the first time in his life, he had no idea what to say after being with a woman. With his former mistresses, he would have made plans for another evening or perhaps a trip to the opera. And with the few widows he slept with, he might have suggested another rendezvous if they both agreed.

But Sophie was not a mistress and not a widow. She was an unmarried woman, apparently living alone and with no man to defend her honor. He should have proposed marriage after taking her innocence, but she'd left him in the middle of the night.

So what was stopping him now?

With her gray eyes wide, her hair disheveled, and a slight tremble to her bottom lip, she looked like a frightened woman. *And we both know marriage is not a possibility.* Her words from earlier ate at him.

"Sophie, why did you say marriage is not a possibility?"

"Because it is not," she said with a shrug. "We come from completely different backgrounds. Besides, you and I don't even know each other, Nicholas. And you love Jennette. I will never marry a man who is in love with another woman."

He could not argue with her logic but something deep inside him wanted to rail at her. Her words sounded more like excuses to his ears. Was there another reason she didn't want to marry him? Perhaps she loved another man and used Nicholas to forget him as he had used her to forget Jennette. He wanted to tell her that he didn't love Jennette any longer. Yet, he said nothing to dissuade her. How could he when there were still some lingering feelings for Jennette?

"I should leave," he finally responded.

"Yes."

Only leaving was the last thing he wanted to do. He wanted to pick her up, bring her upstairs and make love to her again. The desire to be with her overwhelmed his mind. Being with her, made him feel different, alive. And he hadn't felt like that in well over a year.

"Please, Nicholas," she whispered, "just leave."

"As you wish, madam." He walked to the door and then turned with a smile. Holding up her earring, he said, "If you want this back, come to my home tomorrow evening at nine."

The next morning, Sophie sat in the chair where she and Nicholas had made love last evening. She had lay awake most of the night, wondering why she reacted as she did with him. Logically, none of it made sense. But she had never been the most logical of women. She trusted her instinct, her sight, and her feelings. Although none of those things were helping her either.

Her eyes filled with tears but she refused to cry over him. He was not the one for her. Nicholas was . . . was only a diversion.

A wonderful, sensual diversion.

He wanted her to collect her earring tonight. At his home. This could only cause more trouble. They both lusted after each other but if they continued this relationship it would only bring pain. Nevertheless, she wasn't ready to stop seeing him. There was something about him that brought wicked thoughts to her mind and fervent reactions from her body.

Nicholas was a man who might get into her heart if she let him. And she could not allow that to happen. If he were the man for her then she would know it, feel it, sense it. Every time she attempted to see her future she saw nothing, therefore, he was not the man for her.

She felt as if she were going mad. She must talk to someone about this and Avis seemed to be the most likely candidate. Avis was the farthest removed from Nicholas, and the most logical. Plus she had taken Selby as her lover before marriage. So, if anyone could help her it must be Avis.

When Sophie arrived at the Selby home, she prayed her friend would see her without inviting any of their other friends to join them. Entering the small parlor, Sophie heaved a relieved sigh seeing only two cups on the tea tray.

"Lady Selby will be here presently," the footman said, then walked from the room.

Avis crossed the threshold a moment later, and closed the door, cloaking them in privacy. She had her tawny hair pulled into a loose chignon and ink stains on her fingers. "I'm sorry, Sophie. Just as you arrived, I had the best idea for an upcoming scene for my next book. I had to jot down a few notes so I would not forget them."

"I understand."

Avis had one book published and was working on her second. Sophie felt a little stab of envy pierce her heart at Avis's successes. Her friend had a wonderful husband, a beautiful little girl, and a passion for writing.

"What is wrong, Sophie?" Avis sat next to her on the sofa and clasped her hand. "Ever since you matched

Victoria and Somerton you have been acting oddly. And honestly, your behavior has been even more unusual since your return from Venice. You have known me longer than any of our friends. I wish you would confide in me."

Sophie blinked several times. "It's a man, Avis."

Avis smiled broadly. "I had a feeling it might be. Someone you met in Venice?"

"Yes. But he is an Englishman." Sophie glanced down at the pale blue Persian carpet. "And you know him."

"I do?"

"Well, of all our friends, you may know him the least. That is why I came to you."

Avis frowned. "Who is it?"

"Lord Ancroft," she whispered.

"Ancroft!" Avis exclaimed with a broad smile. "That is wonderful!"

Sophie shook her head. "But it's not. Avis, he is not the man for me."

Avis released Sophie's hand and reached for the tea. She handed a cup to Sophie and then sat back against the brocade sofa with her own cup. "Now, tell me why he isn't the man for you."

"I would know," Sophie said, then sipped her tea. She let the flavorful liquid wash over her tongue and its warmth soothed her.

"Explain."

"Just as I knew Selby was the man for you. And Blackburn for Jennette, Kendal for Elizabeth, and even Somerton for Victoria. I don't *see* Ancroft for me."

Avis sipped her tea and then pursed her lips. "Are you certain?" Before Sophie could reply, Avis added, "I mean, perhaps you are not seeing him for you because you don't believe you deserve such a man."

"What do you mean?"

"You are the daughter of an earl who won't claim you. Your mother was an actress and mistress to several men. Is it possible that you do not feel you are worthy of a man who will someday be a duke?"

Sophie stared down at the tea in her cup. Was she intentionally blocking her sight for just those reasons? It was possible. But it didn't explain why she had never seen his face before she knew who he was. Truthfully, she knew she wasn't worthy of being a duchess but it was more than that.

Everyone she ever loved deserted her. Her mother left any time a man made her an offer. Her father had rarely ever visited her in twenty-six years. If she fell in love with a man like Nicholas and then lost him to either a wife or mistress, she doubted she'd recover.

"I don't know, Avis."

"You must forget all those worries. Ancroft is a wonderful man." Avis leveled a wicked smile at her. "Do what you suggested each of us do."

"What is that?"

"Seduce the man," Avis replied with a laugh.

Sophie looked away as her cheeks burned. How did her friend know that seducing him was all she'd thought about from the first time she'd met him? Avis started to chortle.

"Oh, dear," Avis said, laughing and trying to catch her breath. "You already have!"

"Yes," Sophie admitted. "When you went away with Selby you knew you would be his mistress. Did you ever think you shouldn't be with him?"

Avis giggled. "I was certain I shouldn't be with him.

He'd tricked me into choosing him. Plus, he was Jennette's brother."

"But you still went."

Avis looked away with a dreamy stare and a slight smile. "I didn't want to desire him as I did. I was certain it was very wrong."

Sophie glanced down at her pale blue skirts. "Would you have been happy just being his mistress?"

"I wasn't his mistress, Sophie. He was my lover and that was all I wanted from him."

Could she be as bold? The idea of taking Nicholas as her lover seemed to have taken over her thoughts. She'd never met such a fascinating man. Why was she even questioning this? Her mother had been doing it for years. And she had never lost her heart over any of her lovers.

"I'm thinking of taking Nicholas as my lover," she whispered as heat burned her cheeks. "At least until one of us becomes bored with the other."

Avis grinned broadly. "I think that is a splendid idea."

"Oh, Avis, you mustn't tell a soul. It is not like you and Banning or any of the others."

"How so?"

She shouldn't tell Avis his secret. But of all Sophie's friends, Avis was the most circumspect. She would never tell a soul this secret. "Ancroft is in love with another woman." And there was nothing Sophie could do about that.

Avis's smile turned downward. "Then why would you become his lover?"

Why indeed? "I cannot seem to stop myself."

Chapter 6

Nicholas sipped his brandy, letting the heady liquid rest on his tongue for a moment. After Emma left to see Elizabeth for the night, he'd been sitting in his study watching the hands on the clock move far too slowly. If Sophie showed up and wanted what he desired, they would have to locate to a different place for their liaisons. He could not have her here when his daughter was upstairs.

Glancing over at the clock on the mantel, he knew it was time to retire the servants for the night. The fewer people around when she arrived, the better. He walked to the hall and summoned his manservant.

"Lane, tell the servants they may retire early tonight."

"Yes, my lord." Lane cast a glance toward the footman. "Jonathon, too?"

"No, he may stay at the door."

"And me?"

Nicholas smirked. "I won't need your services tonight."

"Yes, my lord." Lane walked toward the kitchen to inform the cook and other servants.

"Jonathon," Nicholas said as he walked toward the front door. "I am expecting someone tonight. When she arrives, show her to my study."

"Yes, my lord."

Nicholas returned to his brandy and clock watching, hoping the next thirty minutes would pass quickly. But when thirty minutes turned into an hour, his patience started to wear thin.

"Where the bloody hell is she?" he muttered in the empty room. He'd been positive that the earring meant something special to her.

He reached into his pocket and pulled out the bauble. Whoever gave her this spent a fortune. The firelight sparkled across the dangling diamonds set in platinum. It couldn't have been from a lover but who else would spend that amount on a woman who wasn't his wife?

A knock sounded on the front door and suddenly his heart started pounding in his chest. He couldn't remember ever feeling nervous about a woman entering his home. But everything about Sophie was different. Never had lust become so overpowering to him.

Not even with Jennette.

"My lord, Miss Reynard is here."

Nicholas stood as Sophie strolled into the room wearing a low cut silver silk gown that displayed the valley of her breasts to his depraved gaze. Dear God, she'd better want to be his mistress. Stripping that gown from her luscious body would be heavenly.

"Good evening, Miss Reynard," he finally remembered to say.

"Good evening, my lord."

"Jonathon, you may retire," he said without taking his gaze off Sophie.

"But, sir, I usually watch the house until dawn."

"The house will be fine without you tonight."

Dragging his eyes away from her, he watched as the footman left for his bed. Once the door shut behind Jonathon, Nicholas moved closer to her. "I wasn't certain you would come."

"You have something I want."

He hoped it was the same thing he wanted. "And what is that?"

She glanced up at him through her lashes as a slow smile lifted her lips. "My earring," she said in the most seductive voice he'd ever heard.

"Is there anything else you might desire while you are here?"

"We shall have to wait and see." She moved closer to the fireplace until her dress shimmered in the firelight.

He walked to the brandy and poured a glass for both of them. Handing it to her, he asked, "So tell me, why is that earring so important to you?"

She laughed lightly. "I cannot wear only one."

"I suppose you can't," he said with a chuckle. "Who bought them for you?"

"My . . . friend."

"Only a husband or lover would buy something that fine."

She sipped her brandy. "Perhaps," she replied with a shrug. "But since I have had only one lover and no husband, I shall call the person a friend."

He realized that no matter how hard he tried, she would not reveal the name of the man who bought the earrings for her. Perhaps they were from her father. After all, he'd heard the stories that her father paid her expenses as long as she never named him. That might explain their significance.

"Do you plan to give me the earring?" she asked, placing the snifter on the table. "Or was this just a ruse to get me to your home late at night?"

He stalked her until reaching her position by the fireplace and then dragged her into his arms. "What would you give me for the earring?"

Her musical laugh tickled his ear.

"I have already given you more than any other man."

"True." He bent his head and kissed the side of her soft neck. "But I believe a reward might be in order."

"Hmm, what do you have in mind?"

He trailed kisses down to her shoulder. Feeling her shudder, he nipped her skin with his teeth. "I think you know what I have in mind."

She pressed her lower belly against his burgeoning erection. "I believe I do."

"Sophie, I want you as my mistress."

Sophie stiffened. Hearing his words had a strange effect on her. A mistress entailed more than she was willing to give him. She didn't want that, but she didn't want to end their relationship just yet.

She wondered if he would reject her offer. Jennette was lost to him, and Sophie doubted Jennette's feelings were ever anything but loving friend. Sophie knew of no man of quality who would ever offer for her. So she could never get what she wanted either. Therefore if neither could get what they wanted would this idea hurt anyone?

"No," she finally replied.

"Why not?" He continued his loving assault on her

shoulder. "I can give you anything you want, a house, carriages, servants."

She laughed. "I already have those items." Quieting her voice to a whisper, she added, "All I want is you."

He fell silent and stopped his hot kisses. "I don't understand, Sophie. You won't be my mistress, but you say you still want me."

She pressed her lips against his strong jaw. "I will be your lover. An equal. With the right to tell you what I want and when. The same as you. With the right to end this relationship if I decide. There will be no gifts and no money. Nothing to make me feel like a prostitute."

He smiled against her shoulder before lifting his head and looking down at her. "I believe we both might enjoy that alliance."

"There will be no talk of marriage or love," she added. She could never allow herself to fall in love with him when she already knew they could never be together. By protecting her heart, she wouldn't feel the bitter taste of abandonment when they ended the relationship.

"How does one stop oneself from falling in love?" he asked with a deep frown.

"Surely, you haven't fallen in love with all your mistresses."

"No, but I never created rules such as yours with my mistresses. We both knew going into the arrangement that I would not and could not marry them."

"Exactly, as is our case. Only that also includes love in our case. We cannot and will not fall in love." She caressed his cheek with the back of her hand.

He shook his head. "It is not always that easy, sweetheart."

"I do understand that, Nicholas. But if we agree in advance, then if one of us feels their attraction is turning into more, that person should end the relationship."

"Very well, if that is how you would like this arrangement"—he paused for a moment as if he had more reservations—"I agree."

"So now what?"

His brown eyes smoldered with gold flecks. He took her hand and led her up to his bedchamber in silence. Firelight danced across the room as he stared at her.

Sophie turned to get a breath before his look burned her to a cinder. His room was exactly how she would have pictured it. A large four poster bed occupied the majority of space with a mahogany nightstand next to it. On the opposite wall, a clothing press and cheval-glass mirror took up most of the space. Two gold velvet wingback chairs were placed by the fireplace. The walls were covered in a dark blue paper.

"Are you nervous?" he asked.

She spun around with a forced laugh. "Of course not!"

"I have wanted to strip that beautiful dress off you since you walked into my study."

Sophie swallowed and watched as he walked to the mirror and turned it toward the bed. "What are you doing?"

The smile he sent her almost buckled her knees. She had heard of many peculiar things men liked in bed from her mother, but Sophie never imagined her body reacting so intensely to the idea of watching Nicholas make love to her. Her pulse thrummed and her folds dampened with desire.

"Come here," he whispered, holding out his hand to her.

She walked over by the bed where he stood. He turned her to face the bedpost and then kissed her neck again. Sophie shivered as his fingers went to the buttons on the back of her dress and slowly slid them through their holes. From the angle of the mirror, she could see his mouth follow the path of the buttons down her back.

He slipped the silk off her shoulders. The dress looked like a glittering pond with the light of the fire dancing upon it. His hands moved to her stays and quickly unlaced them. In only a moment, she was standing naked by the bedpost with the rest of her undergarments strewn across the floor.

She held onto the bedpost for support as he trailed hot kisses down her back to her derrière. He slowly turned her so she faced him again.

"Why am I naked and you are not?" she asked, reaching for his coat.

"That is a problem most easily solved." He tore at his clothing until he stood before her as naked as she was. "Better?"

"Much," she said, reaching for his cock. She skimmed her fingers up the long length of him and watched his reaction in the mirror. Remembering what her mother told her men like the most, she circled her tongue around the velvety tip of him.

"Sophie," he groaned. He reached for her hair and removed the pins, allowing her tresses to fall down her back.

She brought him completely into her mouth. Mimicking the movements they'd made in bed, she slid her mouth up and down his length.

"Oh, dear God," he moaned, staring at her in the mirror. "Sophie, no more." He lifted her up and moved her back against the post. His mouth found her taut nipple and suckled her.

Sophie couldn't take her eyes off the mirror as he tugged and teased her breasts. Bringing her hands behind her back, she clung to the bedpost. The aching in her womb deepened. She needed him, wanted him.

"Nicholas, please."

"Not yet," he murmured. He kissed his way down her belly until he reached her moist folds. He placed one of her legs on the bed board allowing him greater access, and her the ability to see exactly what he was doing.

Watching his tongue on her was driving her mad with desire. When he slid his finger inside her, she almost buckled. He glided his finger in and out of her, imitating the action of his penis. Aching need spiraled deep inside of her until she felt compelled to close her eyes and let the climax wash over her. Shaking as she clutched the bedpost, she moaned his name.

With a laugh, he turned her to face the post again. "Watch as I enter you," he whispered against her neck.

She forced her eyes open again and stared as he slowly entered her depths. Her fingers dug into the bedpost as he filled her. Arching her back, she sighed as pleasure swept over her.

She gazed at the mirror as he slid out and then back into her until she moaned. Pressure built inside her while he continued to fill her completely. Shivers of pleasure radiated and grew until she shattered.

"Oh, God, Sophie, I need to withdraw."

"No, I took care of that," she groaned, sliding her hips against him.

He clasped her hips and stilled her movements as he reached his pinnacle. "Sophie," he moaned against her back.

Sophie woke to the soft sound of a heartbeat pattering against her ear. Nicholas had his arm around her as she rested on his chest. After a magical night of making love, she now wondered if there was any possibility that she would be able to keep her own commandment. There was something about him that made her heart leap when she saw him. How would she be able to keep herself from falling in love with him?

She loved the strength of his arm around her. With him, she felt alive and not lonely.

"What are you thinking about?"

She lifted her head from his chest and smiled down at him. Her heart skipped a beat when he returned her grin. "You."

"Me? Why would you do that? I am a dreadfully boring person."

"Hardly."

"What would anyone find interesting about me?"

She laughed and traced his jaw with her finger. "Other than the obvious physical attributes?" she asked and then let her gaze follow down his stomach to the tented coverlet rising from his erection.

"Yes, other than my better parts."

"Very well," she replied and returned her gaze to his handsome face. "I believe you are a very caring man. Is your daughter home tonight?"

"No. I—"

"Would never bring a woman into the house when your daughter was home," she finished for him. "It would be inappropriate."

"Exactly. And you think that is an asset?"

"Oh, yes. I should hate to think you believe it is all right to make love to a woman who wasn't your wife with your daughter upstairs."

"What else?"

"I do believe you are fishing for compliments, Nicholas," she said with a little laugh.

"Perhaps. But it's not often a woman gives them to a man."

Sophie frowned. "Indeed? Why is that?"

"I believe most women think they are the ones who should be complimented."

"Well that is foolish, indeed. A compliment should be given no matter who the person is." Sophie smiled and then kissed him softly. "For example, you are a magnificent kisser."

"As are you, sweetheart." He brought her closer and kissed her until she desired far more than a kiss. "Now tell me, what is it that you used to allow me to stay inside you?"

"A sponge soaked in vinegar."

"And that works?"

"So my mother told me." Sophie giggled. "Considering I lost count of how many men she's had over the past twenty-six years, and yet only became pregnant once, I think we're safe."

He rolled her onto her back and pressed his body on top of her. "And is it safe for more than once in a night?"

"I believe it is," she replied with a grin.

"Thank God." He brushed his tongue over her pebbled nipple.

"But, Nicholas, I should be leaving."

"Hmm," he said, suckling her. He raised his head and stared down at her. "I believe we have a few more minutes."

Unable to look away or deny him anything, she nodded. "I think you might be right."

And as his head returned to her breasts, she was certain that just this one night might be far more than her heart could survive.

Chapter 7

The roll of thunder rippled through her house, rattling the windows. Never a fan of thunderstorms, she wrapped her arms around Nicholas. Hearing his heartbeat in her ear calmed her irrational fears.

"It's just a small storm," he whispered in her ear.

"I know. Just not one of my favorite things." Sophie smiled against his chest. "Although, I don't mind so much with you here."

"I'll keep you safe, Sophie."

She wondered if that was possible. Almost every night for the past week they'd met in her house and made glorious love. Many of those nights, they would talk until the pink rays of dawn slowly crossed the sky. They wouldn't be able to keep this up much longer. Gossip was bound to happen.

Sophie almost laughed at that excuse. She paid her servants extremely well not to speak of her private affairs. But she might need to use it as a reason to keep Nicholas away. Already, her heart was becoming involved when she had made a promise that love would not come between them. A promise she forced him to make.

How would it look if she suddenly decided she loved him?

The more time she spent in his company, the more her heart ached for him. She would have to end things soon. But not quite yet.

"Sophie," he whispered.

She lifted her head up and stared down into his amber eyes. "Yes?"

He moved his thumb across her lower lip. "Elizabeth has invited me to the opera tomorrow night. There will be an extra seat in their box. Would you care to join me?"

She blew out a long breath. She might be able to keep the gossip down in her own house, but never at the opera house.

Before she could answer, he added, "You would sit with Elizabeth while I sit behind with Kendal. There would be nothing improper about it."

"She asked me if I wished to attend with her yesterday. However, she never mentioned that you would be joining us." Now Sophie had to rethink her attendance. Oh, how she wanted to go. But could she? "Improper or not, it will only cause talk."

"I do not care."

"I do," she replied. "My business depends on how I comport myself. Being seen with you would make people think we are lovers."

"We are," he said with a sensual grin. "Elizabeth will tell everyone that you attended as her guest and I as Kendal's guest."

Sophie frowned as she tried to think of another way

to dissuade him. The only problem was she didn't want to discourage him. She rarely went to the opera except when accompanying one of her friends. Most of those times she had gone with Elizabeth before her marriage so perhaps no one would think improperly of Sophie being there with them. Or maybe she was strictly telling herself this just to have more time with him.

"I suppose as long as I arrive with Elizabeth and her husband it would be all right."

He kissed her lightly. "Excellent."

"This might cause some talk."

"It is an innocent outing to the opera with my cousin and your dearest friend. Nothing more."

She bit down on her lower lip. "You are certain?"

"Yes," he said with a low laugh. "Stop worrying about what others think of you. Now will you attend?"

She supposed a marquess didn't need to worry about such things. But a woman in her position did. She wasn't certain how her father would react if he discovered she attended the opera with Nicholas in the same box. He might even believe she had taken after her mother, which at this point Sophie might agree that she had. Although, Sophie didn't think she would be able to become any man's mistress. It was difficult enough being Nicholas's lover without letting her emotions get in the way.

"Sophie?"

She blinked and realized he'd been waiting for her reply. "Very well, Nicholas. I will do my best to stop worrying about what others think of me."

"Good." He reached over and picked up a book on her nightstand. "Now what are you reading?"

She tried unsuccessfully to snatch the book out of his hand. "Let me have that!"

Nicholas laughed as he kept it out of her reach. "Hmm, what do we have here? *The Wanderer.*"

"Yes. Have you read it?" She highly doubted he would have read such a feminine based novel.

"Actually, I have," he replied with a smile. "I believe Fanny Burney does an excellent job showing the plight of women without families to assist them."

One thing she found fascinating was Nicholas's interest in reading. Although, she could barely contain her surprise at his choice of books. "Now, why would you find that so interesting?"

"My daughter might have ended up just like poor Juliet."

"True, but she has family."

"As did Juliet."

"Yes, but her family refused to claim her." Much like Sophie's own father. She glanced away from Nicholas, blinking furiously. "Perhaps that is why I connected with the story. I have no one."

While not exactly true, no one could learn of her father's identity nor her brother or sisters. But Sophie knew she had wonderful friends here, too.

"I'm sorry," he whispered. He leaned toward her and kissed her slowly. "But I think you are wrong when you say you have no one."

"What do you mean?"

"I think what you need is right in front of you."

"What do you mean?"

"What you're looking for is right here."

She stared at him more convinced than ever that they were getting far too intimate with each other. The idea of falling in love with a man she couldn't have terrified her. She would not end up like her mother—alone and dependent on other men for security. Or worse, dependent on her daughter for shelter.

He moved away and tossed the coverlet off his naked body. "I should leave now."

"Yes," she whispered. Their relationship may have crossed into an area she could not let it go.

Nicholas arrived at the opera house alone. While Elizabeth suggested he drive with them, he knew it would cause Sophie more tension. He wanted this night to be special for her. In truth, he wanted every night to be magical for her.

In thirteen years of being with women, he'd never found one who made him feel so comfortable. They could talk about anything or nothing at all. He'd never felt so comfortable in complete quiet with a woman. Normally the silence meant an argument had arisen. But not with Sophie.

Her rule of not falling in love might be in grave danger. He knew he was halfway there already.

If only he knew how she felt.

He strolled toward the Duke of Kendal's box, nodding to acquaintances as he walked. Hopefully, people would show some deference to Kendal and Elizabeth by not speaking of Sophie and Nicholas.

He reached the box and a liveried footman opened the door for him.

"Good evening, my lord."

With a quick nod to the footman, Nicholas entered the box. Four gilt and embroidered chairs faced the stage. Elizabeth smiled at him as he walked inside.

"Your Grace," he said to Kendal.

"Ancroft."

"Nicholas, I am so glad you decided to join us," Elizabeth said. For appearances, she introduced him formally to Sophie.

Nicholas bowed over her hand with a smile. "It is a pleasure to meet you, Miss Reynard."

"Thank you, my lord."

He couldn't help but notice she watched his every move as he headed for his seat next to Kendal. Once seated, he made some polite conversation with the duke before the orchestra started to play. Instead of paying attention to the opera, he watched Sophie.

Why had he never noticed the length of her slender neck? Or the way her hair shimmered like ebony in the flickering candlelight. The more time he spent with her, the more he was coming to terms with his feelings for her. He'd observed pain in her eyes last evening when discussing Fanny Burney's book. Sophie desperately wanted a family. Something he wanted, too.

Perhaps in a few more weeks, he could broach the topic of marriage again.

He smiled at her mesmerized face. So intent on the opera, she hadn't even noticed his gaze remained strictly on her. But Elizabeth had. She reached back and slapped his thigh with her fan.

"I believe you should give the opera a bit more of your attention, Nicholas," she whispered.

He knew she scolded him only to protect Sophie. If anyone else in the audience perceived his attraction to her, Sophie's reputation might be damaged. And Sophie would rightly blame him if that happened.

Moving his attention to the stage, he attempted to watch the performance. Only his gaze kept sliding to her. He wanted to strip that emerald gown slowly from her body. His thoughts turned to the erotic as he imagined untying her stays and dropping her shift to the floor.

He had to stop. Thankfully, the intermission halted his excruciating ordeal but left him with a slight problem. Being a gentleman, he should offer to retrieve a glass of lemonade for Sophie. But there was no way he could stand up right now.

Sophie turned toward him with a smile. "Wasn't that beautiful, Lord Ancroft?"

She had no idea how lovely she looked tonight. "Lovely, indeed, Miss Reynard."

Elizabeth ordered lemonade from the footman, saving him the embarrassment of standing up while his trousers were tented. The door opened and several young men stood in the threshold, staring directly at Sophie. Nicholas had not counted on this unexpected event.

"Good evening, Lord Riverdale," Elizabeth said as the viscount entered the room.

"Good evening, Your Graces," Riverdale said and then nodded toward Nicholas, "And you, my lord." He looked longingly over at Sophie.

Several other men scrambled into the room, in search of an introduction. Nicholas rose and moved to the back wall to watch the scene from afar. His cousin presented Sophie to each of the men in the room. Several glanced back at Nicholas as if to verify that he was not her protector.

He had no doubt that every man in the room wanted only one thing from her. Flexing his hands in frustration, he waited for the crowd to leave. Sophie blushed at the compliments given her and smiled at all the men. Jealousy rippled through him as he watched her speak directly with Riverdale in hushed tones.

Never in all the years he'd been with women had he felt such protectiveness over a woman, except his daughter. But the way he wanted to protect Sophie felt completely different. He barely stifled the urge to pull her away from all those men and growl at them. Instead, he released a long held breath.

Finally the men shuffled out of the box allowing Nicholas to return to his seat. Sophie and Elizabeth pulled out their fans and waved them in front of their flushed faces. They looked at each other and giggled as the opera resumed.

Nicholas stared at Sophie knowing he was in deep trouble.

Three nights after her trip to the opera, Sophie heard the slow tap of a cane and smiled, knowing Lady Cantwell was here for her weekly reading. The woman usually only wanted to know about her grand-children's lives. But the last time she was here she surprised Sophie with questions about love. Perhaps the older lady had an infatuation.

"That walk gets longer every week," the woman stated as she entered the room.

"Come in, Lady Cantwell," Sophie said with a grin.

"Did you order my tea?"

The woman would only drink her special blend, which Sophie received a shipment of from the lady's housekeeper every month. "Yes, ma'am."

"Good, I am parched." Lady Cantwell ambled toward the table and sat down. "Pour."

Sophie would never stand such rudeness from her other clients, but Lady Cantwell was special. The woman was a little cantankerous but she knew the business of the *ton*, so Sophie never minded. She'd gleaned all sorts of information from the woman. She poured the tea and then sat down across from her.

"Now, I heard a rumor that you were seen in the company of a certain marquess a few nights ago."

Sophie gulped her tea and burned her tongue in the process. "No, ma'am. I attended the opera with the Duchess of Kendal three nights ago. The marquess also attended as a guest of the duke's. I had not met the man before that night."

Lady Cantwell tilted her head and cackled. "Of course. Is he responsible for all the flowers in the entry?"

"No. There were several young men who visited the box during intermission"—she leaned forward for effect—"but I believe most of their intentions are not proper."

"I assure you, Miss Reynard, men have not changed in sixty years. The men of my youth would take one look at you and your background and assume you are only here for their pleasures. Do not be fooled by their advances."

Sophie smiled. "I assure you I know exactly what they want from me."

Lady Cantwell reached over and grabbed Sophie's hand with her own gnarled hand. She gave it a little squeeze. "Hold out for marriage, my dear. There will be a man who shan't care about your background."

"Are you now the fortune teller?"

"No, my dear. I just know that your beauty and kindness will win over some young man." Lady Cantwell squeezed Sophie's hand again. "Now, tell me about this new love in my life."

Sophie cleared her mind and closed her eyes. The usual dizziness swept over her and then nothing happened. The blackness never cleared. Oh, dear God, she really was losing her abilities!

"Well?" Lady Cantwell asked.

"I am not sure today. Nothing is coming to me." Sophie opened her eyes and looked at Lady Cantwell. "Are you certain you are not withholding something?"

"Not at all."

"Very well, let's try again." Sophie closed her eyes and still, nothing came to her. Why was this happening to her now? Ever since hitting her head in Venice her abilities have been acting odd.

Sophie opened her eyes. "I'm sorry, Lady Cantwell. I seem to be having difficulties reading you today."

The older woman shrugged. "Perhaps I should come back in a day or two."

"Yes, that might be the best thing for both of us."

As Lady Cantwell left, Sophie immediately started writing a letter to the only person who might be able to help her. Once finished with the letter to her mother, she sat at her desk checking her appointments for the day when her footman arrived at her study with another large arrangement of roses. She rolled her eyes. "Another one?"

"Yes, ma'am," he said.

"Who this time?"

He pulled out a small note and handed it to her.

She laughed softly. "Riverdale again. I do hope this doesn't mean they will continue to send me flowers until I see them."

"There will be no room left in the house if they do, ma'am. Where would you like these?"

"I have no idea. I'm running out of room." She glanced about her study, which already had two bouquets on tables near the sofa. "Place those in the receiving salon."

"There are already two in there."

"Well, there will have to be three now." The past two days had been a steady stream of flower deliveries to her house. All six of the men she had been introduced to at the opera had sent some large arrangement. Several had attempted to call on her, too. So far she'd sent them all away without receiving any of them.

Hearing Hendricks's slow heavy footsteps, she realized she would be denying callers all day again.

"Ma'am, Lord Ancroft is here to see you," he announced.

Sophie chewed her lower lip. She hadn't seen him since the night of the opera. While she missed him dreadfully, she'd spent the time pondering what to do about him. Already, he was coming to mean more to her than he should. And that scared her.

"Ma'am? Lord Ancroft?"

"Yes, send him in."

As Hendricks ambled down the hall, she wondered if this was the right decision. Her emotions were muddling her mind lately. But one thing she knew, she wasn't ready to give him up yet. Just the sound of his footsteps increased the beat of her heart.

He walked in and observed the flowers in the room. "Just how many damned arrangements have you been sent?"

She smiled slightly hearing the jealous tone of his voice. "I'm now up to seven. Unless you brought a bouquet with you, then it's eight."

His cheeks flushed. "I am sorry to say I did not bring you flowers this afternoon. Although, if I had, I doubt you would be able to even find them."

"Oh, Nicholas," she said with a laugh. "You have nothing to be jealous over. I know exactly why they are attempting to court me."

"Do you?" he said, with his hands on his hips.

She walked toward him with a grin. "Yes, I do." She stepped closer until they were all but touching. "I have no desire to be any man's mistress. They are wasting their time and money attempting to get into my good graces."

"So," he drawled. "How does a man get into your good graces?"

"Hmm," she said, skimming her finger down his waistcoat. "First, by not sending me roses because they make me sneeze."

"Well, that is one point in my favor. I have never sent you roses. Any other ideas?"

She unbuttoned his waistcoat. "Not writing me romantic poems. They are usually most dreadfully written."

"I shall never endeavor to do such a thing."

"Good." She looked into his amber eyes and didn't care about her appointments for today. The only thing that mattered was Nicholas.

"Any other thoughts?"

She smiled up at him. "Knowing when to kiss me."

He returned her smile. "I think I already have managed to figure that out." He pulled her into his arms and brought his lips down hard on hers.

The man was definitely starting to know her too well, Sophie thought.

Chapter 8

Nicholas walked up the steps to his father's home in Grosvenor Square with dread. The only time his father requested his presence was to call him on the carpet for some inappropriate action. Nicholas smiled, remembering the last time involved an actress who thought a night with him meant marriage. She had made a terrible scene and his father had paid the girl off. Nicholas could have done the same but thought she deserved nothing for her tasteless demeanor.

He hoped this had nothing to do with Sophie. While she wasn't his mistress in the most technical meaning of the word, she was his lover. His father might not care for his son taking a woman who professed to be the daughter of an earl.

Then again, Nicholas didn't care. His father had never loved him. His only concern was how Nicholas acted and portrayed himself. The duke wanted Nicholas to be the perfect heir and future duke.

"Good morning, sir," Baker said as he opened the door. "Your father is in his study, expecting you."

"Very good, Baker." Nicholas had deliberately kept

his father waiting for over an hour. It was far past time for his father to realize he was an adult now and would not cater to his every whim.

He walked down the gray marble hall, reminiscing on running down this same hall with his brother Simon. Nicholas grimaced as he thought about his younger brother. Simon would have been twenty-seven this year. Except the smallpox outbreak that took his life when he was only ten. Nicholas had been at Eaton at the time, surrounded by boys so he couldn't even mourn the loss of his best friend and brother.

God, he was in a morbid mood this morning. He hadn't seen Sophie in almost a week and it was driving him mad. He'd tried calling on her several times, only to be told she was not at home. An excuse he scarcely believed. He wondered if he should attempt to propose to her. While the thought of marriage normally filled him with gloom, the idea of Sophie as his wife lightened his heart. But he doubted she would agree. She'd clearly stated there would be no talk of marriage or love.

He approached the study and stopped at the doorway. His father had not heard his footsteps so his head was still bent down as he worked on papers. Nicholas took the moment to really look at his father. He hadn't seen him in months. His father's hair had gone completely white now, but that wasn't so unusual for a man nearing seventy years. Nonetheless, he appeared older and a bit frailer than the last time Nicholas had seen him.

Nicholas cleared his throat. Piercing blue eyes glared over at him.

"About damned time you arrived," his father grumbled.

"Ten is awfully early to make calls."

"Not when your father makes the request. Now sit," he said, pointing to the chair on the opposite side of the desk.

"What is this about? Have I made another blunder you wish to rail at me for?"

His father shuffled through papers and then put his quill away. "No, for once you have not. At least not that I am aware of yet. How was your trip?"

Nicholas narrowed his eyes. His father would never request his presence to have a tête-à-tête about his travels. Could he have heard about his affair with Sophie? "My trip was wonderful, Venice in particular."

His father curled up his lip. "I went to Venice once. It was nothing but stinking canals and lascivious parties. Dreadful place."

"What did you call me here for?"

"Very well, we shall dispense with the pleasantries. My doctor says I may have a year to live at most. Therefore, I have decided that you will marry this Season."

"Indeed? A year, you say?" Nicholas felt only a spark of regret that his father's life would be shortened. His father had never shown him anything but discipline. He had even berated Nicholas for bringing Emma into Nicholas's house and had never met his only grandchild.

"Yes. That should please you since you will then inherit. However, knowing your taste in women, I have decided that your marriage must take place before I . . ."

"I see," Nicholas said, gripping the arms of his

chair. He would never let his father choose a woman for him. His father would pick a woman based on her social standing, just as he had picked his wives. Two had been spiteful women who only wanted him for his title and money. He had no idea about his own mother, as she died giving birth to Simon.

His father lifted a paper from the table and handed it to him. "Here is a list of young ladies I deem acceptable."

"And why would I agree to this? If, as you say, you only have a year, then I shall inherit and be able to make the decision myself."

"You shall inherit the title and the entailed lands. But the fortune I have generated will go to charities if I do not approve of the woman before I pass."

Nicholas tightened his jaw as he stared at the list of names. He had no intention of marrying any of them but for the moment he would humor his father. "Does the woman have to be on this list?"

"No. These are ladies I already approved of, thus making your decision easier. Should you decide on another, then you will inform me and I shall investigate her background."

"Would the daughter of an earl do?"

"I would be most pleased to have the daughter of an earl become the next duchess. Assuming she has no scandals attached to her name. She would already understand her duties." His father's white brows furrowed. "Are you currently courting such a woman? I have not been made aware of this change from your usual course of women."

Nicholas smiled. "Possibly courting. I have not officially started the process." But he knew just the woman.

* * *

"Lord Ancroft is here to see you, ma'am," Hendricks said from the doorway to her study.

Sophie glanced up from her reading and frowned. "Tell him I am not at home, Hendricks."

"Oh, but that would be such a dreadful lie," a deep voice replied from the hall.

Damn him! "Let the cur in, Hendricks."

Hendricks moved out of the doorway only to be quickly replaced by Nicholas. He leaned his tall form against the doorframe in a manner that appeared totally relaxed, but she sensed the tension running through his veins. And for once, it didn't seem to be tension of a sexual manner.

"You wound me, my lady," he said, placing his hand over his heart. "A cur? You called me a cur?"

"Yes, well now you know so you may leave," she said, waving her hand at him in dismissal.

"But I cannot." He walked into the room, closing the door behind him.

"I believe you should open the door. I would not like my reputation ruined at your hands."

"Not just yet." He strolled closer to her in a casual manner, but she could sense his frustration. "Why have you been ignoring me?"

She smiled up at him. "Did you forget already that I am not your mistress? I do not have to abide by your demands to call on me when I am not in the mood for company."

"You are right, of course. However, common courtesy suggests you might have written me a note to that effect."

Seeing the look of anger in his eyes, she knew she

should have done just that. Or at least, let him in so she could be truthful with him. "I'm sorry, Nicholas. You are right, that was dreadfully rude of me. I should have at least sent you a note."

"Or informed me in person." He closed the distance between them and pulled her closer to him. "What is really wrong?"

She looked away from him. There was just so much wrong with their situation. She'd spent the week analyzing her feelings for him. The affection she felt for him was swiftly becoming far too much for her to ignore. "This idea that we can be lovers and keep our feelings out of it might be harder than I realized," she admitted softly.

"Indeed?" He brought his lips down to her ear and kissed the outer shell. "I tried to tell you that."

And he had. But she hadn't believed him. "That is why I believe it might be best if we didn't see each other any longer."

He raised his head and stared down at her with a bemused look. "Because you might actually feel something for me, it is best to stay apart? That makes no sense at all."

"Yes, it does." She drew away from him and sat back down.

"How so?"

Sophie glanced down at her shoes, afraid if she met his gaze, she would never be able to continue. "This way neither of us gets hurt."

He sighed. "If you already believe you might have feelings for me, then one of us is bound to get hurt."

"I understand that. But at some point you will need to marry." She glanced away from him. "I am not certain I can stand by and watch that." And watch him desert her. "Perhaps you should leave now."

"Not until after I have said what I came here for."

"Go on, then."

He dropped to his knee. He clasped her hand in his, and said, "Sophie, would you do me the honor of becoming my wife?"

She gasped. "You cannot be serious! We barely know each other! The majority of the time we have spent together has been . . ."

"Well spent," he interjected.

"I might disagree."

He smiled up at her, which started her heart fluttering. "And yet, in that time, I have taken your innocence and ravished your body."

She closed her eyes in an attempt to sense what had caused Nicholas's sudden proposal. With his emotions running so close to the surface, for once, she had no difficulties determining his reasons. Her lips lifted into a smile. "Nicholas, I know why you are proposing."

"Dammit, Sophie. I want to marry *you*."

"No." Sophie pulled her hand out of his grip. "Your father wants you to marry. I already told you that I will never marry a man who loves another."

Nicholas rose and then looked down at her. "There is more to this than my love of Jennette. I know she is married, Sophie. I know she will never love me other than as a friend. I am starting to accept that. If you are as good a medium as you say, then you already know those things. So, what is the real reason you won't marry me?"

Sophie stood so they were only inches apart. "I do not even know you, Nicholas."

"You know me better than most people."

"But that is not enough for marriage!" she exclaimed.

"Then get to know me. Let me court you properly."

"No, it is not possible."

"Why?"

Sophie brushed his shoulder with hers as she walked away from him. She didn't want to hurt him but she knew of no other way to dissuade him. "You are not the one," she whispered, staring into the fireplace.

"What are you talking about?"

"I have matched many people during the past five years, including some of our mutual friends. I knew they were right for each other. I saw them together." She turned back around and faced him with tears welling in her eyes. "I saw us together only that one night in Venice, Nicholas. Not once since. I think I may have misinterpreted my vision that night."

"Why do you think that?"

"I think I was only supposed to spend the one night with you. We were to be lovers, not husband and wife. I am not the one for you. And you are not the one for me."

He picked up the book on the table next to her chair and hurled it across the room. "Dammit, Sophie. I don't accept that."

"It's true, Nicholas. We might be incredible lovers, but we are not meant to be each other's *true* love."

"I am not certain there is such a thing for me," he muttered, walking toward the book he'd thrown. He picked it up and looked down at the cover. "I apologize for throwing your book."

Sophie breathed in deeply. "I accept your apology, but I believe you should leave now."

"Sophie," he said softly. "This is not over."

"Good day, Lord Ancroft."

"Good day, Miss Reynard." He walked toward the door without a glance backward.

She didn't want him to leave angry. There had to be a way to make him stay longer. If only so she might stare at his handsome face and dream about the wonderful nights she'd had with him. "Nicholas, I might be able to help you."

He stopped at the door and shook his head. "No, you cannot help me."

"I can help you find your true love," she said softly. "The woman you are supposed to spend the rest of your life with. The one who should be your wife."

"How?"

"Come to the table."

He hesitated a long moment before turning around and walking toward her worktable. She sat in one chair while he took the one across from her. A little shiver of excitement caused a tremor to race through her.

"Give me your hands," she said, holding her hands out on the table.

He gripped her hands. Feeling the strength of his hands and remembering the way they skimmed across her naked body, increased her quivers. She had to clear away the tantalizing thoughts.

"Think about love," she whispered, closing her eyes. She focused on his thoughts and the emotions coursing in him. The feeling of being off-centered and dizzy rushed over her as she concentrated.

Instead of the usual images of a person, blackness was all she saw.

Clearing her mind again, she focused solely on him. Again, there was nothing but darkness. She could see nothing. First Lady Cantwell and now Nicholas? She didn't understand why this was happening with only some of her clients. Just yesterday she'd read a friend of Jennette's with no difficulties at all.

"Well?" he asked impatiently.

"Hush. Sometimes this takes a few minutes. Just continue to think about love."

Again, nothing but blackness filled her mind. She must be losing her powers. She could never reveal that her skills were diminishing. To do so would mean the ruination of her small business.

If she truly couldn't see anyone for him, what would she tell him? Even though she didn't want to watch him court another woman, she did want him to find happiness with a proper woman. Quickly she tried to think of one acceptable woman for him. A lady who would love him and help him get over Jennette.

"Miss Amanda Wainscott," she whispered. Amanda was a kind girl of nineteen and would come to love Nicholas. She was perfect for him.

"Miss Wainscott?"

"Yes."

"Are you certain?" He stared at her with a disbelieving frown.

"Absolutely. She is the one for you." Sophie released his hands and opened her eyes. "She is a fine young lady and your father will accept her."

He moved his hand across the table and caught hers again.

Sophie couldn't take her eyes off his face. What was it about him that drew her toward him like a moth to the flame of a candle? He was handsome, but there was more to it than that. There was a loneliness in his eyes that she understood. And pain there, too. Pain that she couldn't divine and he would not tell her about. She should tell him the truth about her vision, but she needed to give him hope.

Something she had lost completely.

"I suppose I shan't be seeing you much now. You will be busy courting Miss Wainscott."

He frowned and nodded slowly but refused to release her hand even when she attempted to pull away. "I suppose I will."

"You should leave now," she whispered. "I have a client arriving in ten minutes and must get ready for her."

"Sophie," he started, then paused. "Neither of us was prepared for our first night at your home. And even though you told me you took precautions after that night, they can sometimes fail. If you find yourself with child, please let me know. I will not betroth myself to another until I know for certain."

She closed her eyes against the pain of that thought. "Of course."

He squeezed her hand a final time then released her. "I shall take my leave now."

"Good-bye, Nicholas."

"Good day, Miss Reynard."

Nicholas spent the next two days attempting to discover some information about Miss Wainscott. Although, he wondered why he bothered. Sophie's reading of him made no sense. He had no desire for Miss Wainscott. Shouldn't true love also mean desiring your partner?

In his heart, he'd known from the first time he met her, that Sophie would never marry him. With her background, she would consider herself below his station. And if that was the case, he should move forward. He still needed to marry. If Sophie had been correct with all his friends' matches, shouldn't he trust her?

With that in mind, he'd attended one ball just to watch Miss Wainscott. She danced with several men but allowed each of them only one dance, except for Lord Claybrook, whom she danced with twice.

Something felt wrong about her but he couldn't determine what. There was one person who could help him with this matter. He walked into White's hoping to find Somerton there. Scanning the room, he found Somerton speaking in hushed tones with Lord Brentwood.

Nicholas strolled toward the men. "Good afternoon, gentlemen. Somerton, when you have a moment, I need to speak with you."

"We're done here," Somerton said, then turned back to Brentwood. "Remember what I said, Brentwood."

"Thank you, Somerton." Lord Brentwood rose and nodded to Nicholas. "Good day, Lord Ancroft."

Somerton leaned back in his seat. "Have a glass of whisky, Nicholas."

Nicholas poured a small amount and then refilled Somerton's empty glass. "What do you know about Miss Wainscott?"

Somerton scowled. "I thought you were interested

in discovering the owner of the earring. I doubt Miss Wainscott was in Venice recently."

"I was but Miss Reynard is now assisting me in finding a suitable match."

"Is she now?" Somerton grabbed his whisky and drank it in one gulp. "And she believes Miss Wainscott is the one for you?"

"Yes."

"Interesting," he said before filling his glass again. "The last I'd heard, Miss Wainscott was all but engaged to Lord Claybrook."

Nicholas sipped his drink as he thought. Perhaps Sophie was wrong about this match. "But is it a love match or a financial match?"

Somerton shrugged. "I would not be privy to that information."

"I see. But I assume they would both attend Northwoods' ball at the end of the week."

"Why don't you ask the man?" Somerton inclined his head toward Lord Claybrook's seat in the corner.

"I believe I shall." Nicholas sauntered over to Lord Claybrook and smiled down at the young viscount.

"Claybrook, how are you?"

Claybrook's eyes widened. "Very well, Ancroft."

Nicholas took the seat next to him and made some staid conversation about the weather and politics. Finally, he directed the conversation toward the Season. "I have heard Northwoods' ball is set to be quite the thing. A perfect time to catch a bride."

Claybrook smiled. "So the rumors are true, then."

Rumors? "To which rumors do you refer? There are so many gossips' tongues wagging."

"That your father will disinherit you if you don't choose a wife this Season. The betting book has already taken a full page of wagers on who will be your bride."

How the bloody hell did that rumor get around so quickly? His father had only informed him of the decision a few days ago. Nicholas supposed there was no denying the truth, not that he had any plans of marrying yet.

"Ah, that rumor," Nicholas said casually. "My father has impressed upon me his desire to see me wed this year. So which beautiful lady is supposed to become my bride?"

"The odds, so far, are in Miss Justine Littlebury's favor."

Nicholas glanced over to the book, where Somerton appeared to be placing a wager. On Nicholas's marriage? He would peruse the book before leaving.

"Miss Littlebury seems an odd choice to me," Nicholas finally commented. "I have met the girl but once."

"Apparently, once is enough to make a marriage." Claybrook laughed. "Besides, you did dance with her twice at the Hartfields' ball."

True enough, but no one needed to learn that he'd done so out of pity for the young lady. The poor girl was standing on the side of the dance floor almost completely ignored by the other men in the room.

"And what about you?" Nicholas pried. "Rumors are that you shall be betrothed before the week is over."

"Speculation, that is all," Claybrook replied, pushing back his chair. "I must be off. Will I see you at the Northwoods?"

"Absolutely."

Nicholas waited until Claybrook left before strolling

to the betting book. He turned the old book around and glanced down at the entries. Claybrook was correct that Miss Littlebury seemed to be the odds on favorite. Curious what Somerton placed a wager on, Nicholas scanned the list until he found the entry.

"Bloody hell," he muttered.

Somerton had wagered one thousand pounds that Nicholas would marry Miss Sophie Reynard before the Season ended.

He was going to kill Somerton.

Chapter 9

"How could you have done this to me?" Sophie shouted at her half brother. "Did you think I wouldn't discover who placed that wager?"

Somerton's smile only increased Sophie's anger. She paced the room in frustration. How could her own brother have done such a thing to her?

"I placed a bet, that is all, Sophie."

"No, you have ruined my life." She'd had an odd sensation in the pit of her stomach since yesterday. Normally, that meant something dreadful was about to happen. But it wasn't until Elizabeth called on her this afternoon and informed her of the wager that Sophie determined the source of her sense of foreboding.

"Since you have told me I cannot uphold your honor, I decided on another way to get the man to pay for what he did to you."

"By trying to ruin me?"

"I am not trying to ruin you."

"Indeed?" Sophie pressed. "Two of my clients have

cancelled for today. Am I supposed to believe that is just a coincidence?"

"Yes." Somerton crossed his arms over his chest.

"By interfering, you are putting my reputation in jeopardy. And risking our father's wrath. He won't take it out on his heir. But he would have no issue rescinding my allowance."

"Sophie, I will support you if that happens."

She threw her hands up in the air. "I don't need your support. All I want is for you to stay out of my personal business."

Somerton stood and then paced the small confines of her study. "I will do whatever I have to in order to protect you, Sophie."

A knock scraped across the door. "Come in," Sophie called.

Hendricks opened the door and glanced inside. "Excuse me, ma'am. Lord Ancroft is here to see you."

Somerton stopped his pacing and glared over at her.

"Tell him I am not at home."

"He is particularly insistent this afternoon, ma'am," Hendricks commented.

The man was always particularly insistent. "I said I am not at home."

"Yes, ma'am."

She glanced over at her brother and noticed the arched brow and smirk. "It is not what your dirty little mind is thinking," she said to Somerton as the door closed again.

"Oh? Knowing Nicholas as I do, I doubt I am far off the mark. He should have asked for your hand."

"He did."

Somerton drew back with a frown. "He did? Then why haven't I heard of a betrothal?"

"Because I rejected his offer." She walked across the room, hoping the frustration spiraling through her body would stop.

"Why would you do that?" he asked softly.

"You know the reason. I cannot marry a man like Nicholas."

"A man with a bastard?"

"No, you fool. A marquess!"

"He won't care about your background," he whispered.

Maybe not, but she knew others would care. "Just leave, Anthony. I cannot bear another minute of your company."

"Very well." Her brother left the room, leaving the door wide open.

Sophie pressed her hands to her temples. This day had gone exceedingly bad. Miss Wainscott had actually called on her today to find out before the Northwoods' ball if Lord Claybrook was the perfect man for her. Instead of the blackness Sophie had seen with Nicholas, the vision for Miss Wainscott was completely clear.

And the only man for Miss Wainscott was Lord Claybrook.

Sophie would have to tell Nicholas that she had been wrong about her vision for him. But this time, she would be prepared. Since Lady Northwood was a client of hers, the woman had insisted Sophie attend her fancy dress ball. Wearing a mask would allow Sophie to remain anonymous and still watch Nicholas.

By studying whom he danced with and spoke with, she could determine a perfect match for him.

A commotion from the hall snapped her out of her musing. She strode to the entrance to find Nicholas pinning Somerton to her front door.

"Is your beautiful wife not enough for you, Somerton?"

Somerton laughed in a low deep tone. "Oh, she is plenty for me, Nicholas. And I would suggest you let go of me now."

"Leave Miss Reynard alone." Nicholas leaned in closer to him. "And never associate my name with hers again."

Somerton angled his head to make eye contact with Sophie. He smirked at her. "And you wonder what made me place the wager?"

"Nicholas, leave Anth—Lord Somerton alone." She'd barely caught herself from using Anthony's Christian name.

Nicholas released Somerton and turned toward her. "Would you like to explain why this married man was in your study with the door shut?"

Sophie glared at Nicholas as her anger surged. "As a matter of fact, no. It is none of your business." She did her best to ignore Somerton's smirking face behind Nicholas.

"Did you hire the footmen as I suggested?" Somerton asked.

She waved her hand at Hendricks who stood like a statue aghast at the gentlemen's behavior. "You can see that I have not. Why?"

"*This* is the very reason," he said, inclining his head toward Nicholas.

"Just go," she said, exhausted with the both of them.

"I believe I was leaving," Somerton said with a laugh. "Good luck, *Sophie.*"

There were days she really wanted to strangle her half brother . . . and this was one of them. As the door closed behind Somerton, Nicholas advanced on her.

"Should I call for another footman?" Hendricks asked, finally recovering from the shock.

Now the man has the sense to ask for additional footmen. Perhaps her brother was right that she should hire a few more. If Hendricks hadn't worked for her since she was a child, she might consider replacing him after this. But she just could not do it.

"I can deal with Lord Ancroft." She hoped. "Nicholas, I believe you should leave now."

His slight smile brought a stab of fear to her. "First, we will talk."

She backed up a step. "No."

"Oh, yes." He reached her position and clasped her elbow in a tight grip. "We have much to discuss."

"Very well." She walked into the study.

Nicholas slammed the door behind him. Anger and frustration coursed through his veins. He could think of only one reason why Somerton would have been here behind closed doors. And why he used her Christian name.

"Are you having an affair with your best friend's husband?" he demanded.

Instead of the look of shock at his discovery, she only laughed. "Oh, yes, Nicholas. I have known Somerton for almost ten years, but I would wait until he married one of my dearest friends before falling into bed with him."

Hearing her sarcasm, he felt like a fool. "I had no idea you've known him for so long."

"I have known him far, far longer than I have known you."

And obviously, they had not been lovers, he thought. So why did they seem so close? Their interaction was intimate and Somerton appeared protective of her. There was something between them, but what?

"What is Somerton to you?" he asked quietly, hoping she would offer him the truth.

"A very good friend," she replied. "A man I can talk with who gives me advice when I need it since I don't have a father to guide me."

He glanced down at the rug and then back up to her. "You can come to me."

"No, I cannot," she said adamantly.

"Why not?"

"Nicholas, there is too much between us."

Nicholas sighed and dropped into the same wing-back chair where he'd made love to her only weeks ago. "Sophie, I assume you heard about Somerton's wager at White's."

"Yes, Elizabeth told me."

"I see. Why would a man you consider a friend place such a bet?"

She pressed her hands to her temples as if fighting back the pain. Pacing the room, she said nothing for several moments. He wondered if she was trying to determine an acceptable lie to tell him.

"He knows about us," she finally whispered.

"You told him?"

She stopped pacing and glared at him. "No, you told him."

"I most certainly did no such thing," he said, coming to his feet.

"Somerton gave me a pair of earrings as a birthday gift last year. The same earring that I lost in your bed in Venice. That is why he told you to come to me."

Nicholas muttered a curse. "Well at least that explains both the wager and his protective attitude. I suppose he wants to call me out."

"No, he would not do that." She pressed her lips into a frown. "What are we to do, Nicholas?"

"Since you will not marry me, we apparently do nothing," he said in a resigned tone. He brushed his hands through his hair. "The wager will blow over as long as we are not seen together. No one will believe that it is anything but an odd bet by Somerton."

"Considering how few balls and parties I attend, it should not be difficult to stay apart. As long as you stop showing up on my doorstep and pinning viscounts against my front door."

Her words make perfect sense, and yet, he had no desire to stop calling on her. He was drawn to her, fascinated by her. But she was right. They needed to have no gossips inventing stories about them. And the more time he spent in her company, the more he ached for her. Separating was the only option. No matter how much that hurt.

"Very well, then. I shall leave."

She nodded and pressed her lips into a thin line. "Good-bye, then."

Nicholas sighed and then walked out of her house. The only thing on his mind was getting mind numbingly drunk. He didn't want to think about Sophie anymore. And he certainly didn't want to desire her again.

He laughed harshly as he entered his carriage. The yearnings he felt for Sophie were unlike any he'd ever had for another woman. Even his infatuation with Jennette seemed like a distant memory. The only woman he could think of was Sophie. The only woman he wanted was Sophie.

He wondered how long it would take before he could crave another woman.

Would it be possible to want another after having Sophie?

Sophie arranged the mask on her face before stepping out of the carriage. The dark purple feathers of her mask accented the pale lavender silk gown Sophie wore. She was certain no one would recognize her. At least she hoped one particular man did not notice her tonight.

She had already decided that she would be as inconspicuous as possible. She hadn't even told her friends that she would attend the ball. Her only reason for being here was to watch Nicholas mingle with some of the ladies during the evening.

She hadn't seen him in a few days and missed the wretch already. She supposed watching him from afar would have to suffice tonight . . . and the rest of her life.

Walking up the steps to the Northwoods' home, she wondered at her ability to stay unassuming when she arrived at the ball alone. Normally, her mother would pretend to be her aunt and chaperone her when attending such functions. Not that she went to many balls, mostly those of her closest friends.

Sophie quickly walked into the ballroom and to the refreshment table. A few people inclined their heads toward her but no one made a point of conversing with her. If only her father had acknowledged her. Then attending such a glorious ball would be part of her regular routine. No one would give her the cut direct at a ball and then run to her for advice the next day.

"Now, why didn't you tell any of us that you were planning to be here?"

So much for remaining anonymous. She turned toward Avis with a smile. "Good evening, Avis."

"Sophie?" she replied with a grin.

"It was a last minute decision."

"I see. Did anyone in particular help you make this decision?"

"Avis, you are never this restrained. Ask me what you want to know." Sophie picked up a glass of wine from one of the footman walking past.

Avis clutched Sophie's elbow and led her to a deserted section of the room. "Are you still involved with Lord Ancroft?"

"Not in the manner you mean. I am only helping him find his perfect match."

"Really? You're helping your lover find a wife."

"Yes," Sophie replied. "Is it truly that hard to believe?"

Avis stared at her until Sophie felt forced to glance away. "So Somerton's wager at White's means nothing?"

"Not at all. You know how odd Somerton can be. He

must have seen Nicholas and I talking and assumed the worst after all that nonsense about Ancroft's father demanding his son marry this Season."

"Are you certain?" Avis asked softly.

Sophie tilted her head and stared at her best friend. "We have been through this already, Avis. He is in love with another woman, and I will not be a party to that."

"Very well," Avis said in a resigned tone. "So there is no chance you and he . . . ?"

"No."

"Have you seen Jennette?" Avis asked, obviously attempting to change the subject.

"No, why?"

"I'm worried about her. She hasn't been herself for the past few weeks. The last time I spoke with her she said that she'd had an argument with Blackburn."

Sophie shrugged. "Oh, Avis, most married couples fight at times. I would hazard a guess that even you and Selby do, too. What did they fight about?"

"She wouldn't tell me." Avis sipped her lemonade. "And that's what has me concerned. It's not like her to keep so quiet about something."

"Of course it is. Think about how long she kept quiet about her fiancé's death. Perhaps she felt her argument with Blackburn was too personal to discuss with her brother's wife."

Avis laughed. "That has never stopped her."

"True enough."

"There's Banning. I must be off."

Sophie scanned the room for Nicholas and found him immediately. Even with his mask on, she knew his form. The large expanse of shoulders, the breadth of his muscled chest, the deep dimples of his cheeks when he smiled. Oh, damn. Just the sight of him across the room sent her heart pounding and warm sensations flowing through her body.

She moved away to find a secluded spot where she could watch him undisturbed. He was having an animated conversation with Elizabeth's husband until Elizabeth interrupted them. The duke took his wife to the dance floor, leaving Nicholas alone.

He glanced about the room, his gaze landing on her for a brief moment. Thankfully, he continued to look around. His gaze finally landed on Miss Amanda Wainscott. The young woman stood next to her mother on the edge of the dance floor. Her face was flush with excitement but as Nicholas approached, she paled.

If only she could hear the conversation, Sophie thought. Amanda's mother all but pushed her daughter into Nicholas's arms. The young lady stared at the floor as they walked toward the dance floor. Guilt speared Sophie when she noticed Amanda gaze longingly at Lord Claybrook.

She would have to stop this madness. But, not yet. Instinctively, she knew Claybrook might need this to force his hand with Amanda. A little jealousy would not hurt their situation.

A stab of envy poked her when she watched Nicholas take Amanda to the dance floor. Sophie wished she could be in his arms, floating across the floor. But she couldn't. He wasn't the right man for her. If only she knew who the right man was.

She could not take her eyes off them as they glided with the music. Amanda finally smiled up at Nicholas as they made polite conversation. As the music slowed, he positioned them near the terrace door. Sophie's hands fisted as she watched them walk out on the terrace alone.

How dare Nicholas do such a foolish thing!

Could he truly be that desperate to marry? She hadn't felt his anguish when she discovered that his father wanted him to marry. He'd seemed resigned to the idea but not worried. She marched across the room and noticed Claybrook doing the same. Oh, God, she had to get to them before Claybrook.

She reached the door and walked out into the cool April air. "Ancroft," she whispered, strolling along the path. "Where are you?"

"What do you want?"

She peered around a hedge of roses and found them both on a bench. "Claybrook is coming."

Amanda blushed and stood up quickly. "Thank you, Lord Ancroft. Your words were a tremendous help." She ran from the scene.

Nicholas stood and stared down at her. Sophie could feel his fury emanating from him even though she was steps away. She forced her feet to step backward until he caught her arm and brought her close.

"Why did you follow me out here, Sophie?"

"Why were you out here alone with her?"

"What I do is none of your business. Besides, you told me she was the woman for me so why are you upset that I brought her out here?"

"Miss Wainscott is not the woman for you," she whispered, staring at his brown eyes behind the mask. "And I am not upset!"

"You told me she was the perfect woman for me."

The grip on her arm tightened. "Were you lying to me?"

"No . . . yes . . . I didn't mean to," she admitted. She had to tell him the truth. "When I tried to ascertain the right woman, I didn't see anyone. So I told you it was Miss Wainscott because I felt she might come to love you."

"Why did you change your mind?"

"The other day Miss Wainscott came to me for a reading and it was clearly Lord Claybrook whom she should marry."

He released an angry breath. "Then why didn't you tell me days ago?"

She glanced away from him until he tipped her chin upward. "I had to be certain. I knew if I saw you dance together then I would know."

"And now that you have?"

"Miss Wainscott belongs with Lord Claybrook," she replied softly. "I'm sorry, Nicholas."

"I didn't need you or your sense or intuition or whatever you want to call it to come to the same conclusion. I realized it the moment I took her to the dance floor. That is why we came out here, to make him jealous."

He released her and walked back to the stone bench. After sitting, he stared at the ground for a long moment and finally said, "So there is no one for me?"

Her heart went out to him. She understood his feeling of rejection and loneliness, and the wondering if there is anyone out there for him. The only time she hadn't felt that way was with him.

"It may be too soon, Nicholas. Perhaps your perfect woman hasn't entered your life yet. Maybe that is why

I can't see her yet." Although, she knew it didn't work that way. She had seen Kendal for Elizabeth before he returned to England. She just couldn't determine his name then.

"Or maybe it just isn't meant to be." He stood and looked down at her. "And if that is the case, I will not bother you again. It doesn't matter who I marry."

He started to walk away, but this time, she caught his elbow and stopped him. "It does matter, Nicholas. Tell me about your parents' marriage."

"Why?"

"Did they love each other?"

He looked away from her, staring at the small petals opening on the rosebush. "I do not know."

"What do you mean?"

"My mother died in childbirth with my younger brother. I was only two at the time. If not for the portrait at the estate, I would not know what she looked like."

"I had no idea." Sophie bit down on her lip. Why did she sense there was more to this? "I did not know you had a brother. Tell me about him. What is he like?"

She felt his muscles tense under her hand. Closing her eyes for a long moment, she knew what had happened to his brother. "Smallpox," she whispered.

"Is there nothing I can keep from you?" he asked roughly.

She shrugged. "When you try, I can't read you. In fact, most of the time I cannot read you. It's only when you let your guard down that I can."

"None of this matters. I need a wife. You don't want to be my wife. So I am going back into the ballroom to find one. Good evening, Miss Reynard."

Sophie watched him walk away and her heart

ached with sadness. He had lost so much in his life. She wondered briefly what it would be like to marry him. Shaking her head, she knew she could not let her thoughts wander such a dangerous path. She was a bastard. A nonentity in the eyes of Society.

Chapter 10

Nicholas danced with a few beautiful, young women but none of them held his interest for the short time they danced. He wanted more out of a woman than the latest gossip or fashions. Unfortunately, most of the ladies he knew who could carry on real conversations were married. He sipped a brandy and glanced around the room. His gaze immediately found her.

Surrounded by her friends, Sophie appeared content and smiled at them. But as he studied her, he noticed her smile never reached her eyes. She looked lonely. Before he could stop himself, he walked over to the group of ladies.

"Nicholas, I would recognize you anywhere," Jennette said with a forced sounding laugh.

For once, the sound of her voice didn't affect him. Odd. Normally just hearing her speak would send warmth all over his body.

The rest of the ladies murmured their greetings, except Sophie. Her gaze darted between him and Jennette. He could feel Sophie's jealousy from the short distance between them. A slight smile raised his lips. He wanted her to be jealous. At least that meant she felt something toward him.

"Jennette, would you do me the honor of a dance?"

Jennette's dark brows rose, but she nodded. "I would love to, Nicholas."

Sophie's gray eyes turned cold as stone. "I'm sure he would love that, too," she mumbled.

Nicholas choked back a laugh as he held out his arm to Jennette. Walking to the dance floor, he said, "You look lovely tonight."

And she did. Her sapphire gown matched her eyes. The low décolleté of her gown emphasized her full breasts. While a few weeks ago it would have been torture to hold her so close, knowing he could never go farther than a dance, tonight his mind and gaze remained on Sophie.

"You are very quiet tonight, Jennette. Are you well?"

Jennette blinked and then nodded slowly. "I am well, thank you."

"I have known you too long to accept that distressingly polite response."

"Not now, Nicholas. Not here."

Nicholas wondered what could possibly be wrong. Glancing around, he realized he had yet to see Blackburn. "Where is your husband tonight?"

"He wasn't feeling well and stayed home."

Perhaps that was all there was to it. If Blackburn was ill then Jennette might be coming down sick, too. Or she might be worried about her husband as a loving wife should.

"Enough about me. What lady has caught your eye tonight?"

Nicholas smiled, feeling strangely comfortable with Jennette. It had been several years since he felt this way with her. And the sensation was lovely without the tension of his attraction getting in the way. "I am a gentleman, Jennette. I would never dishonor another woman by discussing her with another."

Jennette laughed. "Of course you are, Nicholas. Nonetheless, I cannot help but wonder if you are dancing with me only to make another woman jealous."

"I would never do such a thing," he replied with a smile. "Besides, you are married."

"Oh, I am quite certain you would do whatever it took to win a woman."

"Perhaps."

"Will you tell me who she is?"

Nicholas shook his head. "No, I will not. She doesn't believe she is the right woman for me."

"And you do?"

"I am beginning to believe she is exactly what I need."

Sophie blinked to keep her eyes from welling with tears. Watching Nicholas and Jennette dance together, left her feeling dejected and more alone than she'd ever felt. She had to leave before her tears fell. As she gazed at them, she wondered if the reason she saw nothing for Nicholas was because Jennette was the right woman for him.

Could two men have the same perfect woman?

She had never encountered this before but it appeared to make the most sense. She wished her mother were here. She would be able to give Sophie advice since she had the same gift.

Maybe she had mixed up Blackburn and Nicholas. That wasn't possible. She had clearly seen Blackburn for Jennette, not Nicholas.

"Perhaps we should get some refreshments," Avis said, clasping Sophie's elbow.

Sophie nodded.

Instead of leading Sophie to the refreshment table, Avis walked them both outside. She found a quiet place to sit and then turned toward Sophie. "He's in love with Jennette?"

Sophie couldn't swallow down the lump stuck in her throat. Tears tracked down her cheeks as she nodded her reply.

"Oh," Avis whispered. "I always thought that they considered each more like siblings."

"Jennette did," Sophie managed to answer. "But at some point his feelings changed."

"And he never told her?"

"No. He was certain Selby would be angry that his best friend wanted his little sister."

Avis shook her head. "Banning would not have minded. He has nothing but respect for Nicholas."

"Perhaps."

"Maybe Nicholas was afraid of Jennette's rejection."

Sophie frowned in concentration. Could that have anything to do with it? He had told her about his mother's death but nothing about his life after that. She'd sensed his brother died young and Nicholas's loneliness. If he didn't have a good relationship with his father, perhaps fear of rejection was the reason he'd gone no further with Jennette. Yet he'd shown no such reticence when he proposed to her. Perhaps his proposal had been nothing but the demands of honor.

"What do you know of his family, Avis?"

"Not much. I know he never wanted to go home during the holidays from school so he spent a great deal of time with Banning's family. He and his father do not appear to enjoy each other's company."

"Why not?" What would make a man not love his own son? From what she knew of Society, the most likely cause was an affair by his mother. Although, it was unusual for the wife of a duke to have an affair before the heir and spare were born.

"They think differently on many subjects," Avis replied. "When Nicholas decided to take his daughter in, his father was most vocal in his objections."

Sophie's lip trembled. "Well, his father's opinion is not that unusual."

Avis put her arm around Sophie's shoulders. "I'm sorry for the reminder."

Sophie still believed there was so much more to Nicholas than he showed the world. She wanted to discover his secrets. Even though she knew, she shouldn't. "I should leave," she muttered.

"Why not stay a little longer," Avis urged. "You don't get the chance to attend many balls."

Sophie nodded slowly. Not because she wanted to enjoy the ball but she needed to watch Nicholas's interaction with women and find him the perfect match. Now that she was certain Miss Wainscott wasn't the right woman, she had to find a woman who would love Nicholas.

She and Avis walked back into the warm room.

Nicholas and Jennette were still dancing and they both had smiles on their faces. Sophie could not stand to watch them a moment longer. She walked to the refreshment table and grabbed a glass of champagne from a footman.

"That really won't help matters."

She took another long sip and then turned to her

brother. "Indeed? I believe you have been known to imbibe to forget something."

"Something? Or someone?" Anthony asked with a smirk.

"You are becoming rather tiresome since marrying, Somerton."

"Perhaps the answer is to make him jealous."

Sophie looked up into her brother's hazel eyes. They danced with amusement. "What are you talking about?"

"You need to dance," he said, holding out his arm. "Shall we?"

"No, he won't be jealous of you." She sipped more of her champagne. "He now seems to understand that we have a strictly platonic relationship. And the last thing I want to do is make him jealous. I am trying to find him a wife."

"Of course, you are. I still say you must dance with someone." He glanced about the room. "Brentwood."

"Brentwood is young," Sophie complained.

Anthony smiled. "Even better. Brentwood is three and twenty—young and very virile."

Sophie looked longingly at the dancers. She rarely had the chance to join them. "Perhaps a dance would not hurt."

"Not a dance," Anthony said with a low chuckle. "A waltz."

Sophie bit down on her lip. Many people did still not accept the scandalous waltz. "I am not certain that would be the best dance."

"I will arrange it." Anthony walked away with a wide smile.

As her annoying brother deserted her, Sophie glanced back at Nicholas and Jennette on the dance floor. How she wished she could determine with whom he should be matched. She needed to finish this obligation quickly so she could stop thinking about him.

Anthony returned with Brentwood at his side. The younger man smiled at her in such an immature leering manner, she almost laughed at his attempt. Since he had taken her brother's position working for a secret arm of the government, Brentwood had visited her several times when he needed her services as a medium.

"Good evening, Miss Reynard," he said, bowing over her hand.

"Lord Brentwood," she replied with a nod.

"Would you care to dance?"

"Certainly."

She took his outstretched arm and they walked toward the dance floor. The younger man was handsome with his blond hair and blue eyes, but he did not affect her as Nicholas did. The musicians stopped and waited for the dancers to gather on the crowded floor.

She and Brentwood waited for the musicians to start the next piece. Sophie scanned the room for Nicholas. He had escorted Jennette to her brother and then walked away. She'd lost him in the crowd. It mattered not, she scolded herself. She highly doubted dancing with Brentwood would make Nicholas jealous.

As the music started, Sophie relaxed and enjoyed the moment. Dancing with Brentwood was far more pleasant than she had expected. He was a lovely dance partner who smiled down at her and made polite conversation without the tension associated with other men.

"Miss Reynard, thank you again for your assistance with my last assignment."

"You are very welcome," she replied.

"Is it true that you can find the one person you are meant to be with?"

"Yes." Most of the time.

He tilted his head slightly and smiled. "I shall keep that in mind when the time is right."

She laughed softly. "Love does not always happen when the time is right, my lord. In fact it is usually when both people believe the timing is completely wrong."

"Is that a warning? Is there a woman about to enter my life?"

"I cannot do a reading here. If you are truly interested, then you can call on me."

"Perhaps I shall."

Once the dance ended, she picked up a glass of wine and headed for the cool air on the terrace. A few torches lit the gravel paths but Sophie decided it was far safer to remain closer to the house. Until a firm gloved hand landed on her elbow and led her down the path.

"Why are you taking me away from the house?"

"We need to talk."

She glanced over at Nicholas's dark face and a quick flash of nervousness came over her. "Why?"

Nicholas continued walking to a seat far away from the house. He wanted no disruptions. He only wanted answers. He led her to the small stone bench.

"Sit," he demanded.

Instead of listening to him, she continued to stand

only now she had crossed her arms in front of her chest. "You stand to ruin my reputation, Lord Ancroft."

"Oh, so formal, Miss Reynard. Did you enjoy your dance with Brentwood?" He had been utterly jealous when he'd seen them dancing a waltz together. He'd almost gone out on the dance floor to interrupt their dance, until he realized how foolish that would make him appear.

"Brentwood is a fine dancer and conversationalist. So yes, I did enjoy my dance with him."

He clenched his jaw. "I'm glad."

"Did you enjoy your dance with Jennette?"

He slowly smiled at her. "Indeed, I did."

"Excellent. Now that we have both determined that we enjoyed our dances, I will return to the house," she said, then started to walk past him.

He caught her arm and brought her closer to him. "He is terribly young," Nicholas commented nonchalantly even though jealousy spread through his veins.

"Are you speaking of Brentwood again?"

"Of course!"

She tilted her head and smiled. "Jealousy does not become you, Nicholas."

Damn her for sensing his feelings. She'd said if he tried, he could conceal his thoughts from her. He wondered if that would work.

"And you felt nothing when I danced with Jennette?"

She pulled out of his grip and walked toward a holly bush. With her back turned, she answered, "Perhaps I was envious. If you haven't noticed, Brentwood was the only man who asked me to dance tonight. And that was only because Somerton forced him."

"I'm sorry, Sophie." His heart ached for her. People

refused to dance with her just because her father had never claimed her. Thankfully, his daughter would not be in the same situation.

"I do not want your pity," she said roughly.

"Will you honor me with a dance?" he asked in a soft tone. He should never have asked her that question. If she agreed then he would have her body far too close to his. If she refused, he knew she would believe he pitied her.

She looked over her shoulder at him. A shock of desire pierced him. Slowly, her full lips lifted into a shy smile. "I would enjoy a dance with you. But think what that would do to the betting book at White's."

"What if I don't give a damn about that book?" Nicholas stepped closer to her. "Dance with me, Sophie."

"I really should leave," she whispered.

"Dance with me, Sophie." He leaned in closer. "If you don't, I shall be forced to kiss you to get near you again."

Her eyes widened. "Very well, I shall dance with you. But we cannot be seen walking back into the ballroom together."

"You go first and then I will follow."

She nodded and walked swiftly down the path as if she couldn't get away from him fast enough.

This was foolish. He should forget the dance and go home. Instead, he ambled back to the ballroom to face the temptation she presented. Perhaps he could convince her to come back to his bed. God, he missed her.

Scanning the room, he found her standing near Somerton. Nicholas almost laughed. Did she think that would stop him? Staring intently at her, he walked toward her position. Some day he would discover why she and Somerton appeared to be so close.

"Somerton," he said with a nod.

"Ancroft." Somerton glanced over at Sophie with a frown.

"Lord Ancroft, it is a pleasure to see you tonight," Sophie said.

"Would you honor me with a dance?"

Somerton's eyes narrowed on him. "Do not feel compelled to comply with his request, Miss Reynard."

She smiled up at Somerton. "But that would be extremely rude, don't you think? Besides, with the amount of money you wagered at White's, I would think a dance with Ancroft would be in your best interest."

"I only want what is best for you, Sophie."

Nicholas wondered again at their closeness. Somerton's manner was almost brotherly. But that wasn't possible. Somerton's father was not the type to take a mistress. Nicholas still remembered the night he took Somerton to Lady Whitely's for his eighteenth birthday. Somerton had warred with his conscience and his moral upbringing.

"I would love to dance with you," Sophie finally said with a smile.

Somerton growled. "One dance."

Nicholas led her to the dance floor. As the slow waltz started, he brought her closer. It took all his control not to bring her up against his body. Desire rose within him until he ached to have her again.

"Come home with me tonight," he whispered in her ear.

"That would not be wise," she replied.

"Have we been wise yet?"

"No," she answered with a little laugh. "So we must start now."

"If you insist," he finally relented. Just having her this close would have to suffice.

"Nicholas, I would still like to help you find a wife."

He stiffened slightly. "Why?"

"Because you need to marry, and you must find the right woman. And be happy."

He was truly starting to believe that the right woman was already in his arms. But how could he convince her of that? If he continued to let her attempt to find him someone then he could still see her, talk with her, perhaps even touch her.

The longer it took for her to find his match, the longer he would have in her company. They could discuss other topics and learn more about each other. Perhaps then he could convince her that she was his perfect match.

"Very well, I shall call on you tomorrow."

Chapter 11

Sophie held the hand of Miss Justine Littlebury, attempting to ascertain her true love. The images in Sophie's head made no sense. A cloudy likeness of a man who reminded her of Nicholas emerged. But behind him came a hazy picture of a man with blond hair and green eyes and a slight scar on his chin. So who was the man for Miss Littlebury?

Once more Sophie was struck by the haziness of her intuition. What would she do if she'd truly lost her abilities as a medium? Then she'd have nothing. Even yesterday, Lady Cantwell returned for a third time and all Sophie saw was blackness.

"Well?" Miss Littlebury asked impatiently. "I need to know who my true love is before the ball tomorrow night."

"Hush," she reprimanded the younger woman. Sophie concentrated on the darker image that reminded her of Nicholas. Was it him? And who was the other man? She focused on names.

"Miss Reynard, can you help me or not?"

Sophie blinked her eyes open and stared at the

young woman. At only twenty, Miss Littlebury was the daughter of a viscount and by all accounts, a shy retiring lady. But that was not the impression Sophie gleaned from her. It was all an act to get what she wanted.

"What I am seeing is not making sense to me yet."

"Why not?" Miss Littlebury demanded.

"I see two men but both are very unclear. I cannot determine any names."

"It's just as I thought," Miss Littlebury commented. "You are not able to see anyone's future."

"Miss Littlebury, sometimes these things take more than one session. As I come to know you better, you will open your mind more freely to me so I may determine the man for you."

Miss Littlebury pursed her bow-shaped lips as she scraped back her chair. "I think you are a charlatan. Of course my return would be good for you since you charge for every session."

"Miss Littlebury, this is not an easy thing," Sophie explained. "If a person truly wants to hide something from me they can. Until you and I build a little trust it can be difficult to get an accurate reading."

Miss Littlebury dug through her reticule and then tossed a coin on the table. "That is the last coin you shall see from me."

With a huff, she walked toward the door. Sophie shook her head but followed her to escort the young lady out of her house. Miss Littlebury stopped at the receiving salon.

"Lord Ancroft!"

Nicholas stood and walked over to Miss Littlebury with a smile. "It is a pleasure to see you again, Miss Littlebury."

"And you, my lord," she replied in a seductive voice.

She looked back at Sophie, and said, "I would not waste your time or money with this charlatan. She is nothing but a fake."

He smiled over at Sophie. "On the contrary, Miss Littlebury, Miss Reynard has helped me immensely."

Miss Littlebury narrowed her eyes and glanced between them. "Has she now?"

"Yes." Nicholas returned his gaze to the young woman. "Will you be attending the Blackburns' ball tomorrow night?"

"Of course, I shall be there." She looked back at Sophie. "At least there I will be surrounded by Society." With a little huff, she walked toward the door.

Sophie walked back toward her study. "That woman is horrid."

"I am assuming she has no idea that you are good friends with Jennette," Nicholas said, trailing behind her.

"I should think that was apparent." She stopped at the threshold and giggled. "I do wonder how she will react when she sees me there tomorrow night."

Nicholas chuckled. "I would so like to watch."

"Come along, Nicholas." Sophie took her seat and placed her hands face up on the table. Ignoring the shock of awareness that skipped up her arms when he placed his hands on hers, she said, "Now I need you to really concentrate on love. Don't think about anything else."

She waited until Nicholas closed his eyes before she did the same. There was the normal sense of dizziness but once more, she saw nothing for him. She had never felt so ineffectual in her life. It was as if there was a dark unmovable wall blocking access to his thoughts. There had to be a reason she could not see a woman for him.

Unless she could not read him at all. But that made no sense. She had read his thoughts when they were intimate. So why couldn't she see his true love? Why did she see nothing with him as she'd seen with Lady Cantwell?

"Nicholas, do me a favor and think about your daughter."

"Why?"

"I am just testing a theory."

"Very well."

The moment he started to think about Emma, images flooded Sophie's mind. "Does she have light brown hair?"

"Yes," he replied.

"And your beautiful brown eyes."

"Yes," he answered slowly with a hint of amusement.

"She is beautiful, Nicholas." Sophie had seen her from a distance that day at Gunter's but the image she had in her head was of a very pretty young girl.

"Yes, she is. But what does this have to do with my true love?"

Sophie opened her eyes to see him staring at her with his amber eyes. She pressed her lips together trying to develop a reason she could not see a woman for him.

"You didn't see anyone again, did you?" he asked softly.

"I'm sorry, Nicholas. I just do not understand it."

"It seems obvious to me." He stood and walked to the window that faced the small courtyard. "There is no woman who will ever love me."

Her heart went out to him. "We do not know that for certain."

"Yes, I do," he said, staring out the window. "I don't know why I let you talk me into this. There hasn't been a single woman who loved me."

"I would bet your mother did," she whispered.

"Well, I don't remember her."

"Nicholas, come sit down and talk with me." Sophie looked at the two chairs near the fireplace and opted for the one they hadn't made love in.

He grimaced as he noticed the chair she'd left for him. "What do you want to talk about, Sophie?"

"You. I believe if you tell me more about yourself then I might be able to get through whatever pain your mind is holding on to."

"What pain?"

"It is perfectly obvious that you do not feel any woman has ever loved you. Because of that, it may be difficult to read you. So the question is why do you feel no woman has ever loved you?"

He tightened his jaw as he looked away from her. "Perhaps my mother loved me. I do not remember. But none of my stepmothers did. They were pleased when I left for Eton and thrilled when I returned to Selby's home instead of my father's home."

"What about mistresses? Emma's mother?"

"They were mistresses, nothing more. They enjoyed my company but loved my money more. Every woman has been interested in me for the bragging rights of sleeping with a future duke, or the possibility of becoming the future duchess. Nothing more."

Sophie blinked to keep from crying. She wanted him to know love. Real love. Not some woman who would say the words just to become his wife and the future duchess.

"Were you ever in love with anyone other than Jennette?" she asked, ignoring his question.

He folded his arms over his chest defiantly. "I thought I was but learned quickly that it was nothing more than infatuation."

"Who was she?"

"Emma's mother," he said softly.

"Ahh," she mumbled. She thought back to the two times she'd tried to read him. Not once did she get any feelings of love for this woman. "When did you realize that you didn't love her?"

"When she took my father's money and tried to leave London with Emma."

"But I thought . . ."

Nicholas looked away as his face grew dark. "You thought I paid Maggie to leave Emma with me."

"It was the common rumor." Heat crossed her cheeks. After knowing him even this short time, she should have realized he was not the type of man to do such a thing.

"I was furious at her for taking my father's money. But I wasn't going to let her take my daughter away. I caught up with Maggie before she left. She told me that was for the best because she'd had no intention of keeping Emma."

Sophie's mouth dropped. "What was she going to do?"

"Drop Emma off at the first church she came upon."

Sophie slapped her hand over her mouth to hide her revulsion. While her own mother would have been pleased if her father had taken her in, at least her mother had kept her when he refused. "I'm so sorry."

"It's been ten years. I have no feelings at all for Maggie. Except possibly pity. She lost the chance to discover what an amazing daughter we had together." Nicholas looked back at her and frowned. "Why do you look as if you are about to cry?"

She shook her head, blinking her eyes quickly. "I don't know. Perhaps my situation is not that different from Emma's. Although, had my father taken me in, I would have been accepted far more than I am."

"Why doesn't your father want his name associated with you?" Nicholas reached over and clasped her hand in his. "Was he married at the time?"

She nodded. "He was married but also put on a front of being morally righteous."

"I'm sorry. Did your mother raise you, then?"

"When she had the time. Mostly my father paid for nurses and governesses. My mother would live with me when her current protector tired of her."

"Where is she now?"

"In Venice with some count." She glanced away from him, as memories of Venice ran through her mind. Closing her eyes, she imagined him as she had seen him there, wearing nothing but a towel over his hips. "I thought you were Italian," she whispered.

"I beg your pardon?"

"When we first met in Venice."

He laughed. "I thought *you* were Italian."

She looked back at him and giggled. "I was actually a little angry when I read Jennette's letter and realized you spoke English."

Damn. Seeing the far-off look in his eyes made her

understand that she had done it again—mentioned Jennette's name.

He blinked and glanced over at her with a slight smile. "I should take my leave now," he said as he stood.

"Please stay," she whispered. "I don't have another client until four."

Nicholas stared down at Sophie, unable to move. He knew the right thing would be to leave now before they started discussing things far too intimate. But her gray eyes were clouded with tears, and he found himself returning to his seat.

"So why were you angry when you read Jennette's note?" he asked softly. While he had no desire to speak of the woman he once loved, he wanted Sophie to talk with him again.

"I find writing in Italian much harder than speaking the language. So I struggled just to write you a good-bye note in Italian. When I had finished it, I found the other note in English." She picked at an imaginary thread on her skirt. "Of course, that is also when I discovered who you were and threw my note into the fireplace."

"Ah, yes. That was such bloody bad luck on your part." He smiled over at the astonishment on her face. "Next time you should get to know your lover a little better before taking him to bed."

"Perhaps you should leave now," she said stiffly.

"Tell me," he said, ignoring her request, "how did you meet the other spinsters?"

A smile lifted her full lips upward. "Avis came here seven years ago. She wanted to know why a man kissed her. At the time, I thought it was an odd question. But as I read her, I realized she and Selby were meant to be together."

Nicholas frowned. "But they didn't marry until almost two years ago."

"The timing wasn't right for them then."

"So who kissed her?"

She arched a brow at him as she smirked. "Don't you know?"

"Well, it wasn't me."

Sophie laughed. "Of course not! It was Selby. He won the bet and melted the Ice Maiden."

"I'd heard no one won that wager."

"Selby is an honorable man," Sophie whispered.

Nicholas wondered if Selby would agree. By not telling anyone about kissing her, he missed out on five years with Avis. "Why wasn't the timing right for them seven years ago?"

She tilted her head. "They were not ready yet. Had they married then, they never would have been as happy as they are now. They both needed to mature."

What if he and Sophie were meant to be together but it wasn't their time? Could that be the reason she didn't see anyone for him?

Sophie rose and left to order tea as he considered her words. He just didn't believe they were not meant to be with each other. Sitting in this room with her felt right.

She was wrong about them.

And he would prove it to her.

"The tea will be here shortly," she said, entering the room again.

"Thank you."

He picked up the book on the table. Seeing the

bookmark, he smiled. "You have not read *Pride and Prejudice*?"

Her cheeks reddened. "I am reading it again."

"Oh? And how many times have you read it?"

"Four."

"Four times! It was a good book but not worthy of reading four times." Nicholas almost laughed at the look of outrage on her face.

"It is a marvelous book. Maybe you should read it again."

"Perhaps I should." He opened the book as if he meant to start reading it right now.

"Not now," she said in an exasperated tone.

"Very well, then," he said, placing the book back on the table. "Whatever will we discuss over tea?"

As the footman brought in the tray with tea, Nicholas sat back and watched Sophie. She poured two cups and handed him one. Once she sat back, they spent the next hour discussing topics that made Nicholas smile. From the Greek philosophers to modern politics, she was an extremely educated woman. And yet, until today, he'd had no idea. He wondered why she kept her intelligence such a secret.

The hour closed in on four and he knew he had to leave. But he had no desire to depart. He had enjoyed this afternoon more than any other he could remember.

"I should take my leave now."

She glanced away and nodded slowly. "I'm sorry I couldn't help you more."

He held out his hand to assist her from her seat. A spark of desire raced up his arm with the gentle contact. He should not kiss her but as she looked up at him all thoughts of being honorable fled. Dragging her up against his chest, he stared at her.

"Please don't kiss me," she whispered.

He smiled down at her. "Why not?"

"You know why. It will lead to more than a kiss and we cannot do that again."

"And that would not be good?" he asked with a seductive smile. He wanted to take her upstairs and make love to her all night. But he also knew it would only cause more problems. He admired her being the morally strong one, because he most certainly wasn't.

"It would be good," she said with a hint of a smile. "Too good. And cause far too many problems."

"You are right, of course." He could wait to kiss her again and during his waiting period, he would court her. He took her hand and kissed it softly. "Good day, Miss Reynard."

"Good day," she whispered.

The Duke of Belford sat in his overly large leather chair and tapped his fingers on his cherry desk. It had been well over a week since he'd given his son a list of appropriate women. In that time, his source told him that he had not called on a single woman.

"Lord Witham is here, Your Grace."

Belford glanced up with a grimace. "Send him in."

Witham's call was not unexpected. There was a reason Miss Littlebury's name was on the top of the list of eligible women. A match between the families would benefit both men. The sound of footsteps preceded Witham's arrival.

"Your Grace," Witham said with a bow.

"Come in, Witham." Belford sat back and waited

for Witham to take the seat across the desk from him. "What did you discover?"

"He danced with several women at the Northwoods' ball. Lady Blackburn, Miss Wainscott, Miss Holden, Miss Smythe, Miss Randall, and Miss Reynard."

"I know of all of them except Miss Reynard," Belford said. "Who exactly is she?"

"A matchmaker, Your Grace." Witham nervously pulled at his waistcoat. "It is said she has the power to read minds and find people their perfect husband or wife."

Belford laughed sharply until a coughing fit stopped him. Pulling the handkerchief away from his mouth, he noticed a few more specks of blood. "But who is she that Lady Northwood would invite her?"

"People say she is the bastard daughter of an earl and some actress. But no one has actually claimed to be her father. Rumor is he pays for her expenses, but she probably fabricated the story to appeal to the ladies of the *ton*. Most likely she has a protector paying her expenses."

Belford's ire grew. "The daughter of an earl?" Nicholas's parting remarks were something about the daughter of an earl. He had better not be thinking about Miss Reynard. The duchess needed to be a woman from the right type of family and not some bastard.

"That is what people say. Personally, I do not believe she is anyone of consequence. But there is more, Your Grace," Witham mumbled, looking down at his hands.

"What?"

"My daughter Justine went to Miss Reynard's home yesterday." Witham paused and looked up at him. "As she was leaving, she noticed Lord Ancroft waiting to speak with Miss Reynard."

"Did she learn his business?"

He shook his head. "She assumed that he must be there for a reading. She thought he might be trying to find the right woman for him."

Belford tightened his jaw. He knew his son's taste in women and doubted he was only there for a reading by a medium. "What does she look like?"

"I have only seen her once, Your Grace. She is a beautiful woman with dark hair and gray eyes."

"Her age?"

"I believe she is in her middle twenties."

Exactly what his disreputable son would want in a mistress. Belford hoped that was all there was to this relationship because he would never stand for such a woman becoming the next duchess. His son could take as many mistresses as he wanted, once he was properly married.

"Anything else?" he asked.

"No, Your Grace." Witham rose to leave.

"Wait, Witham." There was at least one way to make sure his son married the right type of woman. "Would your daughter be willing to compromise herself with him?"

"Your Grace?" Witham's face paled.

"Don't look so innocent and shocked. It is done all the time. She need not lose her virginity to him. She just needs to be caught in a serious kiss at a ball. As if she was about to be ravished."

Witham nodded with a smile. "I will make certain that she agrees to it. My daughter will be your son's wife and the next Duchess of Belford."

A slow smile crossed his lips. "Excellent."

Chapter 12

Sophie awoke the next morning and checked the bed sheets again for any sign of her monthlies. Now close to a fortnight late, she worried that she may have repeated her mother's mistake. As she sat up, a wave of nausea forced her to lay back down on the bed.

"Oh, dear God," she whispered once the initial wave passed.

She rolled on her side as tears wet her cheeks. What was she to do now? Her options were limited. She could get rid of the baby, but that wasn't an option for her. She could have the child and give it to Victoria's home for orphaned children. Again, she knew she could never do such a thing. Giving up her baby was not a choice for her, which left her with raising the child alone as her mother had done.

Or telling Nicholas.

She brushed away another tear. The only option was to inform him. She would never be able to withhold the fact from him. Nor did she want to. Even if he wasn't her true love, she was coming to love him already. She had no doubt that he would offer to marry her again. So the only issue that remained was could she marry a man who still loved another woman?

Did she have a choice?

No.

She could only pray that some day he might start to love her as much as he did Jennette. And if not, Sophie would shower her child with all the love she had in her heart.

Sophie sipped her lemonade as she watched the dancers floating across the floor. Thankfully, her sickness this morning didn't last long, which only strengthened her suspicions. She would have to tell Nicholas soon.

Jennette's party was a crush but not one person other than Sophie's immediate friends had even nodded at her. She felt as if she were invisible in the crowded room. Scanning the room, she had yet to see Nicholas, though he'd said he would be here.

Why did she miss him when she'd seen him only yesterday? Perhaps if she had accepted his kiss she would have been satisfied. She almost laughed aloud. His kisses were more intoxicatingly potent than any spirit she'd ever tried. Of course, if she truly were with child, then she could have him again without worrying about the consequences.

Glancing about again, her heart fluttered as she noticed him standing at the threshold of the ballroom. He wore a black jacket, with a burgundy waistcoat shot with gold thread, snowy white cravat and black breeches. Just seeing him stand across the room made her knees weak.

As she watched him, he moved toward Miss Randall

and her mother. Why would he be chasing Charlotte? She would never do as duchess. Her dreadful shyness kept her on the edge of the dance floor most balls. Perhaps he was just being kind to her. Or maybe he was one of those men who wanted a retiring woman for a wife so he could dominate her.

Sophie highly doubted that. He seemed to like her show of intelligence yesterday over tea. Their talk had been refreshing. The only person she ever had such stimulating conversation with was Avis. And talking with Nicholas was much more enjoyable.

He bowed over her hand and then led her to the floor. They danced a quadrille, which gave them precious little time to speak with each other. Although, even when they had the chance, they didn't seem to talk.

"You really must stop staring at him," said a whispered voice near her ear.

Sophie turned her head to see Avis standing next to her. "When did you get here?"

"A while ago. There are so many people here I could barely make it across the floor to find you."

She smiled at her friend. "But that is a good thing. A year ago, not even half these people would have been here. Jennette and Blackburn are making good progress with both their house and their position in Society."

"I agree," Avis said. "But back to you. The staring must stop. If you don't marry him, someone else will. And I know I speak for all your friends when I say we would much prefer you over any other woman."

Sophie turned to her friend with a frown. She didn't dare mention anything about her pregnancy concerns. Instead, she would pretend she could not marry him. "Marry him? I cannot marry him."

"Why not?" Avis sipped her lemonade.

"I am not one of you," Sophie whispered.

Avis tilted her head. "How many people in this room have you matched?"

Sophie looked around and shrugged. "Near twenty. Not that they care. Once they are matched, I am invisible to them."

"Not to me."

She squeezed Avis's hand. "Thank you."

Even with Avis's kind words, Sophie realized that she wasn't part of this crowd and never would be. Nicholas should find a woman who was already a member of Society. As duke, he would need a wife who understood how to move in the *ton*. Something she could never do. She feared she would be an embarrassment to him and hated that thought.

If only life were easier. If only they could wait until the baby was born to discover its sex. Then he could support her if she happened to be delivered of a girl. But she knew he would never take the chance that she might be carrying his heir.

She would tell him of her worries tonight.

Jennette approached them with a tight smile on her pale face. Something was wrong. And Sophie was determined to discover the cause so she could help her friend.

"I'm so glad you both made it," Jennette said as she reached them. "I cannot believe how many people decided to come."

"You look a bit overwhelmed," Avis commented. "Are you all right?"

Jennette smiled. "I am well."

Sophie clasped Jennette's hand in greeting or so Jennette would believe. "Thank you for inviting me, Jennette."

As she held her friend's hand, she sensed why Jennette appeared so pale. She was pregnant. Early in her pregnancy but definitely with child. Sophie smiled. If she was with child as she strongly suspected, then her baby and Jennette's would be very close in age.

"Avis, Lady Cantwell asked me to retrieve you. She needed to ask you a question but was too tired to move from her chair," Jennette said.

"Of course."

Once her friends had left her alone again, Sophie glanced around the room. She still wondered what had caused him to dance with Charlotte Randall. She walked closer to where Nicholas stood speaking with a man to whom she was not acquainted. Slowly he walked away until she lost him in the crush again.

A few minutes later, sensing his presence behind her, she said, "Miss Randall is not the woman for you."

"Indeed?" he whispered and stepped closer. "And why not this time? Is she already betrothed? Already in love with another man?"

"No. She is painfully shy. She would be a detriment to your position."

"Now you sound like my father." He walked away without saying another word to her.

Sophie bit down on her lip. By not telling him about Miss Wainscott earlier, she had lost his trust in this matter and obviously gained his ire. She would need to apologize to him again before telling him about the possible baby.

Seeing him walk out the door to the gardens, she believed this would be the perfect opportunity. She casually strolled toward the door as her heart pounded in her chest. Once outside, she breathed in the fresh scent of a May evening. She tiptoed down the path, searching for his hiding place. Hearing the low murmur of voices, she stopped and listened.

"What is wrong, Jennette?"

Sophie clapped her hand over her mouth to hide her gasp. He was with Jennette in the gardens . . . alone! What was wrong with him?

"Oh, Nicky, it's awful."

"What is awful?"

"I'm with child," Jennette whispered with a sniffle that made Sophie believe she was crying.

"You told me you knew how to prevent a pregnancy from happening. When did this happen?"

Sophie stood unable to move from the shock. Why would Jennette tell Nicholas something so personal? Could Jennette and Nicholas be lovers? But that was impossible! Sophie had matched her with Blackburn.

Although, that might explain why she couldn't read Nicholas. His feelings were too confused about Jennette.

"It was that night you returned from Venice. We were both so drunk," Jennette said.

"Have you told Blackburn?"

"How can I tell him? He'll be furious!"

Sophie couldn't listen to another word of this sordid conversation. She ran from the gardens and from the party.

* * *

Nicholas walked back into the Blackburns' ballroom determined to find Sophie and dance with her tonight. After thoroughly scanning the room, he walked toward Lady Selby.

"Lady Selby, how lovely you look," he said as he bowed over her hand.

"Thank you, Ancroft."

"Have you seen Miss Reynard? I needed to speak with her about something."

She smiled. "I did not realize you were acquainted with Miss Reynard."

"She is trying to match me."

"Of course."

She told him Sophie had been here but she hadn't seen her in quite a while.

After waiting several more moments, he decided to try the garden again. Perhaps she had gone out for some cooler air. He snatched a glass of brandy and headed outside again. But he never found Sophie. Perhaps she'd left early. He sat on a bench wondering why he couldn't seem to get her off his mind.

"So have you picked one yet?"

Nicholas looked up to see Somerton standing by the brick wall with a half empty glass in his hand. How the bloody hell did Somerton sneak up on him when there was a gravel path he had to walk on? "Pick one?"

"A wallflower to marry." He sipped his drink slowly.

"Why would you assume that is what I am doing?"

Somerton laughed. "Actually, I don't believe that is what you are doing at all. I think you are attempting to make a certain matchmaker jealous by dancing with others."

"And if I am?" Nicholas sipped his brandy, savoring the heady flavors.

"She may not believe it. After all, she has quite the talent for reading minds."

"So I have discovered," Nicholas stated. "But why do you care? What is she to you?"

Somerton narrowed his eyes. "A very good friend. Nothing more."

Nicholas still didn't quite believe him. Somerton was far too protective of Sophie to be nothing more than a friend. But knowing Somerton as he did, Nicholas knew he would get no information from the man.

"Ah, friendship," Nicholas said before sipping his brandy. "Interesting how concerned you are over just a friend. Even more protective than I was of Elizabeth. And she is my cousin."

"Leave it be, Nicholas," Somerton warned. "There are some things that should never be inspected too closely."

"Indeed. However, should I desire to marry her, would you object?"

Somerton crossed his arms over his chest. "I do not believe it is my decision to make."

"True," Nicholas replied with a nod. "But in order to marry her, I might just need to discover her father's identity in order to placate my father. Would you happen to know?"

Somerton's jaw tightened. "I suggest you question Sophie in that regard."

"I could do that. But we both know you can discover information on any person."

"I am retired from that business, Nicholas."

"Are you? Or is there another reason you would prefer not to get involved?" Nicholas stared at Somerton's tight stance. He knew Sophie's secret. Nicholas had no doubt. But he also knew that Somerton would take her secret to the grave if necessary.

"Both." Somerton turned on his heels and walked away before Nicholas could question him further.

Chapter 13

It had been four days since the Blackburns' ball and Nicholas had still not seen Sophie. He attempted to call on her several times, only to be turned away. He'd visited all of her friends' homes with vague excuses for calling. He had even ventured to the opera and spent the entire time combing the audience for a glimpse of her.

His valet brushed out his jacket and then slid it over his shoulders. Tonight was the Tilsons' soiree. He wondered if she would attend. Without calling on her, he had no way of knowing. Perhaps he could drive by her home on the way.

It was exceedingly difficult to make a woman jealous if he never saw her.

"All set, my lord."

"Thank you, Lane."

"The carriage is waiting for you."

"There is no need to wait up for me tonight," Nicholas said.

"Yes, my lord."

Nicholas walked up to Emma's room and knocked on the door.

"Come in," she said.

He entered the room to find her sitting at her dressing table, brushing her dark hair. "Good evening, Emma."

"Papa, you look very handsome tonight."

He took the brush out of her hand and grazed it through her tresses. It had been a long time since he brushed his daughter's hair. He'd missed it. Before her governess arrived, this had been their time together. After brushing and braiding her hair, they would read together in her bed.

He placed the silver brush down. "Do you think I can still put your hair into a queue?"

She laughed. "You haven't done that in years."

"I know." He separated her hair and started braiding the locks. "I believe I have remembered."

"Thank you, Papa."

As soon as he finished, he kissed the top of her head. "I am off to the Tilsons' party. I shall see you in the morning for breakfast."

"Assuming you don't stay out too late."

"And miss our breakfast together? Never."

"Good, because I must hear about all the beautiful gowns the ladies wore."

He rolled his eyes deliberately. "You are going to force me to remember what everyone wore?"

"Yes." She smiled at him. "But only the ladies."

"Very well, then."

She stood up and hugged him before he left. "I love you, Papa."

"I love you too, Emma."

He instructed his driver to take a detour down

Clifford Street before heading to the Tilsons' party. No matter how much he tried to tell himself he should attempt to put her out of his mind, he could not do it. Truthfully, he didn't want to erase her from his mind. Passing her house slowly, he noticed a number of candles lit in her receiving salon and two carriages near her home.

He knocked on the carriage to stop the driver for a moment. As he pulled up a few houses away, he saw another coach halt before her home. Selby and his wife clamored down and walked inside the inviting home. Nicholas smiled slowly.

"I am getting out here," he announced.

The carriage door opened and a groomsman was there to assist him. He walked down the street whistling softly. As he approached the house, Hendricks opened the door in his usual stoic manner.

"Good evening, Lord Ancroft."

"Good evening, Hendricks. Is she at home?"

Hendricks's mouth gaped slightly before he recovered. "Please wait in the receiving salon and I will see if she is at home."

Nicholas sauntered into the room with a smile. He heard Hendricks open the door and the familiar voice of his cousin Elizabeth sounded. Nicholas turned as Elizabeth and Kendal walked into the entryway.

"Nicholas!" Elizabeth walked into the room and hugged him. "What are you doing in there? Come with us to the upstairs parlor."

"As you wish," he replied. "Good evening, Your Grace."

"And you, Ancroft. But you know I would prefer you call me Kendal."

"Of course." Nicholas still cringed at the strange accent Elizabeth's husband had picked up in America. He followed his cousin and Kendal up the steps. As they reached the hall, Elizabeth waited for him. She held out her arm for him.

"Now what could be better than walking into a room with two handsome men?"

Nicholas chuckled. They stepped over the threshold and everyone in the room went silent.

"Look who I found in your receiving salon, Sophie. You should have told him you don't stand on formalities when it's just your friends."

He could have sworn Elizabeth held back a laugh. When his cousin had first seen him, he believed she must have thought he'd been invited, too. But seeing the slight smirk on her lips, he knew what she was about now.

He glanced at Sophie's bemused face and almost laughed himself. Her eyes turned to slate as her shock turned to anger.

"Good evening, Miss Reynard. Thank you for inviting me this evening."

Her jaw tightened as if she held in a stinging retort. "Good evening, Lord Ancroft," she replied stiffly. "If you all will excuse me a moment, I must tell the servants there will be one more for dinner."

"I am truly sorry if I forgot to reply to your invitation," he whispered as she passed him. "I might have thought you would *sense* my desire to be here."

Her cheeks flushed red before she left the room without a word.

"You are a dreadful person, Nicholas," Jennette reprimanded him. "She had no idea you were coming, and I would wager she never invited you either."

"I only came to speak with her. Elizabeth invited me up."

"Well played, Elizabeth," Avis said with a nod. "I would have done the same."

"She is going to be furious with you," Victoria said to Elizabeth.

Nicholas looked over at Victoria and said, "No, she will save her fury for me."

"I have no doubt about that," Somerton added.

Sophie walked back into the room looking far calmer than when she had left. As she passed him, she cast him a little glare, but Nicholas didn't mind at all. He was here with friends instead of a ball filled with people with whom he had no desire to socialize.

He watched as Sophie walked to the small table in the corner filled with decanters. Her blue silk gown had small embroidered lilies at the hem. She turned and walked toward him.

"Sherry, Lord Ancroft?"

He took the proffered glass and gave her a quick salute. She returned to her seat, ignoring him. But he knew she wasn't disregarding him. Every few seconds, her gaze would slide to him and then back to someone else in the room.

While his friends spoke pleasantly, he and Sophie added little to the conversation. Finally, a footman announced dinner. With all the married couples paired off, he waited to escort Sophie to the dining room.

She took his arm but held him back as everyone left. "How dare you!"

"I only came to call on you this evening. I had no idea you were hosting a dinner party for *our* friends."

She narrowed her gray eyes on him. "I do not believe you. One of them must have told you about this."

"No one said anything to me about your party."

"Well," she huffed, "you should be at the Tilsons' soiree instead of here."

Nicholas smiled down at her. He felt her breath quicken. "Why is that?"

"Because you are supposed to be looking for a wife. You won't find one amongst the married women here. Unless of course you are seeking one of the married women for something nefarious."

He pulled her closer to him. "I did not come here to see Jennette," he whispered. "I didn't even know she was here . . . but I knew you were."

She stared up at him with her lips slightly parted. He wanted to feel her sensual lips against his, but it was not the right time. She had to come to him this time.

"Still," she said harshly, "you should be where the available unmarried women are—the Tilsons' party."

"There is *one* unmarried woman here," he whispered as he arched a brow at her.

"But she is unavailable."

"We shall see."

He led her down to the dining room, trying his best to ignore the alluring scent of her jasmine perfume. And the soft touch of her bare hand on his arm. Watching the shallow rise and fall of her breasts, he was certain she felt the same way. The urge to make love with her again continued to increase.

One way or another, he would have her again.

Sophie stopped as they entered the dining room. Since this was an informal dinner with just her friends, she hadn't assigned seats. Seeing the two empty chairs next to each other meant she would be near him all through dinner. She would be close enough to inhale the clean scent of his soap. He might even brush up against her.

She shook her head slightly and moved to an open chair. He took the seat next to her, which suddenly felt far too close. She could do this, she reminded herself. It was just a dinner.

She had wanted to confront him about his affair in the salon but did not dare with Jennette and Blackburn in the house. All she had to do was manage to get through dinner with him next to her.

As she sipped her soup, she listened to the conversation. Avis and Jennette spoke of their children while Elizabeth and Victoria listened intently. The men talked of politics. Yet, she and Nicholas remained oddly quiet.

"Nicholas, did you know that you and Sophie were in Venice at the same time?" Elizabeth asked before sipping her wine.

Heat streaked across her cheeks. Sophie glared down at her friend. How could Elizabeth do this!

"I did not realize that," Nicholas said evenly.

"Yes," Elizabeth continued. "Wouldn't it have been interesting if you had met there?"

"Interesting, indeed," he replied before turning to Sophie. "What do you think, Miss Reynard?"

She cleared her throat softly. "Since we had never been introduced before that trip, I doubt we would have even noticed each other."

Nicholas smirked at her. "Oh, I think we would have noticed each other," he muttered so quietly only she heard him. "True enough," he added loud enough for the others.

She attempted to think of some topic to change the

conversation. "The weather has been quite lovely lately, don't you agree?"

Everyone murmured their agreement. Thankfully that seemed to have worked . . . until Jennette spoke up.

"I am not sure I agree with you, Sophie."

"On the weather? But we have scarcely had any rain—"

"I meant about you and Nicholas meeting in Venice." Jennette played with her food but ate almost nothing. "After all, you were both English in a foreign country. I believe you would have been drawn to each other just to hear your native tongue."

Sophie choked on her meat.

"Are you all right?" Nicholas asked.

She nodded and then sipped her wine. "Perhaps you are right, Jennette. However, since we did not meet in Venice the topic is meaningless."

Thankfully, Avis steered the conversation back to some gossip running through the *ton*. But as she did, Sophie suddenly felt Nicholas's knee brush up against her leg. A rush of desire washed over her. How could she feel desire for a man who had gotten a married woman with child? He looked over at her and excused himself, but she noticed the humor in his eyes.

When the footman cleared the last of the plates, she rose and said, "Ladies, let the men enjoy their port or brandy while we have tea in the salon."

Her friends agreed and followed her into the salon. All four of them burst into giggles the minute the door shut behind them.

"I cannot believe you find this amusing!"

"Oh, come now, Sophie," Avis said as she sat on the sofa, "you have to admit the man is interesting."

Sophie could never deny that. She found Nicholas interesting, handsome, quick-witted, and so much more. "I suppose he is."

"I apologize for what I said about you and Nicholas meeting in Venice," Elizabeth said. "I just think it would have been so romantic to meet in a foreign land. And Venice is such a beautiful city."

"Yes, it is," Sophie replied, staring into the empty fireplace. She would never forget that night in Venice with him.

"Why are your cheeks getting so red, Sophie?" Victoria asked with a smile.

Sophie blinked and looked over at her sister-in-law. "What are you talking about?"

"You appeared to be daydreaming and staring at the fireplace," Jennette added. "Were you thinking about that man you met in Venice?"

This time, Sophie felt the scorching heat on her cheeks. "Perhaps," she replied vaguely.

"If only it had been Nicholas," Elizabeth said in a dreamy voice.

"You know, don't you?" Sophie demanded and then looked at Avis. "Did you tell them?"

"Oh, my God! It *was* Nicholas?" Elizabeth exclaimed. "That is perfect! You will be my cousin by marriage. Our children will be related just like Avis and Jennette, a little more distant cousins, but still related."

"I did not tell them," Avis said, smiling over at Sophie. "You just did."

"I already knew," Victoria commented.

Jennette frowned. "How did you know?"

Sophie glared over at Victoria who only stared back

with a frown. No one else knew they were related by marriage.

"I—I could just tell by how you were reacting," Victoria lied.

"Hmm, I have known Nicholas forever and I didn't see it." Jennette picked up her tea and sipped it. "How did I miss it?"

"Perhaps you were preoccupied with other thoughts," Sophie said in a testy tone.

Jennette tilted her head in confusion and then the realization dawned on her. Her mouth gaped open in surprise.

"He's my cousin and I didn't see it," Elizabeth added. "So, did you do what you have always advised us to do?"

"What do you mean?" Sophie asked.

"Did you seduce the man?"

Chapter 14

Sophie glanced at Avis and Victoria who both nodded their heads to her. She had never withheld the truth from her friends, except for her father's name. But she had never told anyone about that and they had always understood her reasons. Victoria had figured it out when she and Anthony became lovers.

"Yes," she admitted, then stared at her blue silk skirts.

"And yet you didn't know who he was?" Elizabeth asked.

"We were both speaking Italian. I had no idea he was even English."

"But you let him into your bed?" Jennette said in an odd voice.

"Well, it was his bed, not mine."

"Excuse me," Jennette said as she walked across the room. She blinked quickly as if attempting to hide her tears. "I need a moment."

"When did you meet him?" Elizabeth queried.

Finally, Sophie knew she had no choice but to tell her friends the entire story of how she and Nicholas had met. She'd never felt so embarrassed in her life. Admitting she'd had an affair with a man she just met was mad.

She had barely finished the story when the men returned from the dining room. Blackburn entered first and explained that Jennette was feeling unwell and he was taking her home. Sophie wondered if it was the pregnancy or the topic that made her ill.

Her breath caught as she glanced over at Nicholas. Why did the man have to look so handsome? She needed to remain angry with him for his betrayal, not gazing at him like a swooning adolescent. The men took seats near their wives or perched on the arm of their chair. Nicholas looked oddly uncomfortable. He finally took a seat across from her.

"So what were you ladies discussing before we entered?" Selby asked. "The latest fashion? Gossip?"

"Children, my dear," Avis replied. Selby took her hand in his and squeezed it.

As Sophie glanced about, she noticed other loving endearments the couples made toward each other. Sometimes it was just a long look, or a little hand squeeze, or a gentle caress. She pressed her lips together and slid a glance toward Nicholas. His slight smile caused her heart to pound.

"Is Jennette all right?" Selby asked in a caring tone. "She hasn't been herself for the past few weeks."

Avis smiled. "I believe your sister will be perfectly well in a few months."

"Months?" Selby looked down at his wife. "Another child? Already?"

Sophie looked over at Nicholas. His face had gone pale with the conversation. "Are you all right, Lord Ancroft?"

He frowned and tilted his head. A lock of brown hair fell over his forehead. "I am fine, thank you for asking, Miss Reynard."

"Sophie," Victoria said, "is it true about Jennette?"

"Yes," she answered, staring at Nicholas. He finally looked away as color tinged his cheeks. "I realized it the night of their party."

"I cannot believe Blackburn would be happy about this development," Selby said.

"Why wouldn't he be pleased to have another child?" Somerton asked. "Her first went smoothly enough."

Selby nodded. "He wanted more time to get his estates in order. They have only just finished the town home. He had hoped to finish with the estate in Lancashire before another child came along."

"Well, sometimes these things just happen," Nicholas mumbled.

"I have tables set up for cards and other games," Sophie announced to move the conversation away from Jennette.

Quickly, the couples paired up for cards, leaving her and Nicholas without partners. Sophie knew her friends had deliberately left her without a partner so she would have to choose him. Nicholas stood and walked toward the table with the chessboard.

"Would you care to play, Miss Reynard?"

"Thank you, but no," she replied coldly. She would have words with her friends tomorrow. They most likely assumed she and Nicholas would marry. She doubted any of them knew about Jennette and Nicholas.

She had no idea what she would tell them. She couldn't speak of Jennette's illicit affair. They would hate her for it, if they even believed her.

"But if you don't play I shall grow terribly bored. As hostess, you should want to fulfill my needs," he said just loud enough for her to hear.

"Oh, let us play, then. I would hate for anyone to learn what a dreadful hostess I am for not fulfilling the needs of a man who wasn't even invited."

Sitting on the side with white pieces, she lifted her pawn and moved it.

"Why are you angry with me, Sophie?" he whispered.

"I am not about to get into this with you tonight."

"Then when?" he pressed, before moving his black knight. "I am quite certain this is not just about me inviting myself to your party."

"You are correct about that." Sophie glanced around the room and noticed Avis and Elizabeth looking over at them. She had to change the subject of their conversation before she garnered even more of their curiosity. She needed a neutral topic that would keep them talking without the sexual undertones usually present.

"Tell me about your daughter," she said, then moved another pawn forward.

Nicholas saw the pain in her eyes and wanted to take it all away. But looking around the room, he noticed more than just a few gazes on him and Sophie. He was taken aback by her sudden change of subject and her request. Not one woman he'd ever courted or even kept as his mistress had taken an interest in Emma. Most preferred to pretend she didn't exist.

"Emma is doing quite well, thank you." He took a moment to study the board before moving a pawn.

She arched a brow at him. "That is all? I have heard stories from Elizabeth about what a proud father you are."

"Do you really want to know or are you just making polite conversation?" Although, there was nothing polite in asking about a bastard child.

She tilted her head at him and paused for a long moment before replying, "I would really like to know."

"Emma is ten and already thinks she is quite a lady. She is far too intelligent for her years. I was tasked tonight with taking note of all the ladies gowns and reporting back to her in the morning."

She laughed. "I was the same way at that age. It only gets worse as she gets older. She will start to pester you for all the latest fashions."

"One more thing to look forward to," he mumbled.

"I do hope you have a good governess for her to keep her mind occupied."

Nicholas sipped his brandy as she captured one of his pawns. "Her governess is very impressed with her intelligence. Mrs. Griffon already has her learning Latin and Greek."

"Mrs. Griffon? Eliza Griffon?"

"Yes," Nicholas answered. "Do you know of her? Is she one of your clients?"

"No," Sophie answered, blinking quickly. "She was my governess for eight years."

"Was she?" Nicholas smiled to himself. He really must review Mrs. Griffon's references. Perhaps he might discover the identity of Sophie's father.

"She is a wonderful teacher," Sophie gushed. "You must be sure to have her take Emma to the British Museum several times."

"Why is that?"

"I have never met anyone who knows so much

about the contents of that museum. She made me come to love it and history in particular."

"I shall insist she do that then."

She glanced down at the board as he captured one of her pawns. She smiled and he realized his mistake. He'd been so preoccupied with her that he'd put his rook in danger. She held up the marble piece with a smile.

"I believe I should pay more attention to the game and not the beautiful woman across from me," he remarked.

"Be warned, Mrs. Griffon taught me to play."

As the others finished their games, they walked over to watch the game in progress. Nicholas finally had Sophie on the defensive, but she was a challenging player. And he thoroughly enjoyed the competition. The few times he had attempted to play chess with other women they either had no idea of the rules or had no skill.

She furrowed her brow as she stared at the board. Finally, she picked up her knight and moved him to defend her king. "I believe that will just about be the end of the game," she said quietly.

"I think you are correct," he replied, taking her knight. "Checkmate."

"Well played, my lord."

He nodded and stood. "I should take my leave now."

Leaving was the last thing he wanted to do now. He wanted to stay and determine what had her angry earlier so he could ease her mind. But mostly, he wanted to stay and take her to her bed. At some point soon, he had to find some time alone with her again.

He pushed his chair under the table and nodded to her. "Good evening, Miss Reynard."

"Good evening, Lord Ancroft."

He walked out with her friends trailing behind. Overall, he was pleased with the evening. Once she had recovered from her anger at him for attending her party, they had been able to have a lovely conversation. And he had learned a little more about her.

Once he arrived home, he strode to his study and searched out his file on Mrs. Griffon. According to her letter of reference, she had worked for Lord Westbury for twelve years. Westbury was Somerton's father, which meant nothing because Somerton's sister Genna was almost one and twenty.

Still, something niggled at his mind. Mrs. Griffon had been Sophie's governess for eight years. And the governess had been with Lord Westbury for twelve years, plus four years here. That meant Mrs. Griffon had twenty-four years of experience as a governess. But that didn't add up. Mrs. Griffon had told him she became a governess at the age of thirty after being widowed. He was positive that she had just turned forty-six this past year.

Had Mrs. Griffon lied to him?

It made no sense. Why would she say she had less experience? Or perhaps she had lied about her age. He was too tired to think about any of this tonight. He would discover the truth tomorrow.

Sophie grabbed the biscuit from her nightstand and prayed it would keep the nausea at bay. This morning had been the worst so far. She'd been positive that she wouldn't be able to keep her stomach settled. Perhaps it had been the larger than usual dinner last night.

Just remembering the dreadful night made her stomach roil again. She tried to breathe in deeply and forget how that scoundrel invaded her home and her party. But no matter how she tried, she could not forget the look of guilt on his face when Selby brought up Jennette's pregnancy. How could she have fallen for such a bastard? He'd made love to her in Venice, returned to an affair with Jennette, and then made love to Sophie again.

She was such a fool to think he was a softhearted man. He was nothing but a hardened rake. And she was a fool for thinking there was good in him. Well, never again would she make such a mistake.

Somehow, she would get through this mess she found herself in. She just didn't know how. Once her condition became known, there was a good chance her father would stop his allowance payments. Perhaps, she could manage with her clients. As long as she moved, of course.

Lying back against the soft pillows, she shut her eyes and another wave of nausea struck. She didn't want to move away. Her half brother was here, her half sisters, Genna and Bronwyn. She had her friends in London, too.

But this town was far too expensive to live in just on the small amount her matchmaking skills earned her. Somerton would support her, but she hated the idea of taking money from him and Victoria.

"What am I to do?" she whispered.

There was one other answer but she could never do it. If she told him about the baby, he would insist on marriage. She could not marry a man who treated women as he did. He was obviously not the type of rake who would reform. And she wasn't the kind of woman who would marry a man who kept mistresses or had affairs with married women. Not after seeing the effect it had on her mother and Somerton's mother.

She might just have to leave the country and start her life over. Take a new identity. Abandon her friends and family and be alone in a new city. She wasn't sure she could do such a drastic thing. However, if she did, at least it would be on her terms and not those of her parents.

How could she have been so wrong about him?

A knock scraped across the door and then her maid peered into the room. "Ma'am, you have callers this morning."

Sophie glanced over at her clock. It was only ten. Who could be calling at this hour? "Who is it?"

"Lady Genna and Miss Bronwyn."

She smiled hearing her half sisters had managed to pay a call. "Show them into the salon and return to help me dress."

"Yes, ma'am."

Sophie slowly eased out of bed. Her stomach seemed to have settled . . . finally. She quickly dressed in a blue and white striped muslin gown and put up her hair before visiting with her sisters.

"Genna! Bronwyn!" she said as she entered the room. "What are you both doing here?"

Genna rolled her eyes. "She," Genna said, inclining her head toward Bronwyn, "insisted something was wrong and that we needed to see you now."

Sophie cautiously turned to her ten-year-old half sister. Bronwyn was Genna's true sister, though only a few people knew it. She'd been raised by Victoria in her home for orphans. Once Somerton discovered his sister, he brought her into his home with Victoria.

Bronwyn had some abilities that Sophie had, only Sophie had no idea how strong her sister's intuition was yet. She assumed Bronwyn's sense would be weaker like Somerton. Sophie had always believed she received the majority of her abilities from her mother.

"Why would you think something was wrong, Bronwyn?"

"I had a dream that you were hurting," the younger replied. "Are you all right?"

"I am perfectly well," she lied.

Bronwyn's eyes narrowed. "No, you are not."

"Bronwyn, if Sophie says she is all right then she is!"

Sophie sat on the pale green chair and smiled at her sisters. "Genna is right."

Bronwyn looked up at her with curiosity. "I dreamed you are with child. My dreams are always correct."

Genna laughed. "Sophie's not even married, Bronwyn."

Sophie knew if she didn't tell her sisters the truth, Bronwyn would never stop pestering her about it. If she spoke about it to the wrong person, such as Victoria or Somerton, things would only get worse. "Girls, you mustn't tell a soul about this."

Genna stared at her. "You really are with child?"

Sophie pressed her lips together and nodded. "I believe I am."

Bronwyn sat back down in her chair and folded her arms over her chest. "I told you something was wrong, Genna."

"I need your solemn promise that you won't speak a word of this." She looked at Genna. "Not to your father," she said and then looked at Bronwyn. "And not to Victoria or Anthony."

Genna frowned but slowly nodded while Bronwyn just shrugged.

"Bronwyn, why don't you go ask Mrs. Holmes for some biscuits," Genna suggested.

"All right." Bronwyn skipped out of the room and down the hall.

Genna immediately moved to a chair closer to Sophie. "Who is the father, Sophie? Have you told him yet? Do you honestly believe you can keep this from Father for long?"

Sophie laughed at the questions. "One at a time, Genna. I shan't tell you the father's name."

"Does he know about the babe?"

"No. And I know I can't keep it from him or from Father for more than two months. I just haven't decided what I should do yet."

"Oh, Sophie," Genna cried. "You must tell the man . . . unless he is married. Please tell me he isn't married! That would be dreadful."

"He is not married." Sophie looked down at her skirts and played with the folds. "But he is in love with someone else."

"Perhaps, he is currently, but he might come to love you once you marry and have the child."

Sophie looked over at her innocent half sister. "Would that be enough for you? Hoping your husband *comes* to love you?"

Genna's blue eyes welled with tears. "I suppose not. Nevertheless, you are in a delicate position here. You rely on Father to pay most of your expenses, and your clients for extra money. Both of those sources of income may disappear if you think to have this baby without being married."

For only being twenty-one, Genna was a very intelligent young lady. "I have already thought about that, Genna."

"Then what will you do?"

Sophie wished she knew. After overhearing Jennette and Nicholas talk about her pregnancy, Sophie had thought of little else. The sense of betrayal from both of them wouldn't leave her. In her heart, she knew there was only one option.

"I shall most likely have to leave the country."

Chapter 15

Avis waited for Elizabeth to sit before she began. She had called them all to her house for only one reason. Something was going dreadfully wrong with their plan.

"Now," Avis said, adjusting her skirt. "Does anyone know why Nicholas and Sophie appeared to be angry with each other last night?"

"Actually, it looked far more like Sophie was mad at Nicholas than he at her," Elizabeth said. "It takes quite a lot to make Nicholas angry."

"But not so much for Sophie," Victoria added with a laugh.

Jennette nodded. "Perhaps one of us should pay a visit to Sophie to determine her ire."

"Brilliant idea, Jennette," Avis said with a smile. "But Sophie is very smart and will see right through us. One of us must have a valid reason to visit her. Otherwise she may become suspicious of us."

All the women glanced over at Jennette. Pink tinged her cheeks. "Am I to presume you have all figured it out, then?"

Avis laughed. "I do remember how the evening sickness affected you with Christian. While I could not get out of my bed until after ten and then only after eating dry toast and tea, you were up early and feeling wonderful until late afternoon. It wasn't difficult to determine your cause of illness the other night."

"Well, you all guessed correctly. Blackburn surprised me with his reaction. I'd thought he would be angry to have another child so soon after Christian, but he is so pleased." Jennette paused and sipped her tea. "So I will call on Sophie tomorrow to talk to her about the baby."

"Excellent," Avis said. "And do find out what has her so angry with Nicholas. I am certain it was not just the fact that he came to her party uninvited. There was something else going on and we must determine the cause so we can get them matched."

Nicholas sat down behind his desk and tapped his fingers impatiently against the cherry wood. He'd summoned Mrs. Griffon over ten minutes ago, and she still had not arrived for their meeting. Pulling out her references, he stared down at the letter from Lord Westbury. It definitely said she'd been in his employ for twelve years.

So who was lying?

Sophie seemed far too sincere about her praise of Mrs. Griffon. The obvious answer was Mrs. Griffon had lied about her age and previous employment. But either way, Mrs. Griffon had been in service as a governess to Sophie therefore she must know Sophie's father.

A soft knock rapped at the study door. "Did you wish to see me, my lord?"

He turned to look at the older woman. With gray strands lining her light brown hair and a few wrinkles around her eyes, she appeared close to fifty. "Yes, Mrs. Griffon," he said, rising at her entrance. "Please have a seat."

She furrowed her brow. "Is something wrong?"

"I have a few questions that I would like to speak with you about."

"Very well," she said as she sat.

Nicholas returned to his seat and picked up the letter from Lord Westbury. "Mrs. Griffon, when you came into my employ you told me you had married at twenty, and nine years later your husband died. A year after that you went into the employ of Lord Westbury as a governess."

"Yes, my lord. All that is correct."

"So, if you don't mind my asking, you are forty-six years old?"

"Yes."

He stared at her but only saw honesty shining in her eyes. "And you were only in Lord Westbury's employ?"

"Yes, sir." She looked down at her hands as she spoke.

"Who did you teach for Lord Westbury?"

"Lady Genna, of course."

"For all twelve years?" he pressed.

Mrs. Griffon sat up straight and stared at him. "What exactly are you implying, my lord?"

"I met a woman who told me you were her governess for eight years. And it wasn't Lady Genna." Nicholas watched as Mrs. Griffon's face drew pale.

"She told you?" she whispered.

"She was very excited that my daughter had you for a governess. She praised your intelligence and teaching methods. And she told me to insist you take Emma to the British Museum because you have a wealth of knowledge about it."

Mrs. Griffon clapped her hand over her mouth as she blinked away tears. "How is she, my lord? I haven't seen her in over four years."

"Very well. Can I assume the reason Lord Westbury paid you to teach Sophie was because he is her father?"

"My lord, I apologize for not telling you the exact truth. I did work for Lord Westbury for twelve years. Eight years with Miss Sophie and then I replaced Lady Genna's governess for four years."

Mrs. Griffon bowed her head and nodded. "Please, my lord, if anyone discovers the truth Lord Westbury will cut her off financially."

"I have no plans to announce that he is her father."

"Then for what purpose do you need the information?"

"Leverage, Mrs. Griffon." Seeing her frown, he added, "It might be enough to persuade her to marry me."

"Oh, my lord, she would be such a splendid marchioness."

Nicholas smiled fully. "I believe she would indeed, Mrs. Griffon."

The next morning, Sophie finally made it downstairs by eleven. The morning sickness seemed to be getting worse with every passing day. Her breasts were so full and tender, even putting on stays bothered her.

She had never been one to cry much but every little thing seemed to make her eyes water.

Glancing down at her calendar, she was relieved to see she had no clients today. She sat down behind her desk and finished her correspondence before picking up her book and returning to the salon. A nice day of reading would be just the thing to return her spirits to normal.

Only as she attempted to read the words on the page, the letters blurred together as her mind wandered back to her condition. She would have to make her decision soon. If leaving was her one option, then she would be forced to deal with her father's wrath.

Perhaps she could convince him that this was the best for both of them. By leaving the country, no one would ever discover her father's identity. That should please him enough to continue giving her an allowance. Then she could let a small apartment in Venice and build her business there. Without his money, she had no way of supporting herself and a baby.

But the biggest obstacle to leaving was Nicholas. No matter what had happened between him and Jennette, he deserved to know about his child. He would be furious if she had a boy. And worse, she wondered, if boy or girl, he would want to keep the child as he'd done with Emma. Sophie could not leave her child.

God, what a horrible mess this was.

"Ma'am, you have a caller," Hendricks announced from the threshold. "Lady Blackburn is here to see you."

Sophie stared down at her hands as anger filled her. Perhaps she should just confront Jennette and be done with this mess and her. "Send her in."

"Shall I ring for tea?"

"No, Lady Blackburn will not be here long enough for tea." Even as Sophie said the words, her eyes blurred with tears. While she had not been as close with Jennette as the others, the idea of losing a precious friendship was like a knife to her heart.

"Sophie," Jennette said with a smile as she entered the room.

"Jennette," Sophie said tightly. "What are you doing here at this hour?"

Jennette sat on the pale yellow chair. "I have some news I wanted to share with you."

"I already know of your news."

Jennette frowned and tilted her head. "I assumed you determined my condition but you don't seem pleased about it."

"Are you? Pleased that is?"

"I am now. At first I was concerned about what Matthew would say. He had wanted to wait a little longer so we'd been using the sponges you recommended."

The same vinegar soaked sponges that Sophie had completely forgotten about with Nicholas that night in this very room. Had she used them the time they made love in the chair, she might not be in this condition. "So, Blackburn is fine with raising another man's child?"

Jennette shot out of her seat. "What are you talking about?"

"I know, Jennette. I know the truth. I heard you and Ancroft talking in the garden at your party."

Jennette's blue eyes widened. "I have no idea what you are talking about, Sophie. There is nothing between Nicholas and I but friendship."

"And a child."

"A child? Sophie, what is this about?"

"I know the baby is his, not Blackburn's."

Jennette's mouth gaped. "I cannot believe you would think such a thing! You are the one who matched us! You are the one who told me he was my true love."

"You wouldn't be the first married woman to have an affair once the heir is born," Sophie said bitterly. She'd had such a good feeling about matching Jennette and Blackburn. How could she have been so wrong?

"I would never do such a thing, Sophie. And you offend me with your insinuation."

"Enough, Jennette." Sophie rose from her chair and folded her arms over her chest. "I don't want to hear your lies any longer. Just get out of my house."

"Gladly," Jennette said, then turned and strode from the room.

Nicholas walked toward the receiving salon in Sophie's house just as Jennette stormed down the stairs. Knowing Jennette's wild nature, he wondered what had set her off this afternoon. He stopped to greet her.

"Good afternoon, Jennette."

She glanced up with a look of fury in her sapphire eyes. "You are here to see her?"

"Yes, why?"

"Good luck. She is positively mad. Perhaps her skills as a medium have addled her mind." Jennette retrieved her bonnet from the footman and quickly tied the hat under her chin.

"What is this all about?" Nicholas asked softly in an attempt to calm Jennette.

"She actually thinks you are the father of the baby I carry."

Nicholas tried not to laugh but failed miserably. "She thinks that you and I . . ."

"Yes." Jennette walked toward the door. "Good day, Nicholas."

He mumbled something but took the opportunity to run up the stairs as Hendricks opened the door for Jennette.

"My lord!" Hendricks called from the hall. "You cannot go up there unannounced."

Nicholas heard Hendricks shout for some footmen but nothing would stop him from seeing Sophie today. He walked into the salon and halted. She stood in front of the window with tears streaming down her cheeks. He had never seen anyone look so forlorn in his life.

"Sophie?" he whispered.

She turned toward him with fire in her wet eyes. "Get out of here right now, Nicholas. You caused all this mess."

Instead of doing as she requested, he slowly approached her. "Sophie, what have I done?"

"You have ruined everything!"

"I don't understand," he said softly. "What have I ruined and how?"

"Jennette's marriage and my life," she cried.

"What are you talking about?" He heard the hard footfalls of footmen running up the stairs. If he didn't get her calmed soon, she would force him to leave.

"You had an affair with Jennette. She is carrying your baby."

"What?" he shouted.

Two footmen raced into the room. "Would you like us to evict the man, ma'am?"

"Yes." She stared at Nicholas. "You know what you have done. Now get out of my house and my life forever."

"How could you think for one moment I would dishonor Jennette that way?" Nicholas attempted to shrug off the footmen's hands on his arms to no avail. They started to drag him out of the room. "Don't think for one moment that this is over, Sophie. I will be back."

"Do not bother," she said, furiously wiping tears off her cheeks. "I will not allow you entry into my home again."

Once out of the salon, he yanked his arms out of the footmen's grip and strode down the steps and out of her house. He stopped before entering his carriage, wondering how she could have come to this odd conclusion. There was one person who just might know.

"Sir?" his groomsman asked. "Would you prefer to return home?"

"No, Lord Blackburn's home, if you please."

"Yes, my lord."

While the carriage rolled down the cobbled streets, he examined the situation from Sophie's point of view. She knew he'd loved Jennette. But why would that cause Sophie to make such an obtuse supposition?

It made no sense to him.

Upon entering Jennette's home, he waited for her in the small parlor. The room always made him smile. While Sophie's home was filled with warm pastels, Jennette's home reflected her vivid artistic personality. Instead of pastels, the rooms were painted or wallpapered with rich jewel tones.

"What did she tell you?" Jennette said as she entered the room with an angry swish of silk.

Nicholas turned around and smiled at the woman he once thought he loved. In truth, he would always love her, just not as he once had. Something had changed in him since meeting Sophie.

"I believe she thinks you and I have had an illicit affair."

Jennette threw her hands in the air. "Why would she think such a thing?"

Nicholas frowned. He'd wondered the same thing on the trip here. "I have no idea."

"She told me that she overheard us talking in the garden the night of my party. We were discussing my condition but how did she make the leap to this being your baby."

"Perhaps she didn't stay for the entire discussion. Or for the part where your husband joined us."

"I still don't understand why that would make her jump to such an odd conclusion. You and I have never been anything but friends."

Nicholas blew out a breath. Perhaps it was time to tell Jennette the truth. "Jennette, sit down with me," he said, patting the cushion of the sofa.

"What is wrong, Nicholas? You looked a little apprehensive." Jennette sat down next to him.

He took her hand in his. "Jennette, Sophie knows something about me that no one else knows. It's the reason she believes what she overheard is true."

Jennette's black brows furrowed deeply. "What can she possibly know that I do not? I have known you forever."

"When Sophie and I first met, she found a letter you had written me several years ago." He paused, dreading this conversation but understanding he had to have it. The time had come to put his feelings for her in the past.

"And?"

"I had kept the letter because it reminded me so much of you. It was filled with your enthusiasm about the social season."

Jennette shrugged slightly. "I don't understand how her finding a letter like that would matter."

"Because with her abilities, she was able to read my emotions on the letter."

"Again, how does that relate to her wild assumptions?"

Nicholas sighed. "She knew that I was in love with you."

Chapter 16

Nicholas had never wanted to run from a room as badly as he did at that moment. Heat scorched his cheeks so he turned his head away from her amazed stare. Telling Jennette had been a mistake. He felt it immediately as she pulled her hand out of his grip.

"Oh, Nicholas," she said with a sigh.

"Jennette, it was years ago," Nicholas said, finally turning back to face her. "Before Blackburn returned to your life."

She gave him a slight smile. "Why didn't you tell me?"

"How could I?" He rose and walked to the window. "You were Selby's baby sister. I had known you since you were eight. How was I to explain that my feelings for you had changed from brotherly to something lascivious?"

"I thought we could talk about anything," she whispered. "I had told you how I felt about every little thing that happened to me."

He turned. "You never told me about Blackburn."

"Touché. But that doesn't explain why you didn't tell me."

"After your betrothed died, I just didn't think you would be interested in me. And truthfully, I didn't have the courage." Nicholas walked back to the sofa. "I was certain you didn't feel the same way for me."

Jennette stared at the rug. "You might have been right. I felt so guilty over John's death."

"Because you didn't love him. You loved Blackburn."

Jennette only nodded. "You are most likely right that even if you had confessed your affection for me, I would have turned you down."

"Because you loved Blackburn," Nicholas said again. As uncomfortable as this conversation was, it felt good to clear the air. While he would always love Jennette, since meeting Sophie, his feelings for her had changed.

"I suppose so." She smiled slightly. "What are you going to do now?"

Nicholas leaned back against the cushion and shook his head. "I have no idea. How can I convince her that I don't love you that way any longer?"

Jennette giggled. "You could tell her the truth."

"What do you mean?"

"Tell Sophie you love *her*, not me."

He closed his eyes in thought. Did he really love Sophie? Or was it just lust? He honestly didn't know. He felt certain that if he married her, they could be happy. But was that enough? Was that love?

"It's not that easy, Jennette."

"So what are you going to do?"

"Make her see reason." And the only way he could do that was to talk to her without her henchmen throwing him out of her house. His lips lifted slightly.

"Oh, I know that smile," Jennette said. "What devious thoughts are you thinking?"

"Nothing at all." At least nothing he could tell her about. Tonight he would get into Sophie's house, one way or another.

Sophie placed her book on the table and then snuffed out the candles in the parlor. No matter how hard she'd tried, she could not concentrate on reading the entire day. After Jennette and Nicholas left, her thoughts had remained on them. Jennette had appeared very offended by Sophie's insinuation of an affair.

She said good night to the footman on duty for the night and walked upstairs. Her mind buzzed with questions. Was it possible that she was wrong about Jennette? It seemed as if she seldom got anything right since her trip to Venice.

Maybe she had jumped to the wrong conclusion.

Entering her room, her maid assisted her with her clothing and into a nightgown. Instead of lying on her bed, Sophie paced the room examining the evidence in her mind. All she had was the knowledge that Nicholas loved Jennette and an overheard conversation regarding a baby.

Sophie stopped by the window as a cool breeze fluttered the marigold curtains. She glanced outside at the quiet street. She was right. Jennette had told Nicholas that it happened the night he returned from Venice. And that they both had had too much to drink.

She rested her head against the window frame. In the time she had known Nicholas, she had never seen him drink more than two glasses of any type of spirit. While Jennette could drink most men under the table.

The sound of a floorboard squeaking made her look back into the room just in time to see Nicholas before he clapped his hand over her mouth.

"Not a word. If you call for a footman, I will carry you out of here before they arrive. Then I will take you to my house until we have this discussion. Do you understand?"

Sophie swallowed the lump of fear in her throat. She had never heard him sound so furious. Nor so fierce. With a hand over her mouth, she had no choice but to nod.

Slowly he moved his hand away. She turned to face him and his ire. "Why are you here? And how did you get in?"

"You left a window open in the back of the house."

"But how did you get upstairs without anyone noticing?" She moved away from the heat of his body before her thoughts went in a very bad direction.

"I have been in your house since eight. I just had to wait until your servants went to dinner and then I sneaked up here. Perhaps Somerton was right that you need more footmen."

"Why are you here, Nicholas?" she demanded as her own anger escalated. He had no right to be here, invading her home as he did her thoughts.

"I told you this morning that our conversation was not finished." Spying the key to her room on her nightstand, he grabbed it and then locked the door.

Now she was trapped in her bedroom with the one man she seemed unable to resist. "There is nothing left to discuss."

He strode back across the room until he stood before her. Dressed completely in black, he appeared sinister and cold. "How could you think for one moment that I would have an affair with Jennette?"

She backed up a step until she was against one of the cherry posters of her bed. "It wasn't that hard to determine. You love her. She is with child and very upset by it. I heard her tell you that it happened the night you returned from Venice. And that you both had had too much to drink."

He folded his arms over his wide chest and smirked. "And that was all you heard?"

"That was enough!"

"No, that was enough for you to make the wrong conclusion. Had you stayed longer, you would have heard us talking about the fact that Jennette was only upset by her condition because her husband wanted to start improvements on the estates. He wanted more time between the children, and Jennette was concerned that he wouldn't love this child as much as Christian."

"That doesn't explain how she said it happened the night you returned from Venice."

He sat down on the edge of the bed. "Jennette had invited me for dinner. She and Blackburn were both a little foxed by the time I left. I only had one glass of brandy."

Sophie bit down on her lip as tears blinded her eyes. She should have trusted him. But how could she? Even after two months, she barely knew him. Still, she should have let him explain before jumping to conclusions.

"I'm sorry," she whispered. She glanced back at him and her heart pounded madly in her chest. It dawned on her that all the time he'd been in the room she only wore a thin white nightgown. Her nipples hardened into peaks so tight they almost hurt.

He stood and approached her slowly. He lifted her chin with his warm hand. "The only woman I have been with since Venice is you," he said softly. "The only woman I have wanted to be with since Venice is you."

She felt horrible about how she treated him. She stared into his sensual brown eyes and was lost. Rising on her toes, she inclined her head toward him.

"If you kiss me now," he whispered, "I will not leave your bed until morning."

"Good," she replied, before moving her lips over his.

As his velvety tongue touched hers, all the exciting sensations of being with Nicholas returned even stronger than before. Desire damped her folds as she attempted to push his jacket off his shoulders. He pushed her hands away and yanked off his jacket. In one swift movement, he slid her nightgown down until it fell at her feet.

Standing naked before him, she felt timid about the slight changes in her body that she could already see. Would he notice them too? He pulled her against him and kissed her deeply. His hands skimmed down her bare back until he cupped her derrière.

She worked at the buttons on his shirt, eager to feel his skin next to hers. He released a low growl before moving away from her.

"Lay down," he commanded as he tore at his shirt.

Sophie did as he requested and then watched as he exposed more skin to her wanton gaze. With his chest bared, he sat down on the bed to yank off his boots. She couldn't help but glide her hand up his muscled back as he worked at his boots. He turned toward her with such a deep smile her heart beat faster.

He stood and slid his trousers down his hips until his erection came into view. Her hands itched to touch him everywhere. Moving to her knees, she reached out to caress his chest until he hissed. She moved her hand lower until she reached his curly hair and penis. With a whispered caress, she touched him. She glanced up to see his eyes shutter as she slid her hand over the top of him. She moved closer and let her tongue circle the top of him.

"Oh, God, Sophie," he muttered hoarsely.

Since he hadn't told her to stop, she slipped him into her mouth. She brought him in and out of her mouth. The feel of fullness in her mouth excited her.

"Oh, stop," he moaned. He pushed her back on the bed and covered her body with his. "Do you have any idea how much I want you right now?"

"Mmm," she said as he kissed her neck. "I think I do."

He trailed hot kisses down her neck until he reached her taut nipples. As his mouth enclosed over one, she tried not to wince. Her breasts had never been this sensitive. But as his tongue swept across her nipple the pain turned to exquisite pleasure.

Nicholas tickled his tongue down her belly and farther until he reached her clitoris. As his mouth found her sensitive nub, she bucked her hips. He could feel her muscles tightening as he stroked her. Slipping a finger into her wetness, his control weakened.

"Nicholas," she moaned softly. "Now."

He smiled against her soft thigh. "Anything you say, Sophie."

Positioning himself over her, he entered her silky depths slowly. The desire he felt for her was unlike anything he had with other women. As he filled her completely, he wanted to stay there forever but her wet warmth was like a siren's call to him. Stroking her, he watched her face as desire overtook her.

"Nicholas," she whispered haltingly. She arched her back as her spasms rocked him.

Unable to control himself any longer, he let go to the sensation. His body shook with pleasure. Finally, he eased himself down on her.

"Sophie," he said against her neck. He had done it again. Instead of withdrawing, he'd stayed inside of her. What was wrong with him that he lost control when she was near? This had never happened with another woman. Not even his mistresses. Only one time had he forgotten with Maggie.

Knowing he had to be hurting her, he moved off her to lie on the bed. He pulled her closer until her head rested on his chest.

"Sophie," he said softly.

Her fingers splayed across his chest. "Yes?"

"We really should talk."

Her hand stopped its gentle caress. "And what topic would you like to discuss?"

"Shall we start with your father?" he asked and then pushed a few black tendrils off her forehead.

She shook her head. "No. That is a topic best left closed."

"I already figured it out."

She rose up and then looked down at him. Her face lined with agony. "You could not possibly know."

"My curiosity was raised by Somerton's overprotective attitude toward you. He appeared to be acting like an older brother."

"I already told you that Somerton is a longtime friend."

He smiled at her. "Yes, you did. But you should never have told me you knew Mrs. Griffon," he said, drawing a finger down her jaw.

"She never would have told you who my father was!"

Nicholas caressed her cheek with his palm. "It wasn't hard to determine. She had only worked for one employer before coming into my house. So if you hadn't told me that she had been your teacher, I would have continued to assume she had only been Lady Genna's governess."

She lay back against the pillows and covered her face with her hands. "How could I have been so foolish?"

Slowly he removed her hands from her face. "You weren't being foolish. You were pleased that I had such a wonderful governess for my daughter. You wanted to be certain I knew she was excellent."

"He is going to be furious," she cried. "I might even lose my home!"

"Sophie, I would never tell a soul about this." He picked up her hand and brought it to his lips. "I would never do anything to hurt you."

"How can I trust you?" she whispered.

"Other than our rather peculiar first meeting when I told you my name was Nico, I have not lied to you. You know more of my secrets than any other person."

"Only because I sensed them," she retorted.

"Because I let you sense them," he insisted, then kissed the tip of her nose. "You don't know all my secrets."

"Indeed?" she said as she rolled on her side. "Tell me a secret that no one else knows about you. And not about Jennette because I already learned that one."

Nicholas lay back and watched her gray eyes sparkling in the flickering candlelight. Warmth suffused his body. "Very well, but if this gets out, I will be forced to seek vengeance."

She smiled at him. "Agreed."

"I hate rats."

She cocked her head. "Hate or are you scared of them?"

He closed his eyes and remembered what led to his fear. He'd never told a soul about this. "Terrified of the filthy creatures."

"Why?" Her thumb gently stroked his cheekbone.

"When I was nine, my brother Simon and I were at the estate in the Cotswolds. We were exploring the old dowager house that had fallen into disrepair. As I walked across the room, the floorboards gave out and I fell into the dirt cellar. It was pitch-black and I couldn't find the stairs."

"And there were rats in the cellar?" she asked.

He nodded. "Simon couldn't find anything to help me out. The part of the building where the stairs were had collapsed so he couldn't get to them. He told me he would run back to the estate to get help."

"How long did it take him?"

Nicholas squeezed his eyes tighter as the pain returned. "It wasn't Simon who prolonged my stay in that dank place."

"Then who?"

"My father," he muttered, disgusted again with how his father had treated him as a child.

"What?"

"When my father heard that we had disobeyed

him, he wanted me to face my penance in that cellar. It took them five hours to return for me. As I sat there, I could hear the rats scuttling across the floor and squeaking."

"But you might have been seriously hurt!"

"I know, but thankfully I wasn't. I only had a few scratches from the fall. Still, the sound of those disgusting creatures scared me to death."

She kissed him softly. "You do realize that they were probably only field mice."

"I know that now. But when you're nine and stuck in a dark place with only rodents for company . . ."

She cupped his cheeks and kissed him again. "Shh, I cannot imagine what that must have been like. And I hate your father for putting you through it."

"So do I," he murmured before moving his lips to hers. As much as he enjoyed talking with her, desire flared again with a simple kiss.

She pulled back slightly. "You should leave now," she said breathlessly.

He curled his hand around her neck and brought her closer to him. "You really don't want me to leave yet."

"Are you reading *my* mind now?" she said before kissing him deeply.

Chapter 17

Sophie woke slowly, blinking as she gingerly lifted her head off Nicholas's chest. She looked down at his sleeping face for several moments. What would it be like to wake every morning next to him? Would they lie together and confess to more secrets about themselves? Would they tire of each other after a few years?

Her lips lifted into a smile. The idea of becoming bored with Nicholas seemed impossible. Her heart told her to forget her intuition and admit her condition to him. He would love their child and hopefully come to love her as well. But something stopped her.

Marrying her would cause untold problems for him. His father would never consent to her becoming the next duchess. The only possible chance of gaining his permission would be to tell him the identity of her father. And that would cause countless issues for her and her family. None of it mattered anyway. His father had threatened to disinherit Nicholas for marrying an unacceptable woman.

If she told him about the baby, nothing would stop

him from marrying her. Even if it was the worst thing for him and his family. How could she do that to him?

A wave of queasiness washed over her. She laid her head back down on the pillow and blew out a few deep breaths. Praying she wouldn't disturb him, she opened her nightstand and pulled out a biscuit she'd hidden there. She chewed the biscuit quickly and then reclined her head on the pillow again.

She stared up at the white ceiling and wondered how her life had become so complicated. While she had apologized to Nicholas for her dreadful assumption regarding Jennette, Sophie would have to speak with Jennette, too. She doubted her hardheaded friend would forgive her so easily.

Warm lips kissed her bare shoulder. She closed her eyes and smiled as delicious shivers raced through her body. Perhaps he was the secret to relieving her upset stomach.

He rolled on his side and looked down at her. He brushed a crumb off the corner of her mouth with a smile. "Eating in bed?"

She needed a good excuse for why she would eat something at this hour. "My stomach had been in knots earlier this evening over you and Jennette. I just could not eat."

He stared at her in disbelief. "You keep food in your nightstand?"

"Don't worry, it won't attract the mice. Besides, I have two cats that roam the house and keep the mice in line."

"If you say so." He groaned. "I should leave before we're discovered."

She raked her hand through his thick chestnut hair. "You should," she said with a sigh.

"If you keep looking at me like that, I won't leave."

"But you truly must," she whispered. "I shall be ruined if you stay."

"Ruining you is one of my favorite things to do." He bent forward and kissed her softly. "But alas, I shall leave."

She didn't want him to depart yet. "Nicholas, what am I to say to Jennette? She's bound to tell the others what I said and they shall all hate me for it."

He wiped away a tear from her cheek. "I've known Jennette since she was a child. She is wild and unpredictable but one of the most tolerant women I know. Jennette will forgive you."

"How can you be so certain? You know how stubborn she can be. What I said to her was dreadful."

"She's your friend. And if you speak with her tomorrow, or rather, today, she will understand."

"I can't tell her everything!" Why couldn't he understand that? "I can't tell her that I made that foolish assumption because you love her."

He looked away from her. "Yes, you can."

"She won't believe me," Sophie said bitterly. "She will think I'm mad."

"I told her how I had felt about her," he mumbled.

Sophie's hand stilled on his cheek. "You told her?"

"Yes," he answered, blowing out a long sigh.

She bit down on her lip. "That must have been incredibly difficult."

"Jennette is a gracious woman and understood without making me feel pitied."

She felt terrible about this mess she'd caused. Her damned jealousy was the reason. "I'm sorry my actions caused you to have to confess to her."

"I should have done it a long time ago."

She nodded but knew it would not have made a difference. Jennette was meant to be with Blackburn, not Nicholas. She wondered how he felt about Jennette now. Did he still love her? She wanted him to be happy and find a woman who could make him happy and feel loved. But she still had no idea who was destined for Nicholas. The only thing she knew was . . . it would not be her. She could not let him make such a terrible mistake. Marrying her would make him an outcast.

"Can you make a distraction so I can leave here without being seen?" he asked as he clamored out of bed.

Not trusting her stomach, she stayed in the bed and watched him dress. "I will call the footman upstairs and then you can go out the front door."

"It will be locked," he said flatly. "I shall go out the way I came in."

"Be careful," she whispered.

He turned and looked down at her intensely. "Always."

Sophie blew out a long breath before knocking on Jennette's front door. A footman opened the door and led her into the receiving salon. She bit her lip in anticipation of Jennette's arrival. Instead of sitting on the settee, she paced the room.

"Are you here to apologize?"

Sophie turned at the sound of Jennette's cold voice. "Yes, I am. Jennette, I am dreadfully sorry for the accusation I mistakenly hurled at you yesterday. Will you please accept my apology?"

Jennette slowly walked into the room. "On one condition."

"Oh?"

Jennette smiled. "That you tell me how you came to that odd conclusion."

"Of course," Sophie said and proceeded to tell Jennette everything that led her to such a disastrous supposition.

A heavy silence filled the room as Jennette waited for the footman to bring the tea and then leave. Once he was gone, she said, "Nicholas paid a call on me yesterday. He told me he had loved me. It was before Blackburn, but I don't understand why he never came to me."

"You were his dearest friend's younger sister. He may have felt Selby would have thought it unseemly. He may have been concerned you would reject him."

"Perhaps." Jennette frowned slightly. "Did you ever see him for me?"

Sophie smiled and shook her head. "No. I only ever saw Blackburn for you. He is your perfect match."

Jennette poured tea and then sat back with a sigh. "Oh, did you hear about Lady Cantwell?"

"What about her?"

"I heard from Avis that Lady Cantwell died in her sleep last night." Jennette sipped her tea. "I didn't think she was so near death. She always seemed so cantankerous. I never thought about her dying."

"She's dead?" Sophie's mind whirled. Why hadn't she known? Why hadn't she seen it coming?

"You had no idea? She was one of your clients. I would have thought you would sense something like this."

So would Sophie. Why didn't she sense this? Was

this yet another example of her abilities slipping away from her?

Even as she left Jennette's home, her mind continued to spin with thoughts of Lady Cantwell's death. The carriage rolled down the streets of Mayfair. Sophie had never lost a client before now but she was convinced she should have seen it coming. The last three times Sophie had read Lady Cantwell, she'd seen the same thing—blackness. Could that have been the sign she should have been looking for?

The only people she'd ever seen just darkness for were Lady Cantwell and . . . Nicholas.

"Oh, God," she whispered in the empty carriage. "Is Nicholas next?"

The Duke of Belford tapped his fingers impatiently on his desk, waiting for Witham to arrive. Far too much time had passed since their last meeting. He needed Nicholas married off soon. He covered his mouth with a handkerchief as another coughing fit struck him. Pulling away the white cloth, red specks dotted the linen. Every day more blood appeared. He feared his physician was overly optimistic in his assessment that he would have a year to live.

The only thing he still did not have in order was his wastrel son. He'd be damned if he let Nicholas ruin everything he'd built.

"Lord Witham, Your Grace," his butler announced from the threshold.

"Witham, come in here," the duke ordered.

"Yes, Your Grace." Witham almost ran into the room. "I am sorry to be late, Your Grace."

"Just tell me what you have discovered. Since I have

not heard any rumors, am I to assume your daughter has not publicly kissed him yet?"

Witham sank to the chair across from him. "I am sorry, Your Grace. We had everything planned for the Tilsons' party but your son never attended."

The duke frowned. "Where did he go that night?"

"The man I have following him told me he attended a small dinner party at Miss Reynard's home. The Selbys, Blackburns, Kendals, and Somertons were in attendance, too."

He hated to admit that other than Lord Somerton, Nicholas did keep excellent company. And since Somerton's marriage to that little nothing of a woman, he had settled into marriage nicely. "So Miss Reynard is a friend to them?"

"Yes, Your Grace. She is acquainted with the wives."

This explained why Nicholas thought her to be acceptable. But friends did not make the woman in the duke's eyes. "Do you know if he has spent any other time with Miss Reynard?"

Witham's beady eyes slid downward. "Yes, Your Grace."

"Well speak up, man. When?"

"Two nights ago, my man followed him back to Miss Reynard's home. Your son entered the house through an open window in the back of the house. He stayed until half past three."

Damn that boy. He would never learn. "The Middletons' ball is tonight. I will make certain Nicholas attends. You make sure your daughter is caught in a compromising position with him. If not, you may find my son's interests lie elsewhere."

"Yes, Your Grace. Justine will do everything in her power to entice him."

"No, I want you to arrange this personally. Do not leave it up to your dim-witted daughter to attempt to entice him."

"What do you want me to do?"

The duke sat back for a moment and then smiled. After explaining everything to Witham, he waved his hand in dismissal to the viscount. Now he just had to determine a reason why Nicholas had to attend that ball tonight. As Witham departed, he had his butler send a note to Nicholas.

Nicholas sat down and stared at his father. He had spoken with his father's physician several days ago and understood that consumption was slowly killing him. If he was a better person he would feel some pity for the man. But after a childhood filled with nothing but scorn, Nicholas felt numb toward him.

"I need you to do me a favor," the old duke then coughed.

The hair on Nicholas's neck stood up. "What favor?"

"It has nothing to do with marriage, Nicholas." His father handed him a sealed note. "I would like this personally delivered to Lord Middleton this evening at his ball."

"Why tonight?"

"Because Middleton is busy this afternoon and he needs to see it before tomorrow. If I leave this up to a footman, Middleton won't get it in time. It's about an investment we both have. He needs to act on it tomorrow morning or it will be too late and he will lose money. You will need to wait for a reply."

Nicholas studied his father. Consumption had

taken its toll on the duke. His father had always been a tall, strong man, but now, he appeared feeble. A cane hooked onto the corner of his desk.

"Will you do it?" he asked.

"Of course, Father." Nicholas couldn't remember the last time he'd called the old duke that. After tucking the note into his jacket, he rose. "I take it that is all?"

"No, sit down, Nicholas. There is one more thing I would like to discuss with you."

"Oh?" Nicholas sat back down and waited.

"I have heard a rumor that you are getting far too close with this Miss Reynard. Some people say she is a matchmaker and if that is the only reason you are in her company, then I approve, as long as her match is someone on my list. However, if there is more to this, you had best realize keeping a mistress after you marry requires discretion."

Nicholas shot to his feet. "What I do and with whom is my business, sir."

"True, as long as you do not care about the money you might lose."

Nicholas smiled slightly. "And if I don't?"

"Then expect a hard first few years as duke. The estates have been bringing in far less income the past few years. You will need every pound just to maintain them. I promise you won't get a penny from me."

"You will do what you think is necessary, Father. And I will do what I think is right." If only his father knew just how useless his threats really were. Nicholas rose and walked out of the room before his father could stop him.

* * *

"Miss Littlebury, this is indeed a surprise," Sophie said, entering her study. "I thought you believed I was a charlatan."

A splotchy red blush tinged the woman's cheeks. "My friend Miss Hall said you were correct about her match."

Miss Hall? Sophie thought back to her many clients over the past few years but could not remember one by that name. There had been a few ladies who had tried to deceive her by using a false name. "Is she married now?"

"No, but she expects a proposal this Season."

Sophie frowned. "What are you truly about, Miss Littlebury?"

Her pale blue eyes widened in surprise. "What do you mean?"

"I know of no one named Miss Hall. The last time you were here, you strode from the room declaring me a fraud. So what exactly is your purpose in coming here today?"

Miss Littlebury bristled. "How dare you little nobody accuse me of coming here on false pretenses."

Sophie smiled slightly. The woman wanted something from her, but Sophie didn't know what. Using her softest tone, she said, "I didn't accuse you of anything. I would just like to know why you came here again."

Miss Littlebury blinked and looked up at the plain white ceiling. "My father would like me to marry someone. I am not certain he is the man I should marry." She bit her lip and glanced down at her hands. "You did help a friend of mine make a superior match. Miss Elizabeth Tyson is now the Countess Rotherham. She is so happy, Miss Reynard. I apologize for not speaking the truth before now."

"Very well, Miss Littlebury," Sophie said, holding out her hand. "Take my hand and think about love . . . what you want in a husband."

As Miss Littlebury did, Sophie felt the familiar dizziness and closed her eyes. Just like the last time she read Miss Littlebury everything remained faint as if a sheer fabric covered the scene. There were two men and while Nicholas was one of them, this time he remained farther in the background.

"I see two men in your life right now," Sophie whispered. "One is blonde with green eyes and very handsome." Well, handsome from what she could determine.

"And the other?"

"He is farther in the back. I'm not certain what it means."

"Who is it?" she urged.

"I believe it is Lord Ancroft," Sophie said softly. "I am not sure why he would be so far in the distance."

"What about the other man? What is his name?"

Sophie concentrated but couldn't determine a full name for the man. "I can only get Edward or Edmund. Something similar to that."

"I don't believe I know of any man with that name."

Sophie kept her eyes shut but knew the girl was lying. Edward was a very common name and even Sophie knew several men with that name. She opened her eyes and saw a gleam of satisfaction in Miss Littlebury's blue eyes.

"My father would like me to marry Lord Ancroft," Miss Littlebury admitted. "I would like to be the duchess but after seeing Miss Tyson marry for love . . ." Her voice trailed off as she glanced away.

"Miss Littlebury, I will tell you something only if I have your complete confidence."

Miss Littlebury turned her head back toward Sophie. "Of course, I shall not speak of anything we have conversed about today."

"Very well, I believe the other man is the one for you to find true happiness with. I read Lord Ancroft and you were not the woman for him."

"Then who is?"

"I could not determine his match. With you, things are hazy but with him, there was nothing to see." Sophie still wondered if it was related to death as was the case with Lady Cantwell. Was he fated to an early demise?

"So," Miss Littlebury started, "you don't see any specific woman with Lord Ancroft."

Hearing the scheming tone of her voice caused the hairs on her neck to rise. "What do you mean?"

She smiled as she removed her hands from Sophie. "Thank you for your time, Miss Reynard. I must be off now."

"Miss Littlebury . . ."

"Yes?" Miss Littlebury stood and picked up her reticule. She fished some money out and tossed it on the table.

"Please believe me when I say that there is another man for you."

"Well, if you can ever determine his name, please let me know, Miss Reynard. Good day." She turned and departed the room with a rustle of muslin.

Sophie remained seated as she watched the younger lady leave. She rubbed her tummy. The unsettled sensation would not leave her as easily as Miss Littlebury had.

As the late afternoon turned to evening, the disquieting feeling only increased. She wandered back into her study after supper and picked up the money Miss Littlebury had left on the table. Holding the coins, Sophie closed her eyes.

A vision of Nicholas and Miss Littlebury came to her. The image appeared surrounded in darkness. Sophie dropped the coins as if they had burned her.

Nicholas was in trouble. And Sophie was certain, Miss Littlebury was the cause. Could some action of Miss Littlebury's be the impetus to his death? Not if Sophie had anything to do with it.

Chapter 18

Nicholas waited impatiently as his valet brushed out his jacket. The idea of attending the Middleton ball had left a bad taste in his mouth, but he had no clue why. Well, there was one idea—Sophie. He'd hoped to spend more time with her this evening and possibly well into the night. Perhaps after he had delivered the note to Lord Middleton, he could leave and go to her.

The woman seemed to have become imprinted on his brain, and if he truly wanted to be honest, his heart as well. Since he'd met her, he rarely thought of Jennette any longer. Instead, all his attention focused on Sophie.

"Here we go, my lord," Lane said, bringing the jacket to him.

"Thank you." Nicholas pulled on the jacket and straightened the lapels. A knock scraped on the door. Expecting Emma, he said, "Come in."

A footman opened the door with a frown. "There is a Miss Reynard here to see you, my lord." He lowered his voice to a whisper, "She arrived unattended by a maid, sir."

Nicholas smiled at the idea of Sophie being in his home but then frowned. She knew they could not meet here as long as Emma was home. "That is all right, Liam. Show her to the receiving salon. I will be there presently."

"As you wish, my lord." Liam backed out of the room and closed the door behind him.

"How do I look, Lane?"

His valet brushed at a piece of invisible lint then stepped back. "Very well, my lord."

"Excellent." Nicholas walked down the marble stairs. He stopped at the threshold of the receiving salon and his heart pounded at the sight. Sophie was braiding Emma's hair. Both were giggling about something Sophie had said.

In that instant, he knew he loved her. And he had no doubts that Emma would come to love her, too. Now it was just a matter of convincing Sophie to become his wife. He had to persuade her to not be worried about what the gossips would say. It didn't matter as long as they loved each other.

He would have to tell her the truth about his father's money. Having the money would make things easier, but they would be fine without it, too. He had plenty of money invested.

He leaned against the doorframe just watching them. Sophie had a look of delight on her face as she finished braiding his daughter's hair. He wanted to see that same look every day for the rest of his life.

Of course he had no idea if she loved him. She appeared terribly concerned about finding him the right match. That didn't seem like the actions of a woman in love. What if she rejected his proposal again?

He couldn't think about that right now.

"Now," he said, moving away from the doorframe, "what are you two giggling about?"

Emma giggled again as Sophie gasped.

"Papa, Miss Sophie put my hair into a queue." Emma stood and turned around so he could see the braid. "She made a beautiful braid."

"So she did," Nicholas replied. "But what are you doing down here?"

"I was looking for you," his daughter said with a shrug. "Maria wasn't feeling well so I told her that she must go directly to bed. And you gave Mrs. Griffon the night off to see that play. When I came to see if you were here, I found Miss Sophie."

Nicholas stepped into the room and sat in the gold brocade chair. "I see."

"And," Emma continued excitedly, "Miss Sophie told me Mrs. Griffon was her governess! Did you know that, Papa?"

Nicholas smiled at his daughter. "Yes, I did know that."

"She told me to make certain that Mrs. Griffon takes me to the Egyptian section of the museum because Mrs. Griffon knows everything about Egypt."

He looked over at Sophie and almost felt sorry for her. His daughter was a chatterbox who never knew when to stop. But when he glanced over at Sophie, all he noticed was amusement shining in her gray eyes. "Emma, I do believe you are supposed to be in bed reading now."

"Yes, Papa." She turned and gave Sophie a hug. "Thank you for braiding my hair, Miss Sophie."

"You are welcome, Emma," Sophie murmured.

Emma kissed him and then skipped out of the room, leaving an empty silence in the room.

Nicholas finally cleared his throat. "Now, to what do I owe this honor, Miss Reynard?"

"May we speak in private?" she asked, glancing at the door.

"Of course." Nicholas rose and shut the door. "Is there something you need to tell me?"

Her face drew into a mass of confusion. "What do you mean?"

"Just tell me why you are here, Sophie." He returned to his seat but wanted to take the spot on the sofa Emma had deserted.

"Are you going out tonight?"

Nicholas frowned and shook his head. "You risked your reputation to come over here and ask me if I was attending a ball. Why?"

"Because you should not go anywhere tonight."

"Sophie, did you have a vision in which something happened to me?" He understood that she believed in her visions completely, but he still had reservations.

She grimaced. "Not quite a vision."

"Then what?" he demanded. He glanced over at the clock on the fireplace mantel. It was already after eight. He'd planned on getting there early so he could deliver the missive and leave. Now it looked as if that would not happen.

"I've had a dreadful feeling ever since Miss Littlebury came to see me this afternoon." She stared over at him intensely. "This feeling has something to do with you and her and this ball tonight."

He barely knew Miss Littlebury, although he'd noticed her name on the top of his father's list. Perhaps Sophie had learned about the list and was trying to stop him from marrying Miss Littlebury. "Sophie, I am only going to the Middleton ball to deliver a note to Lord Middleton for my father."

"Don't go, Nicholas," she pleaded. "I know something horrible will happen to you if you attend this ball."

Nicholas leaned his head back against the chair and looked up at the white coffered ceiling. "I must," he whispered. "I made a promise to my father."

Sophie leaned forward. "Please trust me, Nicholas. I have a feeling that this will ruin your life forever. Can you not deliver the note tomorrow?"

"No. It must be done tonight."

"I could go with you," she mumbled, staring at her hands.

"If you do, your reputation will be in tatters. You will lose your clients because they will all believe we have been lovers."

"If it protects you, I won't care."

"I will not let you do that."

Sophie knew she had to do something to keep him from leaving this house. Since her words couldn't convince him, perhaps there was another way. Slowly, she rose and walked toward him.

"What are you doing?" he asked with a smile.

Remembering how they'd made love on the chair in her study, she straddled his hips before he could move. "I just want to kiss you, Nicholas."

"No, you just want to keep me from going to the ball tonight."

She brought her lips down on his hard mouth and kissed him soundly. Finally gaining a slight response, she deepened the kiss and brushed her tongue across his. With a groan, he brought her closer. While she had started this game, he quickly took control.

His hand circled the back of her neck, forcing her nearer to him. Heat radiated downward from his kiss. She moved her hands toward his cravat, only to have him grip her wrists so she couldn't move. Feeling his erection, she rubbed herself against him.

With a groan, he pulled away. "Stand up," he ordered roughly.

Assuming he wanted her to undress for him, she did as he requested. She attempted to reach the buttons on the back of her dress but was unable to grasp even one.

"Would you mind?" she asked as she turned her back.

The chair squeaked as he rose. "As a matter of fact, I do mind."

He swung her around to face him. Sophie cringed as she noticed the anger emanating from his entire body.

"Don't ever come to my house and play games like this again. I told you I have no choice but to go to this ball tonight. Your attempts at seduction won't change my mind."

Sophie blinked back the tears that flooded her eyes. Humiliation swept over her. She couldn't ever remember feeling so foolish. "I'm sorry," she whispered.

He walked to the door and called for a footman. "See that Miss Reynard gets home safely."

"Nicholas, wait!"

He paused for a moment before turning back to her. "What is it now?"

"I fear you may be in peril. Your life may be at risk if you go tonight."

"I highly doubt Miss Littlebury is a killer." He turned back toward the door and muttered, "Good evening, Miss Reynard."

Nicholas watched with only a speck of regret as Sophie left the house. Turning her away had been the hardest thing he had ever done. But he couldn't live his life around her intuitions—good or bad.

He patted his waistcoat to make certain the note to Lord Middleton was still there. Once he delivered the message, he would return and explain things to Sophie. She should understand that he had promised his father he would deliver the note tonight.

As he left the house, her words of warning wouldn't leave him. He knew of no one who wanted him dead. While he had a cousin who would inherit the title should something happen to him, Peter never seemed the type who wanted to be duke. And why would Sophie connect Miss Littlebury to this? It made no sense.

Lord Middleton's daughters were all married so Nicholas doubted this could be any type of attempt at finding him in a compromising position. So if not that, then what would cause Sophie's reaction? He scarcely knew Miss Littlebury, but doubted the shy, retiring woman had any desire to become his wife.

Once he arrived at the ball, he waited for his official announcement before walking slowly through the crush. He asked a footman to give a note to Lord Middleton to meet Nicholas in the study at ten. Then he nodded to several acquaintances before finding Somerton who stood against a pillar watching the dancing.

"Good evening, Somerton," he said as he approached his old friend.

"Nicholas," Somerton said with a nod. "What brings you here?"

"Business for my father."

"I was sent a note this evening stating that if you attended this ball, I was to watch your back." Somerton sipped his whisky. "Any particular reason your back might need watching?"

"I have no idea. Some intuition nonsense." Nicholas grabbed a glass of wine from a passing footman.

"It's rarely nonsense," Somerton retorted. "She tends to get it right most of the time."

"Nonetheless, today she is wrong. I am only here to give a missive to Lord Middleton and then I intend to leave." And then he would return to her home and apologize for getting angry with her.

Somerton smirked. "Sounds simple enough. Still, I believe *I* shall take her advice and watch your back."

Nicholas shook his head. "I am to meet him at ten in his study. Alone."

"Then we shall get there early and make certain the room is empty. And I will stand guard so only Lord Middleton enters the room."

Nicholas blew out a breath. "As you wish."

With a few minutes left before he needed to be in the study, Nicholas watched the couples dancing. Swirls of pale silks blended with the men's darker clothing in the flickering candlelight. A stab of envy punctured him. He wanted to be on the dance floor with Sophie in his arms.

He just had to get through this meeting with Middleton then he could return to her. Perhaps once she saw that everything was all right, she would understand. He hated the wounded look he'd seen in her eyes.

"Come along, Nicholas."

"Very well." He and Somerton walked down the long corridor to Middleton's study. Somerton entered the room with stealth then waved him inside.

"There is no one in here," he commented even as he checked behind the blue velvet curtains. "And the only door is the one we entered through."

"As I said, there is no reason for her intuition tonight. I will give Middleton the note, wait for his reply, and then I leave."

Somerton grimaced. "I certainly hope so."

Hearing the strangled tone of Somerton's voice, Nicholas asked, "What is wrong?"

"I do not know. But suddenly I'm starting to believe she is right. Something feels wrong here."

"We have checked the room already. As long as you let no one in, save Middleton, everything will be fine." Nicholas raked his hand through his hair, exasperated with the conversation.

"I think it's a trap," Somerton said. "Perhaps, I should stay in the room with you."

Somerton could intimidate any man and Nicholas didn't need that tonight. "There is no trap. Nothing is wrong. Just wait out in the hall and only let Middleton inside."

Somerton shook his head. "As you wish."

Once Somerton had left, Nicholas walked to the corner of the room and reached for a decanter of brandy. After pouring a large snifter, he moved to a seat by the window. This way, he would notice if anyone tried to enter the room via the back of the house.

Both Sophie and Somerton had left with him a nervous feeling in the pit of his stomach. Could they both be wrong? A sudden urge to run from the room hit him. Perhaps he should invite Somerton to wait with him.

"God, this is insane," he mumbled, then sipped his brandy down in one gulp.

There was no one in the room with him. There was no way in which anyone could enter without Somerton letting them in. He pulled out his pocket watch again. Where the bloody hell was Middleton?

He refilled his glass and stared out the window. The rain had kept most of the people inside the ballroom tonight. One young woman laughed as she raced down the gravel path followed by a man. He would have to remember to never let Emma out of his sight at balls such as these.

The sound of wood sliding made him turn away from the window. Justine Littlebury silently entered the room with a slight smile on her face.

"Good evening, my lord," she said coyly.

The world around him started to spin. Why hadn't they thought to check for secret passages? Somerton knew better.

Miss Littlebury moved closer to him, holding the bodice of her gown with her hand. "You are dreadfully quiet, my lord."

"You must leave, Miss Littlebury."

"But I was told to come here and be with you. That you are my perfect match." She stepped closer until the overpowering scent of her rose perfume made him sneeze.

"My perfect match?"

"Yes." She started to move her hands up his waistcoat.

Grabbing her hands, he asked, "Who told you that?"

"Miss Reynard, of course. She is the imminent matchmaker of the *ton*."

Sophie told her that she was his match! That made no sense. Sophie would have told him Miss Littlebury was the woman for him. So preoccupied with his thoughts, he didn't notice that she had slipped her hands out of his grip and around his neck.

He blinked and her lips were on his. He grabbed her shoulders only to find that the back of her dress was unbuttoned.

Was this the reason Sophie visited him tonight? Did she suddenly have second thoughts on the scandal this would cause? Wild thoughts crossed his mind. She'd said his life was in peril. Was that just her way of stopping him from going? Or did she already know what Miss Littlebury was planning but had promised not to speak of it. None of the mad ideas in his head made any sense.

The door opened and Lord Middleton entered the room. Nicholas pushed Miss Littlebury away forcefully.

"Ancroft, what is going on here?" Middleton demanded.

"Bloody hell," Somerton exclaimed as he walked into the room. "How did she get in here?"

"A secret passage," Nicholas muttered as he dropped into a chair. He covered his face with his hands.

"Dammit," Somerton muttered. "Why didn't you listen to her?"

Why didn't he listen to Sophie? Because he was a goddamned fool. He only thought to prove to her that her intuition wasn't always right. Instead, he'd been caught in a compromising position by a friend of his father's.

He never felt so angry with another person in his entire life.

Chapter 19

Sophie paced the small confines of her bedchamber until she finally heard a knock at her bedroom door. Her heart pounded so loudly she was certain the maid on the other side of the door could hear.

"Yes?"

"Lord Somerton is here, ma'am."

Sophie dropped to the bed. She glanced over at her clock on the nightstand. It was nearly one in the morning. Deep in her heart, she knew this would not be good news. "Put him in my study. I'll be there presently."

Inhaling a long breath, she slowly exhaled, trying to calm her frayed nerves. She took a moment just to feel the sensation. He wasn't dead, she was certain. Nonetheless, something was dreadfully wrong with Nicholas.

With leaden feet she walked toward her study. Her mind continued to bounce with questions. Why hadn't she just accepted his proposal? Why hadn't she told him that she was carrying his child? Why hadn't she told him that she was falling in love with him?

"Sophie," Somerton said as she walked into the room. "You look like hell. Sit down before you faint."

She barely saw her brother standing in the middle of the room. But quickly, he was there, holding her elbow and leading her to the divan.

"What happened, Somerton?"

"In a minute," he said, fanning her face with a book. She grabbed the book from his hand and hurled it across the room. "I need to know now."

"Very well." Somerton clasped her hands in his. "Nicholas attended the ball."

"I assumed that. What happened at the ball?"

"I did everything I could to prevent it, Sophie."

"Somerton, tell me what happened," she demanded. "Is he alive?"

Somerton scowled at her. "Alive? You thought this was life or death and didn't tell me? Had I known that I never would have left him alone in Middleton's study."

"I wasn't certain what any of this was about," she admitted slowly. She told him about Lady Cantwell's death and the blackness she saw when she read Nicholas. "Tell me exactly what happened."

"He went into the study to give his father's note to the man. I checked the room before I left him and no one was in the room. When Middleton and I entered the study, Miss Littlebury was in the room with him, kissing him. The back of her dress was undone."

"Oh, God," she whispered. "How did she get into the room?"

"A secret panel." He moved away from her. "I blame myself, Sophie. You warned me to watch his back and I failed you. I should have insisted on staying in the room with him."

Sophie stared down at her dressing gown. "You couldn't have known about the panel. I wonder how she knew."

Somerton picked up the book she'd thrown and placed it on the table. "Her father, Witham, is good friends with Middleton. They might have conspired to get the match and told her about the panel."

She nodded. It all made sense now. Miss Littlebury had come to her seeking information on Nicholas. When Sophie had told her that she'd seen Nicholas in her future, Miss Littlebury must have assumed she meant as a match.

"What will happen now, Anthony?" Even as she asked the question, she knew the probable outcome.

"Witham will call him out if he doesn't propose marriage, Sophie."

"I assumed so."

"There might be a way for you," Somerton said and stopped his pacing.

Sophie shook her head. "I have always known that we would never be together. It was a risk I took when I seduced him."

"Tell him you are with child, Sophie."

She looked up at him agape. "How did you know?"

He smiled down gently at her. "I can tell these things," he said with a shrug.

"You mean like I can?" While Somerton had some intuitive sense, his appeared nowhere near as strong as hers.

He tilted his head and smirked down at her. "Your breasts are larger, your skin is radiant, and every time I visit you in the morning you look like hell. I am dealing with the same issue at my own home."

Sophie smiled up at her brother. "Of course. Still,

I cannot tell him, Anthony." She played with the tucks on her gown. "Nicholas is a good man. He will do the right thing by Miss Littlebury."

"He needs to do the right thing by you." Somerton sat down on the edge of the divan. "I can take care of Miss Littlebury."

"You will do nothing. It has been obvious to me since I returned from Venice that we were not meant to be together. You cannot force these things, Anthony. It was no different between you and Victoria. Had you two met before the timing was right, it never would have worked for you. That is why I never told you her name until last year."

"You are still basing everything on the fact that you don't see him for you. You might be wrong this time, Sophie."

"I never saw anyone for him either," she admitted.

"And what about Miss Littlebury? Did you see anyone for her?"

Sophie explained how she saw a very blurred image of Nicholas and a clearer vision of another man. Someone she didn't know. "Which again leads me to believe Nicholas isn't meant to have a long life. After he dies, Miss Littlebury will marry the other man I saw for her."

"What does he look like?" Somerton asked.

She shrugged. "Blond hair with green eyes. He seemed tall to me but other than that . . . wait, I remember, he had a small scar on his chin. I never mentioned that to her, though. She never would stay long enough that I could ascertain his surname. All I discovered was his first name was Edward or possibly Edmund."

Somerton turned away from her. "Hmm, I'm not

certain I know anyone named Edward or Edmund with a scar on his chin."

Sophie yawned. "It doesn't matter. Nicholas will propose and she will accept."

"Go to bed, Sophie. You look exhausted." He kissed her on the forehead and walked out of the house.

There was nothing else she could do now. She'd never felt so conflicted in her life. If she told Nicholas about the baby, he would ruin Miss Littlebury. If she didn't tell him, she would be ruining herself and denying Nicholas his child. But as long as she was the bastard daughter of an earl, she was nobody. Nicholas could not choose her over Miss Littlebury.

And once again, Sophie would be alone.

She wiped away the tear that fell down her cheek. The one time she desperately needed her mother's advice, she wasn't here.

"You will propose to Miss Littlebury this afternoon."

Nicholas crossed his arms over his chest as he leaned against the window frame of his father's study. "No, I will not."

His father slowly rose to his feet with the assistance of a cane. He covered his mouth with a handkerchief and coughed roughly. After his coughing fit had subsided, he stared at Nicholas. "You ruined that girl's reputation."

"No, Father. She ruined herself. The room was empty when I entered it. I had a friend guarding the door so no one but Middleton could come inside. She slipped in by a secret panel. Her gown was already unbuttoned to make it look like I was attempting to seduce her."

His father stepped forward. "You should have been more careful."

Nicholas's ire grew with each step his father took. "No, Father. You should have been more careful." He tossed the note he was supposed to give to Middleton last night toward his father.

He caught the note. "You read my note?"

Nicholas laughed in a low tone. "Yes, it was supposed to be a note about an investment. Instead, it only says thank you for your assistance in this matter."

"Yes, his assistance in my investment."

"You told me that he needed the note before this morning so he could act before losing money."

His father coughed again and then looked up. "I must have given you the wrong note."

"Enough lies, Father," Nicholas ordered. "Why did you and Witham do this?"

"Because you need to marry and Miss Littlebury is a fine young woman. Far better than that little medium slut you have been with."

Nicholas clenched his fists at his sides. "Miss Reynard happens to be the daughter of an earl."

His father laughed coarsely. "Of course that is what she tells everyone. How convenient that he doesn't want anyone to know."

"I know who he is," Nicholas countered. Not that it mattered at this point.

"Then tell me. But it will change nothing. She is and always will be a bastard."

"I promised her I would tell no one."

The old duke sneered. "Again, how convenient."

"It changes nothing, Father. I will not propose to Miss Littlebury."

"Oh?" His father stepped closer then poked Nicholas in the chest with his cane. "And I suppose you wouldn't care if it got out that your daughter might not be your daughter after all."

"Damn you to hell, old man. Don't you dare put Emma into the middle of this."

"Marry Miss Littlebury and no one will know that your daughter might just be your sister."

Nicholas closed his eyes against the painful memories of discovering his father in bed with Nicholas's mistress. He'd never been able to forgive his father for that transgression. His father had said it was the only way to make Nicholas realize that Maggie was nothing but a whore. And he had been right.

Still, there was no way to determine which of them had fathered Emma.

Not that it mattered. In his heart, he would always consider her his daughter. If this became public knowledge, it would only make her life harder. She hadn't faced the biting tongues of the *ton* yet. But once they found out that both Nicholas and his father had made love with the same mistress, the tongues would never stop wagging.

While he could handle the embarrassment it might cause him, he would never do anything that would harm Emma's reputation.

"I will speak with Lord Witham and his daughter this afternoon."

Sophie heard the knock at the front door and her muscles stiffened. After staying up most of the night, she had finally come to the most difficult decision of her life. She had no idea how or why, but she loved him. She could not let him make the wrong decision.

Marrying her would bring him monetary hardship and the ruination of his reputation. Even though men thought less of their reputation than women, it was important. He would become the duke when his father passed.

He needed the right type of woman. A woman who knew how to move about in Society. Miss Littlebury would fill that position. She was the legitimate daughter of a viscount. Other than what had happened last night, she had always kept her reputation without blemish. She would make a proper duchess.

Sophie would manage on her own. While she felt horrible about not telling Nicholas about the baby, she knew it was for the best. He had Emma and would have more children with Miss Littlebury. This would be Sophie's only child. Never again would she trust her heart with another man.

Now that he was here, she would have to face him one more time. Somehow, she had to make him believe that she didn't want to marry him. She had to be strong. This was the best thing for him.

And the hardest thing for her.

She took a long breath in and slowly released it. She finally understood why she saw his image in Venice and not since. He was never supposed to be anything but a brief affair for her.

Concentrating on him, she could feel his anger radiating from him even at this distance. The front door opened and male voices sounded from the entryway. She could feel his anger resonate from the front of her home. Footsteps shuffled along the hall indicating that only Hendricks was coming near.

"Miss Reynard," Hendricks said from the threshold of her study. "Lord Ancroft is here."

"Show him in."

"Shall I bring tea?"

Sophie doubted this would be a casual conversation over tea. "No."

"As you wish."

This time, loud footfalls preceded Nicholas's arrival. The closer he came, the more she felt his anger grow. She wanted to be able to ease his ire, but she was certain this conversation would only increase it.

"Lord Ancroft, ma'am," Hendricks announced before turning and leaving them alone.

Nicholas closed the door behind him. "I can only assume you know what happened."

"Yes." She looked away from his handsome face, desperate to keep herself from blurting out news that would only make this decision harder. "Somerton called on me and explained what happened."

"Of course he would do that for you," Nicholas muttered as he crossed the room. He picked up the bottle of brandy. "Do you mind?"

"Not at all."

He poured a large glass and drank it in one large sip before pouring another. He paced the room with the glass in his hand. "Why did you do it, Sophie?"

He was blaming her? "Why did I do what? Warn you that something dreadful would happen if you went to that damned ball? I did but you didn't want to hear me."

Nicholas sipped his brandy in a casual way that belied the underlying anger she knew he felt. "Why did you try to tell me my life was in danger when you knew for a fact that Miss Littlebury was going to compromise herself?"

"I did not know for a fact that compromising you was her intention. Only that I thought she was involved."

He stopped his pacing by the fireplace and glared at her. The heat from his brown eyes burned her. "Of course you would know that since you told her she was my match!"

"I did no such thing!" No wonder he was so angry.

"Why would she lie about that?"

Sophie laughed coarsely. "Why would she lie? She compromised herself to ring a proposal out of you. And yet you believe her."

He blew out a long breath and dropped to a chair. He leaned forward and raked his fingers through his hair. "You're right," he whispered.

"I did talk with her," she admitted softly. "But I never told her you were her match. In fact, just the opposite." She explained what she saw when she read Miss Littlebury.

"Why would you see me when reading her?"

"It might have been due to her plan to compromise you," she answered with a shrug. "Honestly, I don't know everything about this intuition of mine. I can only tell people what I see. I don't always know what it means."

Like the blackness she saw with him. He was still alive so what did it mean?

"What am I to do, Sophie?"

"You know what you must do."

He stood and stared at her. His brown eyes shone with the pain of his conflict. She wanted to reach up and caress his cheek with her hand, touch his hair one more time, kiss his lips and tell him everything would be all right.

But it wouldn't be all right.

And she would never be able to touch him intimately again.

"I have been thinking about this all day," he said. "I want you to know that I never touched her. She kissed me."

Sophie stared at the rug. "I know. Somerton told me that, too. And that he believed you when you said her dress was undone before she even entered the room."

"It's true, Sophie."

She nodded.

He sipped the rest of his brandy and then knelt before her chair. He clasped her hands and brought them to his warm lips.

She tried not to look at him but she couldn't stop herself. Seeing the tortured look on his face, she almost relented. But that would be wrong. She couldn't harm him. She couldn't be responsible for ruining his and Emma's life.

She had to be strong. No matter how much it hurt. And it hurt more than any pain she'd ever felt.

"Sophie," he whispered against her hands. "I want to marry you."

"No," she mumbled. "We cannot. It would only ruin us all."

"We can tell people who your father is. Everyone would understand."

She closed her eyes to keep her tears from falling. "No one would understand, Nicholas. Besides, unless my father admits to it, nothing will change. No one will believe us. And my father will never let the truth out."

Because doing so might open a much bigger round of gossip. So large that he would look like a fool, and Somerton and his sisters would be ruined.

"You must do the right thing by Miss Littlebury," she whispered.

He rose from his knees and stared down at her. Anger clenched his fists. "You *want* me to marry Miss Littlebury?"

No! "Yes. She will be ruined by her actions. While it's not fair, unfortunately, it does happen."

Nicholas reached down and yanked her to her feet. "You want me to marry a woman you know is not my match?"

"Nicholas, I could not determine who your match is. Maybe it is Miss Littlebury." She tried to keep her voice calm in order to soothe his anger.

"It's not Miss Littlebury but apparently everyone wants to believe it is."

"What do you mean?"

He pulled her close enough that his breath heated her cheeks. "If I don't marry her my father will release a scandalous rumor about my daughter."

"Then why are you even here?" she cried. "You would never let anyone hurt your daughter."

He inched closer to her lips. "Tell me you want to marry me. I will move heaven and earth and damn the consequences."

Oh, God, how she wanted to say those words to him.' "No," she said, pushing him away. "I cannot marry you."

He crossed his arms over his chest and glared at her. "So you want me to marry Miss Littlebury?"

Sophie fought back the tears. She didn't want him to marry Miss Littlebury, but she knew it was the right thing to do for him. "Yes."

"Very well, then."

Chapter 20

Victoria took her seat next to Avis on the sofa. All her friends were in Avis's salon, except Sophie. Victoria waited to tell her friends of the awful news until Avis finished pouring the tea. "We have a very large problem, ladies," she finally announced.

"What is wrong now?" Avis asked, handing a cup to Jennette.

"Ancroft is proposing to Miss Littlebury this afternoon." Victoria took the next cup of tea from her friend.

"What?" Elizabeth exclaimed. "How did this happen?"

Victoria explained what happened at the Middleton ball. "Anthony believes Miss Littlebury compromised Ancroft on purpose to get the proposal."

"You mean become the next duchess," Jennette commented with a shake of her head. "That little bitch."

"So what do we do now?" Victoria asked.

Avis leaned back against the velvet sofa. "There is not much we can do. If they are officially betrothed, Ancroft is bound by the contract to marry her. Miss

Littlebury's father would most likely sue for breach if Ancroft breaks the engagement."

"There has to be something we can do," Elizabeth cried. "I cannot let her marry Nicholas. Not when Sophie is so perfect for him."

"And she is carrying his child," Victoria whispered.

"Oh, my," the other women said with a gasp.

"Are you certain?" Jennette asked softly.

Victoria nodded. She could not tell the ladies that her husband had told her that information without disclosing Anthony's relationship with Sophie.

A loud commotion from the hall forced all their heads to turn. Victoria smiled seeing Anthony surrounded by the husbands of her friends. Even after five months of marriage, just seeing her husband enter the room caused her heart to leap.

"I believe we may have figured a way out of this mess for Nicholas," Anthony announced as the men walked into the room.

Avis laughed. "So, now that you all have been matched by Sophie you are determined to see Ancroft properly matched, too?"

Selby kissed Avis on the forehead and then sat on the arm of the sofa. "No, it's just that Nicholas would be far better off with Miss Reynard than Miss Littlebury. The poor girl would never be able to handle tea with you four."

"Very true, Banning," Jennette replied before leaning against her husband.

"So what is your way to help my cousin?" Elizabeth asked.

"Mr. Edmund Heston," Anthony said.

Victoria glanced about the room to see if any of

her friends recognized the unfamiliar name. Only Elizabeth seemed to nod.

"He is the second son of Viscount Ellington, is he not?" Elizabeth questioned.

Anthony smiled at her. "Yes, he is. He fought with Wellington. And received a scar on his chin."

"Oh," Victoria said, then related the information Sophie had given Anthony about the other man in Miss Littlebury's life.

"So, all we have to do is get them together," Jennette commented. "It shouldn't be that difficult. If they are meant to be together, they won't be able to keep their hands off each other."

"Are you certain?" Blackburn asked his wife.

All the women laughed.

Jennette patted her husband's hand. "My darling, I don't believe any of us made it to our marriages as innocents. That is the power of a perfect match."

Elizabeth's husband looked over at her. "You seriously believe Miss Reynard was responsible for our courtship?"

Anthony smirked. "Without a doubt. But in order for this to succeed, Miss Littlebury will need to break the engagement."

Avis leaned forward in her seat. "Then we need a plan."

Nicholas waited in the small receiving salon at Lord Witham's house. The nauseating pea green color of the walls seemed to match his feelings about being here. After his talk with Sophie this morning, he felt defeated. But he had an idea to give her plenty of time to change her mind.

"Lord Ancroft, it is a pleasure to see you again."

Nicholas turned at the sound of Lord Witham's voice. "Hardly a pleasure, Witham. Let's get this over with."

Witham's plump face reddened. "As you wish. Let us convene to my study and discuss the terms."

As they walked by the music room, Nicholas noticed Miss Littlebury sitting at the piano, looking extremely pale. She did not even smile as he passed the room. He briefly wondered if she was not as much at fault as he previously thought. Perhaps they were both pawns in their fathers' schemes.

"When we are finished, I would like to speak with you, your daughter, and wife."

Witham stopped and looked at him. "Why?"

"I do believe some clarifications are in order."

"Very well, then." Witham opened the door to his study and waited for Nicholas to enter the room. Walking to his desk, Witham said, "I think you will find everything in order, my lord. Justine comes to you as a wealthy bride with a rather large dowry."

Nicholas took a seat in the burgundy leather chair on the other side of the cherry desk. He reached for the documents Witham held out to him. As he perused the documents, he noticed everything was in order. There was no need for a solicitor to review it.

"This is fine." Nicholas signed his name at the bottom of the paper.

"Excellent, my lord. Congratulations." Witham came around the desk with his hand out. "Justine will make you a perfect duchess."

"I am not the duke yet," he reminded Witham.

Witham smiled. "But soon. I talked to your father

only last week. I assume he will be bedridden before the month is out."

He scowled. The man sounded excited by the prospect of Nicholas's father's demise. "You talked to my father?"

Again, Witham's cheeks turned red with embarrassment. "Of course, we had some business arrangements to review."

Business arrangements, Nicholas scoffed. More like marriage arrangements. "Of course."

"Come along, we shall announce the news to the family."

Nicholas followed Witham back into the salon where Lady Witham sat with Justine at her side. Two younger girls sat together on a large chair.

"Lord Ancroft, it is a pleasure to welcome you to our home," Lady Witham said with a deep curtsy.

Nicholas strode toward them and bowed over both ladies' hands. "It is lovely to see you both again."

"It is done," Witham said. "Now you both need to set a date."

"Quickly," Lady Witham commented. "We cannot have Justine's reputation suffer any further damage."

"No," Nicholas interjected. "I have decided a longer engagement is necessary."

"Oh?" Lady Witham said.

"You see," Nicholas folded his arms over his chest. "I know for a fact that I never touched your daughter. Therefore, the wedding will take place after Christmas. I will not make some other man's child my heir."

"But, my lord," Lady Witham said with a cat-like smile. "How do we know that you won't touch her before the wedding?"

Nicholas stared down at the woman. "Because I

shall retire to my estate in a fortnight. Between now and then, Miss Littlebury and I will only be seen with a chaperone in tow."

"Isn't that a tad extreme, my lord?" Lady Witham asked softly. "There is bound to be more talk if you retire to the country, leaving your betrothed in town."

"I do not believe it is, Lady Witham. I have a duty to ensure that my progeny inherit the title. In addition to a seven month engagement, I will have your daughter watched. If she is seen in the company of a man without a proper chaperone, the engagement shall be broken. Does everyone understand this?"

Miss Littlebury's face went pallid as she nodded slowly. "I understand, my lord. I shall be exactly the type of woman you are looking for in a wife."

Nicholas glanced down at the girl and said, "I sincerely doubt that, Miss Littlebury. Good day."

He now had seven months to find out more about Miss Littlebury. The more he'd watched her today, the more he realized that she didn't seem especially excited about the idea of marrying him.

Perhaps Somerton might be able to find out who she may have been seen with before the night of the Middletons' ball.

Sophie stared down at the numbers in her expense book. Without more funds, she could never leave and live on her own. Her father paid for the rent and so many of her expenses, she had never realized how expensive it was to live here. Perhaps Venice would be cheaper.

Although, she remembered the cost of just a few weeks in the city. She would need more money in order to leave. She supposed she could go elsewhere, but being in Venice meant she would at least have her mother there. While Angelina wasn't the best mother, she was family. And she would understand Sophie's predicament.

The possible answer to her money issues seemed to be asking her father for assistance. Perhaps he would be pleased to get her out of the country so his secret would be kept safe. She quickly penned a letter requesting permission to call on him tomorrow.

She asked Hendricks to have a footman deliver the message then resumed her pondering. If her father refused, there was one other she could go to, but she hated the idea. But she would not think of that unless she had no choice.

"Your carriage is ready, ma'am," Hendricks announced.

Elizabeth had invited her to dinner with their friends. Sophie assumed it was because they had heard the news about Nicholas and hoped to cheer her up. She hoped they would have the good sense not to mention his name since she could not stop her tears every time she thought of him.

Arriving at her friend's home, she walked up the steps and the door opened before her. The elegance of the hall established her presence in the ducal home.

"Good evening, Miss Reynard," Elizabeth's butler said. "They are in the salon. I shall have Kenneth announce you."

Sophie followed Kenneth up the white marble steps to the large salon. She breathed a sigh of relief when she entered the room and found only her dearest friends. None of their husbands were present.

"Sophie," Elizabeth said, greeting her with a hug. "Are you all right?"

"I am well." She pulled away from Elizabeth and took a seat next to Avis. "Thank you for inviting me tonight."

"Of course."

"Where are all your husbands tonight?" Sophie asked.

"White's," Avis replied. "We figured it would be a good night for us to get together."

Sophie frowned, hearing the strange tone of Avis's voice. It almost sounded like she was hiding something. Sophie shook her head slightly. Now she was becoming suspicious of her friends. Perhaps pregnancy had addled her mind.

Thankfully, none of the women spoke of Nicholas or his engagement. Their conversation centered on their families and touched on some gossip. The sound of male voices coming from the entrance caused Avis to laugh.

"I believe the gentlemen decided the food would be far better here than at White's," Elizabeth said with a forced sounding laugh.

Oh, her friends were definitely up to something. From her vantage point, Sophie watched the gentlemen as they entered the room. Kendal entered followed by Lords Selby, Blackburn, Somerton, and . . .

Sophie stiffened as Nicholas walked into the room. His face grew dark as he stared over at her. Obviously he hadn't expected to see her any more than she had thought to see him.

"Nicholas, don't stand at the doorway," Elizabeth said. "Come into the room."

"I should be leaving," he said in a low voice. His brown eyes seared her with heat.

"Of course you shouldn't," Jennette chimed in. "We are only having dinner."

Avis reached over and clasped Sophie's hand for support. Before Sophie could think of a decent excuse for leaving, the footman announced dinner.

"See," Elizabeth said. "You cannot leave us now, Nicholas."

Each woman paired up with her husband as an escort into the dining room. Sophie stood, unable to move past Nicholas and unwilling to accept his arm. Everyone left, save them.

"Sophie, may I escort you into the dining room?"

"I believe you should be escorting your betrothed, not me."

Nicholas frowned. "But she is not here tonight."

"Then you should not be either," she replied stiffly.

"Take my arm before everyone becomes suspicious of our behavior."

She reluctantly linked arms with him, trying to ignore the sensual aroma of his sandalwood soap. As they walked down the steps, she could feel the strength of his arm under the wool of his waistcoat. Being near him was such a dreadful thing. It brought back memories of lying in his arms, naked and satisfied.

She couldn't do this. It was wrong.

"Are you all right?" he whispered as they reached the bottom step. "You look a tad peaked."

"No, I need to leave."

He pulled her closer until she wanted to drown in his intoxicating scent. "You will go nowhere."

She yanked her arm out of his grip and stepped away from him. "You have no say in what I do."

Nicholas clasped her hand and led her into the small receiving parlor. Closing the door behind him, he said, "What is wrong, Sophie? Are you upset because I followed your demand and proposed to Miss Littlebury?"

"No," she almost shouted. "I am upset that you are here tonight instead of with her. At the very least, you should have let her accompany you."

He shook his head. "Are you mad? I went to White's where I met the other gentlemen who invited me to dinner. Should I have invited Miss Littlebury to White's?"

"Of course not."

"Do you honestly believe she could handle herself with any of our friends?"

Sophie knew enough about the girl to realize that her friends would dislike her immediately. They would consider her too young for Nicholas and only interested in gowns and fashionable balls. "No," Sophie finally admitted.

"So I should stop seeing my cousin and friends on the off chance you are there, too?"

"No." Sophie turned away from him. "It is not right that you stop calling on your family and friends. Therefore, I should leave. My friends will call on me at my home."

He blew out a long breath. "I never wanted this, Sophie. Besides, your brother is here, too. It's hardly fair to keep you away from him."

"I know that." She turned around and faced him again. "But again, Somerton can call on me. I will take my leave now." She walked past him only to have his large hand grab her arm. "Good-bye, Nicholas."

"Sophie, do not do this," he warned in a low tone. "You have as much a right to be here as I do."

She pressed her lips together and nodded. "That I do. But I just cannot be in the same room as you now. Good night."

Sophie twisted out of his grip and walked out the door. As she rode home, she realized that leaving London, and quite possibly England, was her only recourse.

Nicholas stared at the closed door for a long moment before moving toward it. He was quite certain he had lost her for good. Never again would he see her face brighten as she smiled up at him. Or hear her infectious laugh. Or her glorious cries of satisfaction as her climax washed over her.

"Where is Sophie?"

He looked up to see Somerton frowning at him. "She decided she could not be in the same room as me and left."

"Can't say that I blame her," Somerton retorted.

"She told me to propose to Miss Littlebury."

"Of course she did. Her father won't acknowledge her so she believes you are better off with Miss Littlebury," Somerton said, still glaring at him.

"And yet, we both know who her father is and he is far more influential than Lord Witham."

"You both know who her father is?" a feminine voice sounded behind Somerton.

Nicholas groaned seeing Jennette standing there with a look of amazement on her face. "Yes, Jennette. We both know."

"How?" Jennette asked. "I have known her for over

five years, and she has never told a soul. Does anyone else know?"

"I've known Sophie for ten years. And Victoria guessed it," Somerton said offhandedly.

Jennette's dark brows furrowed. "How in the world would she have guessed it?" Her mouth dropped as she stared at Somerton. "Oh, my God!"

"And now Jennette has figured it out," Nicholas commented with a pointed look at Somerton.

"I never noticed the resemblance until now," she said with a hint of awe to her voice.

"The resemblance?" another feminine voice asked. "To whom?"

This time Somerton groaned as Avis stepped forward. "No one, Avis. Go back to your dinner."

"I believe I would prefer to hear this discussion, Somerton."

"Avis, did Sophie ever tell you who her father is?" Jennette asked.

"Of course not and I never pressed her. Why?"

Jennette waved her hand at Somerton and Nicholas. "They both know. As does Victoria."

"Victoria knows! How?" Avis said.

"Sophie and Somerton have known each other for ten years," Jennette started.

Before she could continue, Somerton blurted out, "Sophie is my half sister. God, what a bunch of gossiping women."

Avis stared at him. "Your sister?"

"Yes, my sister." Somerton flexed his hands. "Now you all know."

"What do we all know?" Elizabeth asked from the threshold of the dining room. "All I want to know is why people are in the hall instead of the dining room. And where is Sophie?"

Both Somerton and Nicholas groaned.

"You might as well tell them all," Nicholas said to Somerton as they herded everyone to the dining room.

Chapter 21

Sophie shuffled through the stack of correspondence on her desk to see if her father had sent a reply yet. Finding nothing, she bit down on her lip. If she didn't hear from him by tomorrow, she would have to use her last possibility.

After her encounter with Nicholas at Elizabeth's house, she could not stay in England any longer. The idea of watching him marry that little tart would destroy her.

"Miss Reynard, Lord Westbury is here to see you, ma'am."

He was here! In her home! The last time he had come by to see her was when she was fifteen and had the measles. The majority of their communication was short notes written when her expenses ran higher than normal.

"Send him in, Hendricks," she managed to say.

Her hands shook as he approached the room. Should she order tea? She glanced down at her dress and thanked God she had the sense to wear one of her better gowns today. Her mind raced with nervousness.

"Good afternoon, Miss Reynard."

"Good afternoon, Lord Westbury." She moved around her desk and pointed to the chairs near the fireplace. "Shall we sit here?"

"Of course." Once Hendricks closed the door, her father sat down and stared at her openly. "You remind me of Genna."

Sophie nodded. "Thank you."

"I didn't mean it as a compliment. She has a head-strong manner about her too." He sat back and folded his arms over his chest. "Your note sounded urgent. Exactly what trouble have you gotten yourself into?"

She swallowed down the lump of fear in her throat. He had changed in the past few years. His dark hair was streaked with gray and his face seemed to hold a perpetual frown.

"I am in trouble, Father."

"Whose is it?"

She blinked and looked up at him. "Whose is it?"

"I can only assume you are with child. I always knew this day would come. Who is the father?" He tapped his finger against the arm of the chair impatiently.

"I would prefer not to say," she replied, staring at her skirts.

He stood and walked to the fireplace. "I can only assume you want my permission to tell him my name." Before she could interrupt, he continued, "Well, I will not give you that. You have known all your life what would happen if our names are connected. Don't think you can toss my name out and expect the bounder to fall to his knees and propose."

"I had no plans to break my promise to you, Father."

He turned and stared at her. "Then what do you want?"

"I need to leave London."

"Why?"

"The man is a marquess," she whispered.

"Who is it?" he demanded.

If her father was half as stubborn as his son, she knew it was pointless to ignore the question. She closed her eyes and said, "Ancroft."

"That bastard. He already has one bastard daughter. Does he plan to take the child away? Is that why you must leave?"

Sophie shook her head. "He doesn't know about the baby. And he cannot find out. He is betrothed to Miss Littlebury."

"I knew you would eventually take after your mother," he muttered and moved toward the door.

Anger flooded her. She rose from her chair and stared at him. "Did I really take after my mother? Or maybe my whoring father who couldn't even remain faithful to the wife who loved him?"

His hand held onto the door handle for a long moment. "You know nothing about my life."

"I know everything about your life. My brother has told me everything he learned from his mother. Your *dead* wife."

"I am finished with this business. I shall continue to pay your expenses while you are here. What you decide is your choice." He finally turned the handle and left the room.

Sophie collapsed into her chair and wept. Now she had only one other option.

* * *

Nicholas watched as Justine danced with Lord Brentwood. This was the last place Nicholas wanted to be tonight. He had become embroiled in an argument with his father about escorting his betrothed to the Huffington ball. He finally relented when he realized the ball gave him the opportunity to watch her with other men. There had to be someone else she had an interest in.

Seeing the bored expression on her face, he doubted she had any attraction to Brentwood. The musicians ended their quadrille and Brentwood escorted Justine back to him.

"Thank you, Lord Brentwood," Justine said as they arrived.

"My pleasure." Brentwood bowed over her hand and then left them.

"My, what a bore that man is," she said with a touch of scorn.

"Why is that?"

"He is dancing with me but telling me I should meet a friend of his."

"What is wrong with that?"

She glared over at him. "I am betrothed."

"Ah, yes."

"Nicholas, there you are."

Nicholas turned his head as Elizabeth and Kendal walked up to them. He noticed Justine immediately stiffened. "Elizabeth," he said and then kissed her cheek. "Lovely to see you tonight."

"And this must be Miss Littlebury."

Nicholas stifled a laugh at Elizabeth's pretentious tone. She knew how to play the haughty duchess to perfection.

"Your Graces," Miss Littlebury said and then curtsied.

"Nicholas, I believe Miss Littlebury and I should take a turn about the room." Elizabeth looked over at Justine. "Come along, young lady."

Justine leveled a worried glance back at Nicholas.

"What is your wife up to?" he asked Kendal.

"I believe she decided that Miss Littlebury must learn how to deal with your relatives and friends."

"She will never survive that, especially not my friends."

"No, but it might be entertaining to watch." Kendal grabbed two glasses of brandy from a footman and handed one to Nicholas. "You do realize that none of your friends want you to marry that girl."

"Nor do I." Nicholas sipped at his brandy wanting nothing more than to escape this room and conversation. But as he watched Elizabeth stop her gait, suddenly Avis, Jennette, and Victoria surrounded them. "What are they up to, Kendal?"

"It is probably best if you don't know."

"You are most likely right." Still, he wasn't happy about the inferring women who had surrounded his betrothed. He'd known those women long enough to be certain they were up to something.

"Who are they introducing her to?" Kendal said, interrupting Nicholas's thoughts.

He glanced back over to the women and stared at the younger man with blond hair. "I believe that is Mr. Heston. Ellington's second son."

Kendal shrugged. "I haven't been here long enough to know either of them. So tell me, Ancroft, if you have no desire to marry the chit, why are you?"

"Surely Elizabeth told you."

"She made some mention of the girl attempting to kiss you and someone walking in on you both.

Nevertheless, I do not understand why that would cause you to marry her. It certainly wouldn't me."

Nicholas chuckled. His cousin's husband had only been in England for a few months and still hadn't learned all the social skills needed to survive. "Her reputation was ruined. No other man would have her."

"Still no reason that you should have to marry her. Break the engagement."

"If I do, her father can sue me for breach."

"And if he does?"

"Again, she will be ruined."

"But again, that was all her fault. You know Elizabeth and I will support you if you should decide to break the betrothal."

Nicholas sighed as he watched Heston escort Justine to the dance floor. It was the first time he'd seen her smile, truly smile, since that night a week ago. He should feel a bit jealous to see his betrothed smiling at another man . . . but he didn't.

He sipped his brandy and wondered what Sophie was doing right now. She was probably home curled up on the sofa reading. Damn it all to hell! Why couldn't he forget her?

"Kendal, I am leaving."

Kendal turned to him with a frown. "What about Miss Littlebury?"

"She arrived with her parents and her parents will escort her home. Good night."

As Nicholas left the ball, a sense of relief washed over him. He hated being seen with Justine. With only seven months to find a way out of this mess, he felt as if a noose were tightening around his neck.

The cool May night smelled of fresh flowers and reminded him of Sophie. He had to see her. Tonight.

But when his carriage rolled to a stop in front of her home, he noticed only one candle lit the house. Could she be out? He highly doubted it, but it was only eleven. Far too early to be in bed.

He scrambled down from the carriage and walked up the steps. The front door opened a crack and a footman peered out.

"Miss Reynard is not accepting callers at this hour, my lord."

"Please inform her that I am here." He pushed past the man to enter the hall.

"My lord, I must insist you leave." The footman leaned closer. "Miss Reynard is already abed."

"Tell her."

Hearing a door close upstairs, Nicholas looked up hoping it was Sophie. She appeared at the rail in her wrapper with her black hair in a queue. Seeing him, her mouth gaped slightly.

"Lord Ancroft, I believe you were informed that I am not accepting callers."

"Sophie, please come talk with me."

"There is nothing to discuss."

Just seeing her again made his heart melt. He wanted to rush up the steps and hold her, tell her everything would be all right. But he couldn't. She wouldn't allow it. And he wasn't sure everything would be all right. It seemed there were too many obstacles now.

"Please, Sophie. I need to know something."

She tilted her head with a scowl. "Oh, very well."

He waited at the bottom of the steps as she descended. He held out his arm for her but she walked past him. Instead, he followed her down the marble tiled hall.

She lit a few candles and then turned to him. "What was so important that you could not wait until morning?"

"I want you to read me again."

"Why? We have been through this before and for some reason that I can't explain I cannot read you."

Nicholas sat down at the table where she always did her readings. "You said you saw me when reading Miss Littlebury. Then you should see her for me if I am her match. Please try again."

She released a long sigh. "Very well." She brought a candle to the table and sat down across from him. "Give me your hands."

Nicholas placed his hands in her soft hands. It felt so good to touch her even this small amount. "I know, concentrate on love."

"Yes."

Blocking everything else from his mind, he thought only of Sophie. He wanted her to know that she was the only woman for him.

"Nicholas, stop that and think of love."

"What do you see?"

"You are only trying to hinder my progress. Now think only of love."

"I am," he whispered as he closed his eyes again and thought of her.

"No," she said, drawing her hands away from his. "I am not the one you are supposed to love."

He leaned back in his chair and watched as she walked away from the table. "Do you realize that you are the only one who believes that?"

"What are you talking about, Nicholas?"

"I believe you are the woman for me. Our friends believe we should be together. My cousin and your brother also believe we should marry." He folded his arms over his chest. "So exactly why do you think we are not suited?"

Sophie paced in front of the fireplace. This conversation was mad. She had to get him out of her house now. "You know why and if that is all you came here for then you should take your leave."

Slowly, he scraped back his chair and stood. She glanced over at him and then resumed her pacing.

"Tell me, what would a man have to do to convince you that he was your true love?"

She shook her head. "There is nothing. If I can't see him then how can I trust that he is my true love?"

He inhaled sharply. "Sophie, that is the most ridiculous thing I have ever heard. How do you think the majority of people in the world fall in love? Do you think they wait until they can 'see' the person in their mind?"

"Of course not," she replied sharply. "But they don't have the ability and I do."

"But maybe you don't."

She frowned. "What do you mean?"

"Perhaps you cannot see your future, only the future for others."

"It doesn't change anything," she mumbled. "You have a young lady to marry."

"Say the word and I will break the engagement." He stared at her for a long moment while she comprehended the implications.

"I cannot do that to you." She blinked and looked at the ceiling. "Marrying Miss Littlebury is the right thing to do. She will be good for your reputation—"

"I don't give a bloody damn about my reputation."

"As I was saying," she said with force. "Marrying her

will give you the duke's blessing. He won't leave you penniless."

Nicholas stepped forward. "I do not need my father's money, Sophie. While my father thought I was out gambling and whoring away my allowance, I was investing it."

She bit down on her lower lip and blinked in rapid succession. "I would only cause you irreparable harm, Nicholas."

"No, you would not." He took the final step closer to her.

Sophie moved away and behind a chair. "I will only bring shame upon your name. I am not good enough to be your duchess or any duchess. My father won't even claim me."

"What if your father spoke out and claimed you as his child? Would that change your mind?" He walked closer to her until only a chair kept them apart.

That would help but she knew it would never happen. Just thinking about it caused something inside her to shatter. "He will never do it. I'm nothing but a reminder of what happened to his marriage. Because of me, his wife left him. Because of me, he doesn't even know that he has another daughter. Because of me, his son hates him. Because of me—"

Suddenly she found herself weeping against his strong chest. "Don't you see, Nicholas? It is all my fault."

"Oh, Sophie," he muttered against her hair. "None of this is *your* fault." He reached down, picked her up in his arms and brought her to the sofa. "Shh, sweetheart."

"It is my fault. If I hadn't been born, none of this would have happened." She couldn't stop her tears or the words from flowing. "Somerton hates our father because his mother left after she found out about me."

"No, Sophie," Nicholas said quietly. "She never left. She died in a carriage accident."

"No, she is still alive."

He pushed her away slightly. "I have known Somerton for twenty years. His mother is dead."

"She lives next to the orphan home that Victoria ran. She runs the brothel. And if not for my birth, she would have lived with her husband and maybe Somerton would have been a different person."

She had never told another person all the things she just told him. And by telling him, she'd broken a promise to her brother and Victoria. "Oh, God, I never should have told you that," she mumbled, wiping away the tears from her cheeks.

His hand stilled on her hair. "Are you telling me the truth? Lady Whitely is actually Somerton's mother?"

Sophie nodded as guilt clawed at her. "You have to promise not to tell a soul, Nicholas. No one can learn of this or it will ruin Somerton and his sisters."

He frowned. "Somerton only has two sisters, you and Lady Genna. What are you talking about?"

"The young girl Victoria took with her from the orphan home is Bronwyn. She is Lady Whitely's daughter with her husband. Only my father doesn't know because she didn't want him to take her away like Genna and Somerton." She looked up at him with tears obstructing her sight. "That is why you must never speak of this to anyone."

"But Sophie, none of this is your fault. Your father has caused this mess." He caressed her face, rubbing his thumb over her cheekbone.

"If not for me, my brother's family would have been normal."

He laughed soundly.

"Why are you laughing at me?"

"Sophie, I have met so few normal families in Society. I think the most normal would be the Selbys. And many people could never understand how the dowager Lady Selby could have loved her husband when he was so much older than she."

"It matters not. I will not ruin anyone else's life." She turned away from him. "I think you should leave now."

"Sophie, I love you."

She spun around and glared at him. "Don't ever say that to me! You love Jennette but now you must come to love your betrothed."

"I *loved* Jennette. But since I met you I realized my feelings for her were nothing compared to what I feel for you. And I will never love Justine."

"Please leave, Nicholas."

He took a step toward her and then stopped. "Do you love me, Sophie?"

Oh, how she wanted to tell him the truth. But this had gone too far. "You need to leave."

He stared at her for a long moment as if making up his mind. "As you wish," he said, and then strode from the room.

She watched him go and knew she had to leave London. He actually spoke of breaking his engagement for her. That would ruin everyone. Tomorrow, she would do what she should have done a few weeks ago.

Chapter 22

The next morning Sophie sat in her office and finished her correspondence. Then she started her lists of things she needed to do before leaving for Venice. There were so many things she had to complete before she could depart. But the hardest thing would be making sure no one discovered her intent before the ship left Portsmouth.

A knock scraped on her door. "Come in, Hendricks."

"Miss Reynard, the Duke of Belford is here. Should I tell him you are not at home?"

"Show him in."

Sophie glanced down at her gown and wished she had time to change into something better suited to meet a duke. Hearing his shuffling footsteps slowly nearing her, she inhaled deeply.

"The Duke of Belford, ma'am." Hendricks bowed out of the room.

"Your Grace," she said with a deep curtsy.

"Miss Reynard." The duke ambled over to the chair on the other side of her desk, leaning heavily on his cane as he went. Once seated, he took a long moment to catch his breath and just looked at her. "I am not sure what he sees in you."

"Excuse me?"

"I said I don't know what my son sees in you." He coughed into a handkerchief. "But whatever it is doesn't matter."

Sophie leaned back in her chair. "And why is that, Your Grace?"

"In case he hasn't told you, he is marrying Miss Littlebury."

"I did indeed know it. Although, I wonder why my knowledge of the situation is so important to you."

He coughed again. "I have a proposition for you."

"Do you?"

"Yes, I know you have attempted to deceive both my son and many of the ladies in the *ton.* Including your closest friends." His gnarled hand tightened on his cane. "But you have not fooled me."

What was the man talking about? "Exactly how have I fooled my friends?"

His icy glare sent a shiver of apprehension through her. "With the lies that your father is some earl. Your friends may have believed you, but I certainly do not. You have the look of some peasant gypsy, nothing more."

She arched an eyebrow at him. "Oh?"

"Yes."

"What is your true reason for coming here today, Your Grace?"

"I will give you ten thousand pounds to leave England and not contact my son again."

Sophie could only stare at the old man. She never could have imagined anyone offering so much money to get her to leave. "You believe you can pay me off as you did Nicholas's mistress?"

A flash of shock crossed his blue eyes and was quickly replaced with curiosity. "You know about that?"

"Of course," she replied with a laugh. "I am a medium." She stood and rounded the desk. "Hold my hand for a moment, Your Grace."

She expected him to balk at her request but he said nothing and placed his hand in hers. Closing her eyes, flashes of his life swirled through her mind. Pity overcame her until she had to release his hand.

"I'm sorry, Your Grace," she whispered, then walked back to her chair.

"For what?"

"Your life. I'm sorry that you feel your wives never loved you. You could have had the love of your son, but you ruined that relationship, too."

The duke rose slowly from his chair and then tossed a large envelope on the table. "Good day, Miss Reynard."

Nicholas watched the excited expression on Justine's face as she danced with Mr. Heston. A proper fiancé would convey his displeasure with the situation to her parents, but not him. If she behaved improperly then the engagement was off and not due to his actions.

It had been a week since he saw Sophie and he missed her terribly. He'd hoped by now Justine would have had a misstep and he would be free of her. So far she has been circumspect.

"Nicholas, there you are."

He turned and smiled at Jennette and her husband. "How are you both?"

"Very good," Jennette replied and then pulled him to a private spot. "Have you seen Sophie?"

"Not in a week. Why?" A sense of foreboding sliced through him.

"No one has heard from her."

"What about Somerton?"

Jennette shrugged. "Victoria said he had to help someone with a problem and he hasn't been home."

Nicholas knew Somerton used to work for a secret agency for the regent. But that was supposed to be in his past now that he'd married. Perhaps they needed his assistance one last time. "Have you called on her?"

"No. I planned to tomorrow." Jennette grimaced. "I think something is wrong."

"Why?"

"I wish I knew."

"I'm quite certain she won't accept my call," he said, then leaned in closer to Jennette. "But please let me know that she is all right after you talk to her."

Jennette smiled at him. "I shall do that."

Nicholas returned to watching his betrothed, only she seemed to be missing. He scanned the room but didn't find her anywhere. Perhaps she wandered to the ladies' retiring room. He waited a few minutes before searching out her parents.

"Exactly where is your daughter, Lord Witham?"

Lady Witham's pale eyes grew large. "What do you mean? She was on the dance floor with Mr. Heston."

"Yes, she was. Now she is gone," Nicholas replied. "Perhaps you should check the ladies' retiring room, Lady Witham."

She nodded nervously. "I shall at that."

While Lady Witham left, Nicholas scanned the room. He finally spied her sneaking back into the ballroom from the terrace. Her cheeks were flushed and her hair slightly messed. As she noticed their stare, her cheeks reddened. She looked far more like a woman who had just returned from a liaison than one out for a breath of air.

"I will speak with her, my lord," Witham said quickly and walked away.

"Do that."

Nicholas continued to watch the terrace doors to see which man walked in alone. After fifteen minutes of waiting, he noticed Mr. Heston strolling through the doors as if nothing illicit might have happened outside. Nicholas knew better than to assume something had happened. But now he knew Miss Littlebury needed to be watched at all times.

Sophie placed her valise on the bed and turned toward her brother. She would never have been able to make this journey without him. He insisted on driving her to Portsmouth where the ship would depart instead of taking a mail coach.

"Thank you, Anthony."

He quickly brought her into his arms and held her tight. "I am going to miss you."

"Please promise me that you won't say a word to anyone."

He moved away from her, his size overpowering the small cabin. "How am I supposed to do that? Especially with Victoria?"

"Just don't tell anyone my exact location. Hendricks is sending a footman out with notes for everyone tomorrow, but I did not let them know where I planned to go. Once I am settled, I shall write and tell them where I am. I just hope they understand why I couldn't see them before I left."

Sophie bit down on her lip. The only person she was truly concerned about was Nicholas. He would be furious that she left without saying good-bye. But it was for the best. With her gone, he could concentrate on his fiancée. While they might not be a true match, she still believed Justine would make him a good duchess.

"Did you inform Ancroft of your condition?"

She shook her head. "If he knew he might do something foolish and break his engagement. I cannot be responsible for that. Once I know he is married, I shall send him a letter."

"He will never forgive you if you do."

She blinked back the tears that had been in her eyes since she'd made her decision. "I know."

"Stay, Sophie. Don't leave your family and friends," Anthony implored.

"I cannot stay and watch him marry." Or worse, watch him die.

"Then don't!" Anthony shouted. "Tell him about the baby and he will insist on marrying you."

"He didn't marry Emma's mother," she whispered.

"Because his father paid her off. The duke gave her a bloody fortune to leave."

She nodded, remembering the envelope of money the duke had left for her. Guilt cut her to the quick. There was so much she should have told Nicholas. She should have told him what she really thought her lack of vision with him meant. But would that be fair to him? Her mother had always reminded her to use care when telling people about their futures. There was always a chance she could be wrong.

"Sophie, you and I could tell the world who your father is. I know Genna and Bronwyn would speak up for us. Even Lady Whitely would stand up for us if I asked her."

"No," she said emphatically. "I will not be the cause of you and your sisters' ruination."

"I don't care about my reputation. Victoria won't either," he commented in a calm voice. "Genna and Bronwyn would be happy to be able to claim you as their true sister."

"But I do care." Sophie had to get him to leave before she weakened. The idea of leaving her family and friends was killing her. "I cannot ruin my family."

"Sophie, the ship doesn't leave for a few more hours. Do you want me to stay?"

She knew he only wanted to stay to continue to convince her to remain in England. "No, Anthony. Please go home to Victoria and love her for the rest of your life."

Anthony blew out a long breath. "Very well." He brought her back into his arms and kissed her cheek. "Stay well."

"Thank you."

She barely contained her tears as her brother left the cabin. Now, she would spend the next three or so weeks alone with just her maid for company. She hoped her mother received her letter informing her of Sophie's impending arrival.

The minutes passed into hours and finally the ship departed Portsmouth. She was leaving England forever.

* * *

Nicholas waited for Jennette to either call on him or send him a note regarding Sophie. Perhaps he should attempt to call on her in person. But he knew she would not see him. It was far better to let Jennette handle this issue.

He scanned the note written by a gentleman in his employ. It appeared that Justine had a penchant for strolls on terraces. Twice more she'd been seen re-entering a ball looking more than a little mussed.

Finally a knock sounded at the door. He stood ready to greet Jennette in his study. But when the door opened, he only heard the low tones of male voices.

"The Duke of Belford is here, my lord," his butler announced from the threshold.

"Send him in," Nicholas replied even though he could hear the slow footsteps of his father approaching. The footsteps stopped only to be followed by a loud cough.

"There you are, Nicholas." His father finally entered Nicholas's study.

"And to what do I owe this honor, Your Grace?"

The duke settled into the chair opposite him and looked askance at the brandy. "First a brandy."

Nicholas sighed and then poured a brandy for both of them. After handing a snifter to his father, he sat down again. "Why are you here?"

"I wanted to find out how your wedding plans are progressing," he replied and then sipped his brandy. "Damn fine stuff."

"The wedding will take place after Christmas."

His father looked as if he wanted to stand up and rail at him. But with his age and condition, rising quickly wasn't an option. "After Christmas! What is that about? I want you married before I pass on.

There is every likelihood that I will not make it until Christmas."

Nicholas smirked. "I am terribly sorry about that, Your Grace. But I will not be made a fool of by a woman. She compromised herself, and I will not take a chance that she is carrying another man's child."

"Of course she isn't. That gel is innocent."

"And how can you be so certain?" he asked. After reading the note about her leaving balls, he wasn't sure she was still innocent.

"Her father informed me," the duke answered.

"Then it must be true," Nicholas said in a sarcastic tone. "I really don't care if the king declared her innocent. Until I know for sure that she is not carrying, I will not marry her."

His father narrowed his blue eyes on his son. "This is about that medium woman, isn't it?"

"This has nothing to do with Miss Reynard."

"Of course it does." His father took a long sip of brandy before continuing, "Not that it matters. She is just like every other whore."

Nicholas shot to his feet and clenched his fists. "She is not a whore."

The old duke laughed scathingly and he stood to leave. "Of course she is. In fact, she never said a word when I gave her ten thousand pounds to leave London."

Nicholas said nothing as his father ambled toward the door. She never would have taken the duke's money. She had her father to pay her expenses. Besides, her friends would have known if she left the country. They would have informed him.

Unless they did not know either.

He refused to believe his lying father. Although, Nicholas knew his father would do anything to keep him from marrying Sophie. Including giving her a fortune to leave.

His world spun around him. There was only one way to straighten this mess out—see Sophie himself. He yelled out to his butler to ready his carriage. Then he paced the room while he waited.

"Excuse me, my lord," Lane said from the doorway. "A letter was just delivered to you."

Nicholas grabbed the letter from Lane's outstretched hand. "Thank you." Seeing Sophie's familiar handwriting, he relaxed his tense muscles. She never would have left without saying good-bye to him and her friends.

He broke open the seal, scanned the letter and then crunched it into a tight ball and threw it across the room. She'd left him. Not only did she leave, but she took his father's money. Pain exploded behind his head and shattered his heart.

She had left him. Without a word of good-bye. How could she have done this to him? He would have done anything for her. He reached for the brandy, decanted it and poured himself another glass of brandy.

He would get drunk until he couldn't feel the pain any longer. Until all thoughts of Sophie were gone from his head. Maybe if he drank enough he would forget how much he loved her, or how beautiful she was, or how she satisfied his every need.

He laughed as he drank a third glass. He didn't have enough brandy in the house for that. He wasn't sure London had enough brandy to help him forget her.

"I am sorry, Lady Blackburn," Nicholas's butler said, "his lordship is indisposed."

"Drunk?" Jennette asked softly. After receiving the letter from Sophie this afternoon, Jennette knew how Nicholas would react. She had arrived as quickly as she could manage.

He leaned in closer. "He's locked himself in his study. He hasn't left his study in three hours except to call for another bottle of brandy. I fear it may have something to do with a letter that Lane left for him earlier."

Jennette was afraid of that. Once she'd received her letter, she knew she must speak with him. "I will talk with him."

"Yes, my lady."

She inhaled deeply and walked toward his study. She pounded on the door, waiting for a reply. When he didn't answer, she knocked even harder. "Nicholas, please let me in."

"Go away, Jennette. I am not accepting calls."

"This isn't a call."

He laughed hoarsely from the other side of the door. "Then what is it?"

"We need to talk about what happened."

"Nothing happened. Sophie left, that is all."

"Nicholas, let me in," she insisted.

"Just go away."

"Maybe she had a reason for leaving." Jennette listened as the room seemed to go strangely quiet. She stepped backward when she heard his footsteps clomping closer.

The door swung open and he stood there in just his trousers and white linen shirt. Looking behind him, she noticed the rest of his clothes strewn across the room. She looked up at him and wanted to cry. The pain in his brown eyes made her remember all the pain she had gone through with her own husband.

"What exactly do you know about her leaving?" he demanded.

"May I come in?" Even as she asked the question, her stomach roiled from the stench of brandy. While she could out drink many men, the smell of alcohol nauseated her terribly when with child.

"Tell me what you know."

"You're trying my patience." She shoved past him and kicked at his waistcoat on the floor. "Lovely," she muttered.

"Jennette, if you don't start talking you might as well leave me to my brandy."

She picked up his cravat from a chair and dropped it to the floor. "Lane is not going to be happy when he sees this room."

"I don't give a bloody damn about what Lane thinks. What do you know of Sophie?"

With deliberate slowness, she sat down and straightened her skirts. "Well, Nicholas, I received a letter today from Sophie stating she felt she had to leave the country because she could not stand to watch you marry Miss Littlebury."

"That is basically the same thing she wrote me." He hurled the crystal brandy snifter at the fireplace. Shards of glass splintered against the firebox.

"Destroying your house won't get her back," Jennette whispered.

He stalked across the room. His anger and frustration emanated from every pore. "I don't even know where she is!"

Jennette smiled as he passed her chair. "You have

no idea where she might have gone. Indeed? I should think it was perfectly obvious."

He stopped his pacing and stared at her. "You know? She told you?"

She laughed softly. "No, she did not tell me. And I doubt she told anyone. Nonetheless, I know where I would go."

Nicholas rubbed his face with his hands, trying to clear some of the muddled feelings from his brain. "Jennette," he said, attempting to control his impatience with her, "I have no idea where she went."

"Now you see, that is what too much brandy will do to you." She rubbed her belly and smiled. "Among other things."

He glared at her.

"Oh, all right," she said. "Sophie is a very romantic person. She loves you dearly."

"I'm not so certain of that," he interrupted.

"I am. She loves you, Nicholas. So much, in fact, that she preferred to leave you than ruin your reputation by marrying you. Being a romantic, she would travel where she can remember the first time she met you."

"Venice," he said with a long sigh. "I should have thought of that. Her mother is there."

"Exactly. She will need to be near family now."

And with the rest of her family here, she would go to her mother. It made perfect sense. Only he'd been too foxed for any logic to sink into his alcohol soaked mind. "I need to go to her."

"And how are you going to convince her to return? What argument will you use that you haven't already employed?"

Nicholas finally sat down in the chair next to Jennette and thought about her words. What would convince her to return? He'd offered to break his engagement. He had offered to marry her. He'd even told her that he loved her. What more was there?

"I honestly don't know," he admitted.

"When I decided to leave England I was running away from everyone. I was terrified that I had ruined Blackburn and my family. I didn't want anyone to discover where I had gone." Jennette bit down on her lip.

"What does this have to do with Sophie?"

"She is running as I did but only because she wants to protect your reputation. And possibly the reputation of her brother and sister."

Nicholas knew far too well that her family's reputation was important. It was the only reason he hadn't confronted her father. But in retrospect, that might have been a bad decision. Perhaps he should have gone to Lord Westbury and asked permission to marry Sophie.

He leaned his head against the back of the chair and closed his eyes. The brandy made his head spin and he needed it to stop so he could think properly. "I don't give a damn about my reputation. I've told her that numerous times."

"She loves you. She doesn't want to see you hurt because of her."

"I know," he muttered. But he still didn't know how to get her back. He'd tried everything he could think of. "I don't know what to do, Jennette."

"I believe the first thing you should do is break your engagement."

"It's not that easy."

"Of course it is," she replied.

"My father has threatened to harm Emma's reputation if I do anything to break off the betrothal." He knew Sophie would be furious if he ruined his daughter's future because of her.

"What can he do?" she asked quietly.

"Emma might be my daughter"—he paused for a breath—"or she might be my sister. I have no way of knowing. But he will make that public knowledge if I break it off with Miss Littlebury."

Jennette stood and crossed the room to the window. Drawing back the curtain, she stared outside for a long moment. "You do realize that your father is dying and in eight years when Emma makes her bow, no one will remember what he said. If you continue to tell everyone that she is your daughter, no one will believe him. Most will simply believe he is going mad with his death imminent."

Nicholas thought about her statement. Would her suggestion really work? There would be talk, but in eight years would anyone of importance remember the scandal? He knew it wasn't his decision to make.

"You have to convince her that no matter what, you are not giving up on her. Blackburn would have moved to America with me if that was the only way I would have agreed to marry him. You must prove to her that no matter what the issue is, you will be her husband."

His lips lifted for the first time in several hours. "Are you certain she went to Venice?"

Jennette shrugged. "I can't be positive. Victoria said Somerton would be gone for a couple of days. If I had to guess, he might know exactly where she went."

Of course! He should have known Somerton wasn't off working for the government again. He'd promised Victoria he would quit. Somerton would have insisted on taking Sophie to Portsmouth.

"Very well. I will wait for Somerton."

Chapter 23

Anthony returned to London with only one thing on his mind. He strode up the steps to the house he despised and then waited for the butler to open the door.

"Good evening, my lord."

"Is he in?"

"Yes, in his study."

Without waiting for an announcement, he stomped down the hall toward his father's study. He walked into the room without even a knock. His father looked up from his book with a grimace.

"Good evening, Anthony. What brings you around at this hour?"

"I just arrived back from Portsmouth." He walked to the whisky and poured a large glass. "Don't you want to know why I was in Portsmouth?"

"I have no idea," his father drawled.

Anthony gulped down his whisky and poured another glass before finally taking a seat. "I was taking my sister there so she could travel to Venice."

"Your sister is upstairs."

Anthony tightened his grip on his glass. He hated how his father would not acknowledge Sophie even to him. "My sister is on her way to Venice with no help from her father. Well, Father"—he stopped to sip his drink—"I think you should know that tomorrow I shall announce the fact that Sophie is my sister."

His father laughed coarsely. "Why would you do that? She is gone. Making that announcement now will do nothing but cause the entire family embarrassment."

"Ah, but you see, I am quite certain a well connected marquess is about to travel to Venice, too. Since I doubt his intention is to live in Venice, I can only assume he proposes to bring her home."

"What have you done, Anthony?" his father demanded.

"Nothing yet. If Ancroft doesn't already know Sophie is on her way to Venice, by tomorrow he will. I am done with the lies you have forced me to keep. If you think to stop me, just remember the one secret I still carry with me. At this point, I would have no issue letting all of Christendom know that my mother is still alive and running the most renowned brothel in Mayfair."

"You would never do such a thing. It would ruin you and Genna." His father rose and walked to the brandy decanter. After pouring a glass, he turned around with one dark brow arched. "Do it, Anthony. No one will believe you, and your mother shall hate you for it."

"Claim her as your daughter. For once do the right thing." Anthony sipped down the rest of his drink. "Do it for your daughters, not for me."

His father shook his head. "I cannot, Anthony. I

have spent my life telling others how to live their lives properly. If I now stand up and say I have a bastard daughter and my dead wife is actually Lady Whitely, people will despise me."

Anthony rose and stared at his father. "The only opinion you should care about is what your family thinks of you. Not strangers. Good evening," he said with disgust.

Nicholas rode to Lord Witham's home eager to be done with this mess. While his head still ached from far too much brandy yesterday, at least his mind was finally clear. Armed with the report of Justine's actions, he knew what had to be done.

As the carriage slowed to a stop, he readied himself for the confrontation. Witham would be furious, but Nicholas knew it was the right thing to do. He could never make Justine happy when he loved Sophie.

Slowly, he climbed down from his carriage and made his way to the door. The butler opened it before Nicholas had put his foot on the first step.

"Good afternoon, my lord."

"I must speak with Lord Witham. It is urgent."

The butler muttered something about more urgent business under his breath but allowed Nicholas entry into the receiving salon. He sat down but just as quickly rose and started pacing the room. He knew exactly what he would say to Witham. Nevertheless, anxiety built within him.

The quiet house suddenly turned to chaos as shouting erupted from the far end of the house.

Nicholas raced out of the room and followed the sound toward Witham's study.

"My lord," the butler said behind him. "Lord Witham will see you in just a few moments."

Nicholas waved him off as he recognized the sound of Justine's voice, screeching at her father.

"I won't marry him!"

"You will do as I say, young lady."

"I will marry Heston even if we have to run to Gretna Green."

Well, there was no sense in that when he had no plans to marry the girl anyway. Nicholas opened the door to find Witham standing in front of his daughter as Heston stood by the fireplace looking peaked.

"Ancroft, what are you doing here unannounced?" Witham demanded.

"I came to speak with you about the wedding," Nicholas replied. "I could not help but hear you and your daughter shouting at each other."

Witham's face turned crimson as he glared at his daughter. "I apologize, my lord. Justine seems to be mistaken about her duty."

"Is she?" Nicholas turned to Justine with a gentle smile. "Miss Littlebury, is it your contention that you no longer wish to marry me?"

Justine nodded. "I am truly sorry, my lord. I thought I could be happy as a duchess." She looked down at the rug. "But then I met Mr. Heston. I am in love with him."

"Love," Witham sneered. "Being a duchess is far more important than love."

Nicholas looked over at Witham. "I would have to disagree. Love is the most important thing. Miss Littlebury, if you would prefer to break the engagement, I would accept your request and harbor no ill will toward you or Mr. Heston."

"You would?" she replied with awe. "My father told me you would never allow this to happen and that you would call out Heston."

"Our parents decided we should marry and forced this situation upon us both. I am not in love with you and nor will I ever be. You deserve a man like Heston who will love you."

"Thank you, my lord. You are more than kind," she said with a little sob.

"This is not up to you both to decide," Witham tried again.

"Yes, it is," Nicholas declared. "Besides, Lord Witham, if you remember, I asked you to keep a chaperone with your daughter at all times. That was not done and I have it on good authority that your daughter and Mr. Heston were seen alone on the terrace of two balls."

Witham glared at his daughter. "Is this true?"

"Yes," she answered defiantly.

"Mr. Heston, do you plan to marry Miss Littlebury?" Nicholas asked before Witham could regain his voice.

Mr. Heston cleared his throat and finally stepped forward. "I should like that very much, my lord."

"Very well, it is settled." Nicholas turned to Witham. "Your daughter will marry Mr. Heston. With your blessing, Witham. I believe if you offer him the same contract as you did me, he will agree to marry your daughter."

"I will not have him for my son-in-law. My daughter will marry a peer."

"My lord," Mr. Heston said, "I believe it is in your best interest to allow me to marry her. At this moment she might be carrying your grandchild."

Witham grabbed a chair for support. "You and he," he sputtered.

"Yes," Justine said with a defiant grin.

Witham went to his desk and pulled out the betrothal contract. He handed it to Nicholas. "Destroy it."

"I shall do just that," Nicholas said. He pocketed the contract and left the three to their business. Now he only had his own father to deal with.

After a short drive to Grosvenor Square, he was ready to face the duke. He walked into the house and the butler escorted him to his father's bedchamber. The duke's face was more pallid than Nicholas had ever seen.

"You don't need to look at me that way," his father complained. "I'm not dying yet. Just tired today."

He bit back a stinging retort. "I only came to give you some bad news, Your Grace."

"Oh?"

Nicholas pulled out the betrothal contract from his pocket and showed it to him. Then he ripped the document down the middle. "I will not be marrying Miss Littlebury."

His father struggled to a sitting position. "You broke the engagement?"

"Actually, no," Nicholas said with a hoarse laugh. "Miss Littlebury did. Apparently, she could not keep one section of the contact that I insisted upon."

"What was that?"

"Staying away from other men." Nicholas pocketed the shredded document and walked toward the door.

"You can still marry her once her monthlies come. Insist her father take her to the country and lock her in the house until they know for certain if she is with child."

Nicholas could only shake his head. "I don't believe you understand me, Your Grace. I intend to travel to Venice and marry Miss Reynard."

The duke slowly climbed out of bed. "Do not think to marry that little slut."

"I will marry whoever I damn well please." He should have said that to his father weeks ago. "Good afternoon, Father."

"If you marry her, I shall disinherit you."

Nicholas turned back with a smirk. "Please do. I don't want your damned money. I have enough of my own."

"Don't lie to me, Nicholas. You have spent your money on whores and gaming."

"No, I have invested the majority of my allowance for the past twelve years. I shall do just fine without your money."

And he would. Once he finally convinced Sophie that they would be all right.

Nicholas had the servants packing his clothing while he waited for Somerton's arrival. The ticket to Venice had been bought but he would not leave until he spoke with Sophie's half brother. He tapped his foot impatiently awaiting him.

"Father, might I speak with you?"

He looked over to see Emma standing at the doorway with a look of apprehension on her face. "Emma, you know I will always find time for you. What is the matter?"

"It's very important that I talk with you." She stepped forward timidly.

This was very unlike his daughter. "Come here and tell me what is on your mind."

She sat down on the chair across from him and breathed in deeply. "I overheard the servants say you were traveling to Venice again."

"Yes, I am. I didn't want to tell you until I knew for certain when I would be leaving."

"I also heard why you were going." She bit down on her lip and frowned.

Nicholas closed his eyes and sighed. He'd never thought to ask Emma what she thought of Sophie. Seeing his daughter's reaction now, he wondered if Emma might not approve of Sophie for her stepmother.

"I think if you are going to Venice to ask Miss Reynard to marry you that I should accompany you," she said in a small voice. "After all, she will be my stepmother. She might want me to tell her how much I would love to have her as my mother."

He opened his eyes and stared at his little girl. She was becoming so grown up. And she might be just the thing to help Sophie make up her mind. He was certain Sophie had a soft spot for his daughter and wanted a family.

"I think that is a fine idea. Go tell Mrs. Griffon that you both will accompany me. That way you can keep up with your studies."

She threw herself into his arms. "Thank you, Papa!"

She kissed his cheek and skipped out of the room. She stopped at the threshold and curtsied. "Good afternoon, Lord Somerton."

"Good afternoon, Lady Emma."

"I'm going to Venice!"

"Excellent," Somerton said and then walked into the room. "So you already know where she is, then?"

"I hope you're going to tell me I'm right in my assumption," Nicholas said, standing to greet his friend.

"You are correct." Somerton walked to the whisky and poured himself a glass. He held up an empty glass and asked, "Do you want some?"

"God, no."

Somerton laughed. "I heard from Jennette you were a little foxed the other day."

"I never want to see brandy again."

"Why do you think I drink whisky? I had one very bad episode with brandy and can barely stomach the stuff now."

Nicholas waited for Somerton to sit before prying. "Where exactly did she go?"

Somerton gave him Sophie's mother's address in Campo Santa Marina. "Her mother is a mistress to a count therefore Sophie may have found her own place by the time you arrive."

"You couldn't stop her?"

Somerton smirked and shook his head. "You couldn't get her to marry you." He paused before continuing, "She felt she was doing the right thing. I tried to convince her to at least stay in England but she refused."

Nicholas sighed. "She could have come to me for advice."

"No, she felt she had to leave."

And with his father's money. The idea that she would go to him for money still irritated him completely. He felt as if she betrayed him by doing so. He understood that she didn't have enough to go on her own, but she might have come to him.

When they returned, he intended to give every pound back to the duke. Once she explained her reasons for taking his money.

"Tell me, Somerton"—Nicholas paused for a long moment—"do you think I can convince her to return home?"

"She believes she would only ruin you, Nicholas."

Nicholas blew out a sigh. "I have told her repeatedly that I don't care about that. I even told her I love her."

"Nicholas, do you know Sophie's biggest fear?"

Thinking back upon their earlier conversations, he couldn't remember her speaking of anything except her fear that her father's identity would get out. "Her father?"

"Not quite." Somerton shook his head. "She would kill me if she knew what I was about to tell you. All her life, she has been abandoned by everyone she loved. First and foremost was the father who would never even admit she was his. Then, her loving mother who left Sophie with a nurse or governess in order to fuck some man until he tired of her. I was another great influence in her life. I would see her when it fit into my plans. Not when she needed me."

"She does have her friends," Nicholas reminded him.

"All of whom are now married and busy with their own lives."

Nicholas remembered the loneliness he noticed in her gray eyes. "She had me."

"Ah, yes. You. A marquess and future duke. In her eyes why would such a man take her for a wife? She's a bastard."

"I offered for her several times. Each time, she refused me."

"Of course she did, you fool." Somerton swore under his breath. "She doesn't want to hurt you. She doesn't want you to abandon her because marrying her ruined your reputation. She doesn't want to watch you die, leaving her heartbroken and alone . . . again."

"Watch me die?"

Somerton told him about her lack of visions with him and what happened with Lady Cantwell.

"She thinks I'm going to die?"

"Yes. So how will you persuade her to come home?"

Nicholas grinned. "I am bringing my secret weapon."

Somerton laughed. "Emma! Of course. She cannot resist a child."

"I didn't think she could. Once Emma tells her how much she wants Sophie to be her mother, I believe Sophie will feel compelled to return. Besides, if I am truly to die, then Emma will desperately need a mother."

"Devious, Nicholas." Somerton smirked. "I do like the idea. And by the way, tell her that I have already informed the dowager Lady Selby that Sophie is my half sister. I'm quite certain Lady Selby will spread the gossip throughout the *ton* in a few days. By the time you and she return, everyone will know."

"She might not be happy that you did that," Nicholas commented.

"Just go bring her home. I can deal with my sister's anger when she gets here."

"I shall do just that."

Chapter 24

After almost four weeks on the ship, with her morning sickness made only worse, Sophie had never been so happy to step on solid ground. Her mother met her at the docks in the count's gondola.

Sophie looked around the city wishing she felt happier about returning. A bead of sweat rolled down her back as she held a handkerchief to her nose. Venice had been much more pleasant in winter.

Once the short ride ended, they walked toward her mother's home through the small alleys that made up the city. Sophie had forgotten how confining some of the passageways were. If she put out both hands, she could reach the buildings on either side of her.

"I still cannot believe you are here," her mother said as she opened the door to her home.

Sophie smiled at her mother's warm greeting. "I am a little surprised that you are still here. It's been a few months, are things still going well with the count?"

Her mother smiled brightly. "Very well."

"Good." And Sophie meant it. While her mother

had never placed Sophie first in her life, she had done the best she could. Surviving on a man's fancy was never easy, especially as a woman aged.

Although, her mother still had her looks. At forty-eight, her black hair had only a few strands of gray. Her face had a few more wrinkles but not as many as most women her age. And the woman had a figure most her age had lost decades ago.

"I want you to rest and have some tea." Angelina brought her into a warm room with very high ceilings and a large crystal chandelier. The room vaguely reminded Sophie of the bedroom she and Nicholas had made love in. "I put you in a room next to me. If you decide to stay, we can find you a place on your own."

While Sophie would love to stay with her mother for a longer amount of time, she understood. This house was only for the count to visit Angelina without his wife knowing. Sophie never realized just how hard a life that must be for her mother.

She sat on the brocade sofa as her mother ordered tea. Finally, the world had stopped spinning. She'd spent the first week onboard the ship doing nothing but crying and vomiting. Once she had cried herself dry, she did her best to convince herself she'd done the honorable thing.

But it never helped the pain in her heart.

Even now, almost a month later, she ached to see Nicholas again. How would she survive never seeing him, knowing he was in London with his wife and they were creating a family together? All the while, she would be here attempting to care for a child alone. Once the count tired of her mother, Angelina would no doubt return to London. Something Sophie could never do.

"Now, I would like the truth," her mother said as she poured the tea. Handing the floral cup to Sophie, she added, "I know you would not be here if everything was going well in your life. Did your father threaten to stop paying your expenses?"

"I think you already know why I am here," Sophie commented.

"Perhaps," her mother replied with a nonchalant shrug. "I would still rather you told me than my sensing it."

"I am with child. By a marquess."

Her mother's gray eyes widened. "Oh my, I thought an earl was lofty when I went after your father. But a marquess?"

"He will be a duke when his father dies, which might be any time as he has consumption."

Angelina shook her head with a slight smile. "All these years you told me you would not end up like me. And yet, here you are."

"I know, Mother." Sophie stared at her hands as humiliation stained her cheeks.

"So your marquess gave you money to leave the country before his wife discovered the truth?"

Sophie sipped her tea. Her stomach was finally starting to settle. "Not quite. He is not married but he is betrothed. I left on my own because I would only ruin his reputation and that of Anthony and the girls."

Her mother frowned as she shook her head. "You have spent your life always worrying about other people. Your protector knew what he was getting into when he made you his mistress. He should have offered to take care of you or at least the baby."

"I wasn't his mistress. We were lovers with no ties that bound us."

Angelina stood and paced the room. "If you were going to take after me you should have paid more attention. A man needs to pay for your favors. He needs to set you up in a proper house with servants and dresses."

"Mother, I didn't want those things from him."

Angelina blew out a long breath that waved her black hair away from her face. "You love him, don't you?"

Tears blinded Sophie as she nodded. "I tried so hard not to, Mother."

"Did you try to read him to see if he loved you?"

"I tried, Mother." Sophie explained how she only saw him in her vision after she was knocked unconscious by the gondola. "I went to bed with him because I assumed he was the one for me."

"But, Sophie," Angelina started then paused. "If you are like me, you cannot read yourself."

"What?"

"I have never been able to read myself. I always assumed it was just the way God made me. He wanted me to read others but not have an advantage on my own life."

"Then why did I see him after I fell into the canal?"

Angelina paused for a long moment before replying. "You said you hit your head on the gondola. Maybe that had something to do with it. Perhaps the injury allowed you to see your own future for a short time until your mind healed."

"Then why couldn't I read Nicholas? I could sometimes read his thoughts but when he wanted to find his match, I could not read him. And then there's Lady Cantwell . . ."

"Who is she?"

Sophie sighed and told her about her lack of visions with Lady Cantwell and her subsequent death.

"Darling, there are several things I've learned over the years about my visions. Perhaps it's time you are taught the same lessons."

"What lessons?"

"First, I have never been able to know for certain when someone is going to die. I've had people I read hours before their death and could still read them and then others, like this Lady Cantwell, where I see nothing for a week or two before their death."

Sophie rubbed her temples to ward off the imminent headache. "What other lessons are you willing to impart?"

Angelina laughed softly. "You cannot read yourself. And you cannot read your true love's future if it involves you."

"Nicholas is my match?"

"I think your heart already knows that answer, my dear. I think it's your head that can't quite accept him as your match."

Oh, God, she had made such a mess out of her life.

Sophie rose and walked to the window, letting her mother's words sink in. She pushed open the wood shutter allowing the heat of the afternoon to filter into the room. Staring down at the small Campo Santa Marina, she wondered if her mother was right.

She turned away from the window and back to her mother. "Can you read me?"

"Does it matter?" Her mother sipped her tea with a secret smile.

"What do you mean?"

"What does your heart tell you?"

Sophie fisted her hands. "You taught me not to trust my heart!"

Angelina drew back. "I never did anything of the like. I only taught you to help others when they didn't trust their own hearts."

"Every time you trusted your heart you ended up getting hurt!"

Her mother shrugged. "Perhaps. But it was usually well worth the hurt. Sophie, if you truly love this man, what are you doing here?"

Sophie explained again how she couldn't be the one to ruin everyone's reputation. "It's just wrong of me to think I'm more important than their name. I am nothing but a bastard."

"No, your father is the bastard for not claiming you."

Sophie could not tell her mother why her father had never claimed her. She had understood how important his standing was in Society. And after finding Anthony, she sensed the secret about his mother. "My father did what he thought was best. It might have been far worse for me . . . and you."

"I suppose you are right." Angelina smiled. "Let's talk of something more pleasant. When do you think you are due?"

While she discussed her pregnancy with her mother, Sophie's thoughts remained on Nicholas. Should she have trusted her heart?

No, it was far more important to keep his reputation and Emma's from harm.

The next two weeks flew as Sophie moved into a small apartment not far from her mother. Thankfully, the home was furnished, saving her some money.

Sophie rubbed her tummy for the second time in just a few minutes. Why did it feel like she had tiny bubbles inside her? She pressed her hand to the spot again and laughed.

"What is it?" her mother asked, drinking her tea.

"I think I feel the baby moving!"

Angelina smiled back at her and then frowned in concentration. "Well, that is about right. You should have a little under five months left. Have you had your maid take out your dresses yet?"

Sophie smiled at her mother's knowing look. "Yes, the bodices were starting to get a little tight."

While not showing much, there was a slight bulge in her belly where a week ago there had been none.

"Mother?" Sophie said and then shook her head. It was wrong to ask this question.

"What do you want to know?"

"Can you sense the sex of the babe?" she whispered. It seemed so wrong to want to know, but she understood if it was a boy, she would have to inform Nicholas. He had a right to his son. Of course, he had the same rights for a daughter, too. And remembering how much love she saw in his eyes for Emma, she knew not telling him was so wrong.

"I can usually sense the sex of the child. But I prefer not to let the parents know."

"Why not?"

"After nine months of carrying a child, it's lovely to have a surprise at the end. I never would have wanted to know what you were." She reached over and squeezed Sophie's hand. "Holding you that first day was the most incredible experience of my life."

"Thank you," she whispered and wiped a tear away. "I only wanted to know because of Nicholas."

"You haven't informed him of his upcoming father-hood?"

"I know I must but . . ." But there was no excuse other than fear. "I thought it best to wait until after he married."

"You will write him today," her mother ordered. "In fact, I believe I will leave you to your writing now. Boy or girl, he should know about his child."

Sophie waited for her mother to leave the house before dipping her quill pen into the ink. She had written to all her friends a fortnight ago to let them know where she was staying. Her mother had found her a small apartment near Campo Santa Maria For-mosa. But Sophie had never felt so lonely.

Her loneliness reminded her of Nicholas. While he had his friends and Emma, Sophie had seen some-thing was missing from his life. And just like her, he wanted love.

Slowly, she wrote, trying to explain why she left him. Why she didn't tell him about the baby. She crumpled five different versions and tossed them into the empty fireplace before finishing the sixth. Every letter reinforced the thought that she was terribly wrong. She should have told him in person about the baby. She should have told him she loved him.

As she reread the letter, tears welled in her eyes. She ached to return to London and see him again. She yearned to feel his strong arms about her.

Would he come to her when he learned of his child? She doubted Miss Littlebury would allow it. Jus-tine would probably tell him not to worry about his bastard because she would give him an heir and a spare. And she would be right.

Nevertheless, Sophie would love this child enough

for both of them. She rubbed her belly again as she felt slight tickling inside her. Soon she would feel real kicks. Movements that Nicholas should feel too, but he never would.

She readied the letter for the post and then gave it to her footman to be sent out. Nicholas would receive the note in about a month. It would then take another month before she might obtain a reply. If she received one at all.

She wiped her eyes and readied herself for her first client. Angelina had recommended Sophie to one of her friends. Thankfully, the woman was English therefore Sophie would not have to translate her thoughts from Italian to English. Starting her business again in Venice was not as easy as she'd thought it might be. Mediums abounded in Venice, and most spoke better Italian than she did.

Lady Sidwell had lost her husband two years ago and moved to Venice to mourn. Now she felt ready to move on and find love again. Angelina had promised her that Sophie could assist her in that matter.

A part of Sophie felt as if she were a fraud for giving people information on their true love when she'd given up her own love.

Within a fortnight of meeting Lady Sidwell, Sophie had five new clients all recommended by the woman. For the first time since she'd left London, she thought her life might return to normal. Every day, she felt the baby move inside her, which caused happiness to swell within.

But today, something seemed different. There was an air of disturbance swirling about her. She just couldn't put her finger on the cause. She prayed everything was all right with her family and friends. Neither Elizabeth nor Victoria should have delivered yet. Feeling a sharp pain in her heart, she understood all too clearly.

It was Nicholas.

Could he and Miss Littlebury be marrying today? Is that what caused her pain? She walked to the window and opened the shutters allowing the humid air inside. She stared blankly down at the church. The sound of bells from various churches filled the late afternoon air.

Were the bells in St. George's ringing out the wedding of Nicholas and Miss Littlebury? Her mind scolded her for such thoughts. But a small part of her knew it could have been her walking down that aisle.

"Excuse me, ma'am," her footman spoke from the doorway. "You have a visitor."

"Did she give you a card?" Sophie asked, knowing she had no one scheduled.

"No, but she said it was urgent." Robert was one of only two footmen who had agreed to come with her to Venice. "She said her name was Mrs. Griffon."

"Mrs. Griffon?" What was she doing in Venice? Sophie immediately sensed something was dreadfully wrong for Mrs. Griffon to be calling on her. "Send her in quickly."

He returned with Mrs. Griffon trailing behind him. Mrs. Griffon moved past him with her arms out wide.

"Sophie," she cried and enveloped Sophie in a hug. "I cannot believe how beautiful you are."

"Mrs. Griffon, how are you?" Sophie asked, slowly pulling away.

Mrs. Griffon looked at her and her gaze remained

on Sophie's slightly rounded belly. "Now, I see why Lord Ancroft was in such a hurry to get here."

Sophie felt heat cross her cheeks. Nicholas was here? For her? "Mrs. Griffon, why are you here?"

"Oh my, of course. You must come with me. Lord Ancroft has fallen ill."

"He's in Venice?"

"Yes, we arrived yesterday evening but by this morning he was not feeling well. He awoke with a dreadful fever. He's staying at the home of a friend across the Rialto Bridge." Mrs. Griffon started toward the door. "Do hurry, Sophie."

Nicholas was sick. That was why she had been feeling so disturbed this morning. "Did someone call for the physician?"

"Yes, but Lord Ancroft needs *you*."

✔"Of course. Just let me get my herbs." Sophie raced to her bedchamber and pulled out her small valise that contained her herbs.

She followed her former governess out the door into the humid air. They walked through the small streets and alleys until they came to the Rialto Bridge. The short walk seemed endless as the heat of the midday sun beat down upon them. Every step she took increased her worry. Mrs. Griffon would not have called on her unless there was something seriously wrong with Nicholas.

"Here we are." Mrs. Griffon stopped in front of an impressive old home that backed to the Grand Canal. They walked up the steps quickly and entered the home. "Come with me, he's upstairs."

As they reached the last step, Sophie heard the sound of light footsteps. Emma ran to the hall.

"Miss Sophie, you're here." She launched herself

into Sophie's arms. "Thank God, you'll know what to do!"

"Shh, Emma," she said, trying to comfort the young girl. "What is wrong with your father?"

"He has a fever and the doctor doesn't know why." She looked up at Sophie with tears in her amber eyes. "You can help him, can't you?"

Sophie didn't want to give any false promises when she hadn't even seen Nicholas yet. And after seeing only darkness when she tried to read him, she still wondered if it was because he was her match or because he was destined for a short life. "I need to see him first," she finally said with a quick caress to Emma's cheek.

"You must see him now, then," Emma said, pulling away from Sophie.

Sophie followed Emma to the same room where she and Nicholas had first made love. Nothing much had changed in the room except the handsome man in the bed looked flushed with fever. She quietly walked toward the bed trying not to wake him. Placing her hand on his forehead, she wondered at the concern everyone had over this fever. He was barely warm.

"What did the physician say?"

"Only that he has a fever."

Sophie turned at the deep sounding voice. A tall handsome man with black hair stood at the threshold.

"Excuse me," he said, walking closer. "I am Nicholas's friend Dominic Santangelo. You must be Miss Reynard."

Sophie drew back slightly. He'd heard of her? From Nicholas? Perhaps Nicholas had told him all about their relationship. Embarrassment seared her cheeks. "Yes, I am Sophie Reynard."

"Excellent." He kissed the top of her hand lightly. "Emma was adamant that Mrs. Griffon call upon you and insist you see Nicholas."

"Did the physician give him anything?"

"Just some laudanum to help him sleep. Nicholas said several of the ship's passengers were ill on the trip over."

Sophie swallowed down her fear and asked the most important question. "Did any of them die?"

Chapter 25

Mrs. Griffon glanced over at Emma and then Dominic. Their hesitation only increased Sophie's frustration and worry.

Mrs. Griffon spoke up first, "Not that we are aware of. Both Emma and I were feeling slightly ill during the final days of the trip but neither of us came down with the fever."

All Sophie knew was Nicholas had a fever. Which meant it could be nothing or something far more serious. What worried her most was the fact that he had only a slight fever but hadn't awakened with all their commotion. But for right now, she had to work on getting that fever down.

She opened her bag and pulled out her willow bark. "Mrs. Griffon, can you please try to find me some cold water."

"I will assist her," Dominic said.

Sophie breathed a sigh of relief to have only Nicholas and Emma in the room. While she readied the herbs, she glanced over at Emma's pale face. The young girl sat on the bed next to her father and held his hand.

Sophie could feel the immense sadness emanating from her.

"Emma, how was your trip?" Sophie asked, attempting to get the girl's mind off her father for a few moments.

"It was all right but long," she mumbled, without looking away from Nicholas.

"Did Mrs. Griffon take you to the British Museum yet?"

"Not yet. She said she would once we arrived back home."

Finally Emma glanced over at Sophie. "Is Papa going to die?" she asked in a small voice.

"Oh, Emma." Sophie closed the distance between them and hugged the distraught girl. Emma's tears dampened Sophie's gown.

"I don't want him to die. Then I might have to go live with my grandfather and I don't even know him."

Sophie closed her eyes and tilted her head to Emma's. She prayed that Nicholas had enough sense to give guardianship to someone other than his father. Then again, if she hadn't been so foolish as to leave London and him, this would never have happened. And if she'd only married him, Emma could live with her.

She'd been such a fool to let her intuition control her life so thoroughly. Her heart had always known that Nicholas was the man for her. Why was she so afraid to listen to it? She'd let fear of people's opinion decide her life.

Whether he'd had only a few weeks to live or another fifty years, she should have stayed with him and enjoyed the time they had together. Now she wondered if she would even get the chance.

"Emma, you should come with me and let Miss Sophie care for your father," Mrs. Griffon said as she entered the room with a basin of cool water.

"I don't want to," Emma said with a sniff.

"You need to go with your governess," Sophie said and then hugged Emma again. "I will let you know if anything changes with him."

Emma pulled away slowly and stared up at her. "Thank you, Miss Sophie."

Mrs. Griffon led her charge out of the room. Sophie focused her attention on Nicholas. She dampened a cloth and placed it on his forehead. He whispered something but she couldn't make out the words.

She sat on the bed and caressed his cheek, rough from the stubble of a day's beard. "Oh, Nicholas, can you ever forgive me for being such a fool?"

He groaned slightly but said nothing.

"I should have trusted your judgment. You weren't afraid of the gossips. You were willing to risk your reputation just to marry me . . . the bastard daughter of an earl who wouldn't claim me."

Tears burned down her cheeks as she stared at his handsome face. "I'm so sorry, Nicholas."

He had to get well. She had so much she had to confess to him. And if he still wanted to marry her, she wouldn't hesitate.

And if all he wanted was the baby?

She couldn't think about that right now. First, she would help him get well. Then she would suffer the consequences for her actions.

"Sophie, perhaps you'd better allow us to care for Lord Ancroft," Mrs. Griffon whispered.

Sophie turned to see both Dominic and Mrs. Griffon looking at her with concern in their eyes. "I need to stay with him."

Dominic shook his head. "I can't let you do that, Miss Reynard. You are putting your life and the child's life at risk."

Sophie frowned at Mrs. Griffon. "You told him?"

Dominic laughed. "No one had to tell me, Miss Reynard. It's perfectly obvious that you are with child. Nicholas's child, I can only assume."

Sophie nodded. Even though she knew they were only being cautious, she couldn't leave Nicholas now that he'd returned for her. "I know I should leave, but I cannot. I know about healing and from what you've told me this is not a long-lasting illness."

"You're still putting your baby at risk."

"I can't leave him . . . again," she whispered the last word.

"He'll be furious with me if you become ill." Dominic looked over at Nicholas and then back to her. "Do what you think is best. I just want him well."

She smiled up at him, seeing the friendship in his eyes. "So do I."

"Do you need anything right now?"

"No, thank you."

Dominic and Mrs. Griffon departed leaving her alone with Nicholas again. She removed the cloth and dampened it with the cool water. After placing it back on his forehead, she moved a chair closer to the bed and sat watch.

The silence of the room gave her more time to think about how foolish she'd been with him. Seeing him again made her realize just how much she loved him. She picked his hand up in hers and brought it to

her lips. She rubbed his hand against her cheek,
savoring the rough feel of his skin against her.

She couldn't lose him now. God couldn't be so
cruel to her.

He blinked his eyes open for a moment and quickly
closed them. "Sophie?" he mumbled.

She moved to the bed and smiled. "Yes, Nicholas.
I'm here."

"Good," he whispered and fell back to sleep.

At least he knew she was here.

As the sun set, Sophie dined with Dominic and
Mrs. Griffon. Emma took a tray in her father's bedchamber. Sophie ate only because she knew the baby
needed the nourishment.

"You will sleep in my bed tonight," Dominic said.

Mrs. Griffon gasped.

He waved his hand at her. "Not in that manner. I
will watch over Nicholas at night while Miss Reynard
sleeps. Nicholas would have my head if I let her stay
awake the entire night in his room."

"Of course," Mrs. Griffon replied.

"Thank you." Sophie knew there was no sense arguing with him. She stifled a yawn. She would never
manage to stay awake tonight. At least she could sleep
knowing Dominic was watching over Nicholas.

Nicholas squeezed his eyes shut as the morning
light hit him squarely in the eyes. He groaned.

"Welcome back."

Nicholas opened his eyes to see Dominic standing
by the window. "How long have I been in bed?"

"Just a day."

"Just a day?" Why didn't he remember it? "Did I sleep the entire day?"

Dominic approached the bed with a grin. "I may have forgotten to tell the physician not to give you laudanum."

"Forgot?" Nicholas sneered. "Damn you, Dominic, I know you too well. You did this on purpose."

"It was the only way to make you stay in bed to get some rest. If the physician hadn't given you the medicine, you would have tried to see Miss Reynard yesterday. Then you would have only become more ill."

Nicholas frowned. Somewhere in his memory, he could have sworn Sophie had been here. At his bedside. But that was madness. She didn't even know he was in Venice.

"I suppose you're right, Dom."

"So how are you feeling?"

"Like hell. And what kind of host doesn't offer his guest some food in the morning?"

His friend laughed soundly. "I suppose I can take care of that for you. Should I send Lane in?"

Nicholas rubbed his rough face with his hands. "Not yet. I may still fall back to sleep. Damn that laudanum. I hate the fuzzy way it makes me feel."

"See how you feel after you eat." Dominic left to order food for him.

Nicholas wondered what Sophie would say when he arrived at her doorstep. Would she be pleased to see him or angry that he followed her? It didn't matter how she felt, she was going to return to London with him.

Except, he could not make her do what she didn't want to do. He'd assumed if he brought Emma along that she would help convince Sophie to marry him.

But what if he was wrong about her? She might not want to have any children after being deserted by her father. They'd never talked about children, except how to prevent them.

He really should marry a woman who desired children. Although, as he thought back to when she met Emma, he would have sworn she enjoyed being with her. There was only one way to determine her feelings. He just wasn't sure he was up to talking with her today.

Damn Dominic for letting the physician give him laudanum. And damn himself for not asking what the physician was giving him. He knew better. As did Dominic. For some reason, laudanum put him into a very deep sleep more so than other people.

A footman brought a tray in for him. Ravenous from not eating and from the dreadful food on the ship, he ate everything on his tray.

"Should I send Lane in, my lord?" the footman asked as he picked up the tray.

"No. I believe I shall sleep a little longer." Nicholas slid back down under the coverlet and closed his eyes.

As he lay there, sleep wouldn't come to him. His thoughts remained on Sophie. Perhaps he should get dressed and attempt to see her today. But with the effects of the laudanum still bothering him, he knew it wasn't a good idea. He needed a clear mind to convince her to return to London as his wife.

"How are you feeling?"

So lost in his thoughts he never heard Sophie approaching. "What are you doing here?"

"Mrs. Griffon told me you were ill and needed my help." Sophie slowly approached the bed.

Nicholas took her form in but stopped as his

gaze reached her belly. Pain exploded in his head. She was with child. *His child*. She left with his child and his father's money.

"Get out, Sophie."

"What?"

"I said get out of here. I don't want to see you." He turned his back to her and faced the wall. How could he have been so foolish? She was no better than Maggie. Or maybe Sophie was worse. She'd known how betrayed he'd felt about Maggie taking his father's money and leaving with Emma. And she did the same thing.

"I'm not leaving, Nicholas. At least not until you tell me why you want me to leave."

"Leave," he ordered harshly. "I do not want to see you now."

He felt the bed depress as she sat down. He turned and glared at her pale face. She looked far too innocent to have done the devious things of which he accused her. Nevertheless, he would not be deceived again.

"I told you to leave. Don't make me call for Dominic to escort you out."

She blinked back tears. "Why?" she whispered. "You obviously came here to see me so why won't you . . ." her voice trailed off. "You know."

"He told me." Not that he'd completely believed his father when he told Nicholas that she'd taken his money. But it made perfect sense that she would need his money if with child.

"He promised me he wouldn't tell you," she said and then brushed away a tear. "I know I should have told you before I left but everything happened so quickly with Miss Littlebury."

"Miss Littlebury has nothing to do with this."

"Yes, she did." Sophie rose and walked toward the large window that overlooked the canal. "I wanted to tell you but I was afraid."

"You know how I felt about what Maggie did. And then you did the same thing."

"I know," she cried. "And I knew you couldn't marry me so what was I supposed to do? I didn't want to ruin your life and reputation. If I had told you about the baby you would have ruined Miss Littlebury's reputation by breaking off the engagement. I could not ruin so many lives."

"This isn't about the baby," he rasped. Why wouldn't she understand how much it hurt him that she'd taken his father's money?

"I don't understand," she whispered, turning back to face him. Her gray eyes filled with tears. "What more is there?"

"My father's money. You left pregnant with my child and his money, just like Maggie."

Chapter 26

"No, Nicholas," Sophie said, returning to his bed. At least now she understood his anger. It had nothing to do with her being with child. "I would never take that man's money."

Nicholas eyed her suspiciously. "He told me he left the money on your desk."

She got up her nerve and sat down at the end of the bed. "He did. He left me a fortune to leave the country. And I had the money returned to him that very day. After hearing the stories you told me about that dreadful man how could you think I would accept anything from him?"

"Then what were we just talking about?" he asked, rubbing his temples as if in pain.

Sophie laughed softly. "I believe we were speaking of two different things. When you said, 'He told me,' I thought you meant Somerton had told you about the baby. I'd made him promise not to tell you or anyone else."

"I was talking about the money." A slow smile finally

deepened the dimples in his cheeks. "You went to Somerton for support, didn't you?"

"There was no one else I could go to," she said, looking down at her skirts. "I hated going to him. I didn't want to take money from him and Victoria."

"You should have come to me," he whispered.

She shook her head. "No, you were supposed to marry Miss Littlebury. It wasn't appropriate. It wasn't as if I'd been your mistress and we had a monetary agreement."

"You were my lover," he said softly. "You were my love. I would have done anything for you."

Sophie heard his words and went still. Tears refused to fall but she recognized the most important word he used—were. She *had* been his love. And wasn't now. Why did he come to Venice if not for her?

Sophie had lost everything she'd ever wanted. The only man she had ever loved.

Nicholas.

Had she stayed in London things might have been different. But she had made a mess out of her life and now the life of her unborn child.

"I'm so sorry, Nicholas," she whispered. "I should have told you sooner about the baby. I've made a mess out of everything. Your life. And my own life."

"Sooner? When did you tell me about the baby? I figured it out when you entered the room a few minutes ago."

She shook her head. "I sent you a note about a fortnight ago. It most likely hasn't even arrived in London yet. I knew you had a right to know the truth."

"Why did you wait?" he asked so softly it almost made her cry again.

"I was afraid," she finally admitted to him and herself.

"Of what?"

Everything, her mind screamed. But one thing more than others. "That you would take my child away from me. That I'd be left alone again."

He shook his head slowly. "What happened with Maggie was completely different, Sophie. Maggie planned to abandon my child. I could never let her do that."

"I never would have abandoned our child, Nicholas."

"I know that. Watching you with Emma made me see what a connection you two have. I'm assuming because of your birth. When I saw you with her I realized . . ."

Sophie nodded, encouraging him to continue.

"You are the only woman I have ever been with who asked me about Emma."

"Indeed? She is the most important thing in your life. You must have been with some very foolish women."

"I believe you're right." Slowly he reached down to the end of the bed and brought her close.

"You should be resting," she said and then felt his forehead. "I do believe your fever is gone."

"I wasn't sick. I think I was overcome from the heat and had a slight fever. A few people on the ship were sick with fevers so I believe Mrs. Griffon and Emma overreacted and insisted that Dominic call the physician. Dominic knows better than to let me have laudanum."

"Why is that?"

"It makes me sleep like the dead for hours. I hate the bloody stuff."

She put her head back down on his chest and sighed. He gently caressed her hair.

"I love you, Sophie," he murmured. "I knew I'd fallen in love with you the night you called on me and I found you with Emma in the salon. But I still felt I had to prove your intuition wasn't always right. That is why I insisted on going to the Middletons' party."

Her throat constricted to the point she couldn't reply. That was the night she met Emma. The little girl had touched her heart so deeply that night. But she had already become aware of her feelings for him. "I started to fall in love with you the night you came to my dinner party uninvited. Listening to you talk about Emma . . ."

She closed her eyes unable to go on.

"But you were furious with me for having an affair with Jennette."

She nodded. "I was. And yet, the way you talked about your daughter touched my heart so deeply. I couldn't help but wonder how different my life would have been if my father loved me as much as you do Emma."

His arms slid down over her slightly extended belly. "I want you to come home, Sophie."

She wanted that, too. She missed her family and friends in London. "I want to go home, too."

"As my wife," he whispered in her ear before kissing the outer shell.

The idea of being his marchioness still terrified her. But after weeks of being alone in Venice, she didn't want that any longer. She wanted him. She wanted to depend on him when she was afraid. She needed to feel his arms around her, keeping her safe and loved.

Slowly, she turned in his arms. She stared into his warm brown eyes and was lost in the love she saw there. "What about Miss Littlebury? You were betrothed. Oh,

Nicholas did you break off the engagement and ruin the girl?"

"I have done nothing untoward. Miss Littlebury discovered she loved Mr. Heston over me."

She stared at him for a long moment before speaking again. "She broke it off?"

"Apparently, Mr. Heston did not wish for anyone else to learn that Miss Littlebury might be carrying his child."

Her black brows furrowed. "Is Mr. Heston blond with green eyes—"

"And a slight scar on his chin? Yes."

"He was the one for her," she whispered. "He was the man I saw for her but was confused because I saw you there, too."

"Apparently, Mr. Heston was her match." He bent down and kissed her softly. "Just as you are my perfect match. Now, will you marry me, Sophie?"

"Are you sure?"

"I'm more certain of this than anything I've ever done in my life. I don't care about the gossips. I don't care that my father will give his inheritance away. The only thing that matters is us."

"I love you," she whispered before kissing him.

The feel of his tongue on hers was sweet agony. Heat built slowly through her body as she pressed herself closer to him. She never thought she could love a man as much as she did Nicholas. Slowly, she drew away with a smile.

"If my daughter was not in the next room, you would be on your back," he said with a sensual smile.

"I think we shall have plenty of time for that."

"Are you all right with this, Sophie? I don't want to push you into something you aren't comfortable with."

Sophie released a long sigh. "I know the gossips will be wagging their tongues over our marriage and the baby. But all my friends have created some type of scandal so it must be my turn. I know they will all stand by us."

"Stand by us." He laughed. "Who do you think introduced Miss Littlebury to Mr. Heston? I believe they were doing their best to match us."

She laughed and let her head drop to his shoulder. "That is why Elizabeth brought you upstairs the night of the dinner party. I thought she was just being kind to you for being left out."

"No, and once offered the chance to be with you and our friends, I wasn't about to leave."

"I'm so glad you didn't."

"But you were furious with me," he reminded her.

"Only because you caught me by surprise." Her brows furrowed. "Do you really think they tried to match us?"

"Absolutely. You matched each of them so they assumed you might need some help with your match."

"They were right," Sophie replied with a giggle. "I had no idea what I was doing."

"Neither did I."

"This will cause a huge scandal," she said with a smile as she rubbed her belly, "especially now."

"The scandal has already started."

She frowned and glanced up at him. "What do you mean?"

"You do not have to worry about your father claiming you because your bother has already admitted to the world that you are his sister."

She clapped her hand over her mouth. How could

Somerton have done such a foolish thing? "Why?" she mumbled. "Why would he do that?"

"Because he loves you. And Lady Genna loves you. She wants the world to know you are her half sister, too. He and all your friends want you to return to London." He brought her hands to his lips.

Tears burned down her cheeks. "Nicholas, you told me that if you married me it might put Emma's reputation at risk."

He sighed. "I already told her what might happen."

"Then perhaps you should tell me."

He nodded. "When I was with Maggie, I told my father that I loved her and wanted to marry her. He told me she was nothing but a whore and only wanted me for my money. He arranged for me to walk in on them while they were . . ."

"Oh, my God," she muttered. "What a dreadful man!"

"He wanted me to see that Maggie only cared about money. He paid her to have intercourse with him." He looked away from her. "Then two months later, she came to me saying she was with child."

She shook her head wondering how this could be scandalous to Emma. His daughter already knew she was a bastard. "I don't understand, Nicholas."

"I have no way of knowing if Emma is mine or my father's child. He threatened to tell everyone the story."

"I am dreadfully sorry, Nicholas. But this just reinforces what I have been saying. Marrying me would only cause you and your family harm."

"I told Emma everything, Sophie. I wanted her to understand what might happen if you agree to be my wife and her mother."

"What did she say?" she asked reluctantly. He would not be here unless he had his daughter's blessing.

"She said that even though she'd only met you once, she believes she loves you and that you would make a perfect mother for her. And she didn't care who her father really was because I am her true father."

Sophie wiped a tear off her cheek. "She is a lovely young girl."

He stopped and looked over at her with love. "And one who needs a mother who will love her regardless of her birth."

She glanced up at the crystal chandelier.

"What are you really afraid of, Sophie?" he demanded.

"Losing you," she whispered. "I thought if I left on my terms it would be better. But it wasn't. I was afraid after Lady Cantwell died that the reason I couldn't read you was because you were going to die. I couldn't stay and watch you die. I know that sounds horrible. I'm sorry I disappointed you."

"You could never disappoint me," he said, approaching her slowly. "All your life people have left you alone. Your father, your mother, and even me. I should have insisted on marrying you the moment I discovered who you were. I should have done more."

She nodded. "I don't know how to be a marchioness, much less a duchess. I've never planned a ball. And I certainly don't know the proper seating arrangements for a dinner party. I will be an embarrassment to you. I should hate to see that in your eyes."

"You would never be that, Sophie. You have friends who can help you with anything you need to know. Just as they did for Victoria." He wrapped his arms around her. "None of those things matter to me, sweetheart. You are the only thing that is important. I want you to be my wife, my duchess, and the mother of my children."

Sophie blinked back the tears. Nothing she could say would dissuade him. And she didn't want to say anything else to do so. She wanted to believe him. She wanted to let herself love him completely.

"I love you, Nicholas," she murmured. "I love you so much that I couldn't stand by and watch you marry another woman. And I couldn't ruin your reputation. I didn't know what else to do. I'm sorry I left you without telling you why."

"Shh," he whispered as he lowered his lips to hers. "I love you, Sophie. That is all that matters now."

"You're right."

Sophie looked up at her perfect match and smiled. He was everything she ever wanted in a husband but had been afraid to dream of because of her background. She snuggled in closer as his strong arms wrapped around her tighter. Right where she wanted to stay for the rest of her life.

The door cracked open and Emma peered into the room. "May I come in?"

"Of course you can, sweetheart," Nicholas replied with a laugh. His arms held Sophie tighter as she attempted to pull away.

Emma walked toward the bed with a wide smile. "Does this mean she said yes?"

"Emma, come over and say good morning to your new mother," Nicholas said.

Emma ran the remaining distance and jumped onto the bed with them. She put her arms around Sophie and said, "I'm so happy you will be my mother.

I knew the first time we met that you would love me no matter that I am a bastard."

"Emma, it doesn't matter how you were born. Your father and I love you. Just like we will love your brother or sister when I deliver."

Emma's amber eyes widened. "You're with child?"

"Yes, and if we don't get home soon, there will be another bastard in the family."

Nicholas laughed. "There is a ship leaving in three days and we will all be on it. As soon as we arrive in London, I will get the special license and we'll be married within a week."

Sophie's heart swelled. Everything she'd ever dreamed of was right here in this room with her. It didn't matter if they created a scandal with their marriage. The only thing that mattered was their family.

Epilogue

Oh, the scandal they had created. Sophie stared down at the gold band on her finger and smiled. The *ton* had been horrified to hear about her condition and subsequent marriage to Nicholas.

Since the wedding four months ago, all the invitations to balls had stopped for Nicholas. She felt dreadful that marriage to her had caused him to be rejected by Society, but Nicholas never seemed to mind. They had each other and their friends.

And she had never been so happy in all her life. She didn't care what they said about her.

Slowly, she picked up her week old son and held him close. He smelled like milk and sweetness. This was what was important. And the man next to her.

"Are you ever going to tell us his name?" Avis asked with a smile.

Looking around the salon of her new home, she was surrounded with love. Nicholas sat on the arm of her chair, holding her hand. All of her friends and family were here.

"We decided on Simon."

Everyone agreed that was a marvelous name. Sophie glanced about the room at all her friends and her heart almost burst. She had matched all of them. Some needed more of her help than others, but all were perfect for each other.

Victoria and Anthony fussed over their little girl, Anne. Elizabeth held her son as Kendal looked on. And Jennette laughed as Christian tried to grab for her glass of wine. She snatched it from the toddler who started to cry.

"I believe he is all yours," she said to Blackburn.

"Very well." Blackburn placed little Rachael in her mother's arms before grabbing Christian.

Sophie glanced over at Avis and Selby. Their little girl sat on the floor playing with a rag doll. Avis's radiant face gave her away.

"Avis, isn't it about time you told everyone?" Sophie asked.

Avis smiled and rolled her eyes. "I should have known you would guess my condition. I am about three months along now."

After a round of congratulations, the butler entered the room. "Excuse me, Your Grace, there is someone here to see you."

Kendal rose with a frown. "Why would someone call on me here?"

The butler cleared his throat. "Not you, Your Grace. I was speaking to the Duke of Belford."

All eyes turned to Nicholas. They had known his father would pass soon and thankfully Nicholas had made some peace with his father. He had even brought Emma with him one time so they could finally meet. It was a pity, Sophie thought, staring down at her son, that the old duke never met his son's heir.

Nicholas nodded and rose to walk out of the room. After several minutes of low voices in the hall, he returned. "My father died an hour ago in his sleep."

"I'm sorry, Nicholas," Sophie said and then kissed his cheek.

"I know. I should feel something but honestly, I don't," he admitted. "Interestingly, his solicitor said my father never changed his will."

"What will you do with the money?" Sophie asked. She'd known Nicholas didn't want his father's money after all they had been through.

"I believe my daughter shall be a very wealthy heiress," he said with a smile. "No one will deny her birthright."

Sophie laughed and then sobered. Now, she was the Duchess of Belford. She blew out a long breath.

"Stop worrying, Sophie," Elizabeth said. "You will make a fine duchess."

"And just becoming duchess will stop much of the gossip about your marriage and son," Avis added.

"I suppose you're right."

"Of course, I am," Avis replied. "Besides, once another woman creates a scandal, the gossip about you will stop. I'm certain that will happen any day now. There must be some young lady out there about to do something scandalous."

They all laughed and Sophie relaxed knowing it didn't matter how long it took for the gossip to stop. She had everything she'd ever wanted but was afraid would never happen for her.

Don't miss any of these passionate
romances from Christie Kelley . . .

EVERY NIGHT I'M YOURS

A woman who wants to know what she's been missing . . . A man perfectly suited to train her . . . Christie Kelley weaves a scintillating novel of one rapturous night of ecstasy . . .

A WOMAN YEARNING FOR A TASTE OF THE FORBIDDEN . . .

At twenty-six, aspiring novelist Avis Copley intends to wear spinsterhood as a badge of honor. But when she discovers a volume of erotica that ignites a searing fire within her, Avis realizes just how much she doesn't know about the actual pleasures of the flesh. Determined to learn more, she devises a daring plan . . .

A MAN READY TO TEACH HER MUCH, MUCH MORE . . .

Avis chooses Emory Billingsworth, a fellow novelist— ot to mention a beautiful specimen of manhood—to instruct her in carnal pleasure. But when the brash Earl of Selby, Banning Talbot, a man she has known for years, unearths Avis's true intentions, he claims she's made a dangerously bad choice. Volunteering his services for one wicked night of reckless, abandoned passion, Banning promises he will satisfy *all* of her deepest longings. Yet Banning cannot begin to imagine the effect his willful, voluptuous, and very eager student will have on him—or how far an innocent lesson in desire can go . . .

Praise for *Every Night I'm Yours*

"Sometimes becoming a fallen woman isn't
as easy as it sounds. Oh! My!"
—Kasey Michaels, *New York Times* bestselling author

"Her appealing characters, sexual tension, and
charming story will enchant readers."
—*Romantic Times*

EVERY TIME WE KISS

GUILT KEPT THEM APART . . .

It's been five years since Lady Jennette Selby's fiancé died. Each courting season since has been filled with suitors eager to win her affection. But Jennette's guilt has prompted her to swear off marriage. For her secrets are as dark as she is beautiful, and the accidental death of her fiancé was tainted by a forbidden attraction . . .

PASSION BROUGHT THEM TOGETHER . . .

Matthew Harris, the new Earl of Blackburn, has been scorned by the *ton* for unintentionally killing Lady Jennette's fiancé. Forced to sell his estates and abandon his tenants if he does not marry a wealthy, respectable woman, Matthew turns to Lady Jennette to help him find a suitable wife. But sharing such close quarters only re-ignites an all-consuming desire neither can resist—even as every shadow of the past threatens to tear them apart . . .

"Rollicking, sexy . . . you'll enjoy this one!"
—Kat Martin

"Kelley knows how to bring a great depth of emotion into a romance."
—*Romantic Times*

"With *Every Time We Kiss*, Christie Kelley has penned an original and enjoyable Regency romance between two complicated, passionate characters."
—*Romance Junkies*

SOMETHING SCANDALOUS

HER SHOCKING PAST . . .

Raised as the youngest daughter of the Duke of Kendal, Elizabeth learns a devastating truth on his deathbed: he wasn't her father at all. And because the Duke had no sons, his title and fortune must go to his only male heir: a distant cousin who left England for America long ago. Anticipating the man's imminent occupation of her home, Elizabeth anxiously searches for her mother's diary, and the secret of her paternity . . .

HER UNEXPECTED FUTURE . . .

Arriving in London with his seven siblings, William Atherton intends to sell everything and return to his beloved Virginia farm, and his fiancée, as quickly as possible. But as Elizabeth shows William an England he never knew, and graciously introduces his siblings to London Society, it becomes clear the two are meant for each other. Soon, Elizabeth finds herself determined to seduce the man who can save not only her family name but her heart . . .

"Kelley reinforces her deserved reputation for page-turning, exciting, humorous plots filled with sexual tension and populated by unforgettable characters readers can't help but fall in love with."
—*Romantic Times*

SCANDAL OF THE SEASON

A DARING CHARADE . . .

For ten years, Anthony Westfield, Viscount Somerton, hasn't been able to forget the woman with whom he spent one scandalous night. When their paths cross again, he's shocked to discover Victoria Seaton is an accomplished pickpocket. But Somerton leads a double life of his own. Working on an undercover assignment, he makes Victoria a proposition: pretend to be his mistress or risk ruin.
Yet soon he's tempted to turn their charade into reality—and surrender to an explosive passion . . .

A HOLIDAY TO REMEMBER . . .

Victoria can't believe the man who almost destroyed her life a decade ago is now threatening to unravel her secrets. But posing as his mistress at a holiday country party is a game she can play well.
For just one look into Somerton's eyes still weakens her with lust. And with Christmas fast approaching, every kiss they share under the mistletoe only makes Victoria fall more deeply in love . . .

"A sexy Cinderella story—racy and romantic!"
—Anna Campbell, author of *Captive of Sin*

"Kelley's fresh and vibrant romances are emotional, fast-paced and intriguing. Her originality captivates readers and grabs their attention."
—*Romantic Times*

Keep reading for a taste of *Scandal of the Season*!

London, 1807

Her smile attracted him like a beacon on this damp, cold night, drawing Anthony nearer to her warmth. But his friends yanked him away from the beautiful woman selling oranges. The force propelled him into the cobbled street. A hackney veered to the left just in time, preventing Anthony Westfield, Viscount Somerton from obliteration before ever giving his father the one thing he wanted—a proper heir.

Anthony stood and then stumbled back over the cobbles, landing at the woman's worn brown boots. Perhaps he shouldn't have had that third, or was it fourth?, glass of brandy. Trey and Nicholas pulled him to his feet.

"Are you all right, sir?" she asked in a small voice. She couldn't have been more than eighteen. Her big eyes looked light, possibly blue, in the pale illumination of the moon. It wasn't the first time he'd seen her. Whenever he passed this street, she was there with her basket of oranges and a shy smile for him. Every time he saw her, he had felt this pull of attraction to her.

She had always favored him with a bright smile, but now her face appeared lined with concern. For him.

"Fine," he mumbled. "Just a bit too much brandy tonight."

Her blond eyebrows lowered in what could only be condemnation. She wasn't the only one who would disapprove of his behavior tonight. Unless he completely sobered up by the time he arrived home, he would catch a severe dressing-down by his father. First gambling, then drinking, and he had an idea of what his friends had in mind next, not exactly proper behavior for the son of an earl. At least in his father's opinion.

Anthony continued to stare at the woman. He wanted to know her name, discover if the scent of oranges was purely from the fruit she sold or if it permeated her skin. Yet once again, his friends pulled him away from her, this time gentler.

"Good night, fair lady," he said as they dragged him away from her.

"Good night, sir." The light sound of her musical voice carried to his ears.

"No more drooling over a woman who isn't about to give you what you want," Nicholas said with a slight slur to his voice. "And we're not about to let you swive some poor innocent." He turned his head and smirked at them both. "One of you should have some experience."

Trey and Nicholas led him around the corner to a house on Maddox Street. After a very successful evening of gambling, his two friends had accomplished the not so difficult task of getting Anthony foxed. Perhaps they knew it was the only way to convince him to come with them. He looked up at the house and shook his head. As a man entered the building, the sound of merriment filled the air.

"Where are we?" Anthony asked, knowing their likely location.

"Lady Whitely has the cleanest girls in town," Trey replied.

The women might claim to be clean, but the last thing Anthony needed was a woman to give him a disease, or worse, a bastard. His father would never forgive him for that dishonor.

"I should be getting home."

Nicholas only laughed. "Don't be nervous, Anthony. We all have to have our first time sometime."

Trey joined in the chortling. "I can't believe you still haven't . . ."

But Anthony hadn't. His father had warned him about the unclean prostitutes around Eton and in town. As the heir to the earldom, Anthony had a responsibility to lead a clean life, marry when the time was right and have his own heir. Besides, Father had been through enough with Mother dying in a carriage accident when Anthony was only ten and his sister only two. Attempting to live up to his father's wishes was the least he could do. Or at least try.

"I really need to go," Anthony tried again. But his friends wouldn't release their tight grip on his forearms.

"Not this time," Trey said. "Lady Whitely will find you the perfect girl. After all the money you won tonight, I would say you could afford any woman you want. But go for experience."

Paying for a woman seemed completely wicked and morally wrong. Women like that only went down the wrong path because they had nothing else. They had no one else.

"I just don't think this is a good—"

"This *is* a good idea. *A very good idea*," Nicholas interrupted. "One of Lady Whitely's ladies will teach you exactly what a man needs to know before he takes a wife."

Anthony frowned. He knew the rudiments of the act, how much more was there to it. "I'm not planning on taking a wife for a few years. And I still—"

"Too late, we're already here," Trey said with a laugh.

They pulled Anthony up the steps, opened the black lacquer door and pushed him into the front hallway. He almost tripped and fell onto the black and white checkered marble floor. Luckily, Nicholas caught him.

"Be a man and do this," Nicholas whispered in his ear. "Your future wife will thank you."

Now his friend sounded like his father. Anthony didn't want a wife yet. He was only eighteen. As he walked into the salon and glanced around, he suddenly realized he did want to learn more about the relations between a man and a woman. Several women walked around in gowns designed to show off all their assets. Lady Whitely offered an excellent selection of women—redheads, blondes, several brunettes, too. Small-breasted women, large-breasted women, and a few in between.

Their arrival brought whispers and giggles from some of the younger ladies, and leering glances from the older ones. Trey leaned over and spoke softly to one of the women while Anthony continued to gawk. His breeches felt confining against his unruly erection.

After blinking to clear his vision, he walked over to the servant selling drinks in the corner and ordered a brandy.

"I haven't seen you here before," a husky voice sounded behind him.

Anthony turned and stared at a woman. Her dress was cut almost to her belly, giving him a splendid view of the valley of her abundant breasts. He picked up his brandy and gulped it down.

"First time?" she asked with a knowing smile. "Well, I do hope you will pick me. My name is Giselle, and I love teaching a man what he needs to know."

"Thank you, Giselle. I'll remember that." Anthony quickly ordered another drink and moved away from the strumpet. There had to be a better way to learn about sex than to lie with a woman who'd been with numerous men.

"Come on, Somerton," Nicholas called to him from the doorway. "We have everything arranged."

Anthony cringed with the thought. But he couldn't back down now, could he? What would his friends think of him? He knew exactly what they would think, that he was a coward. A boy too scared to become a man.

He had to do this at least this once. Then he would do something to help these poor women. He'd find a way of reforming them so they didn't have to work on their backs for a few pounds.

Following Nicholas up the stairs, Anthony took in his surroundings for the first time. When his friends implied they were taking him to a brothel, he'd expected a poor house with naked women prancing about. He had never thought that the staircase would be marble, the railing a burled walnut, that a fine crystal chandelier would hang from the two story ceiling, and there would be beautiful—and completely erotic—paintings on the burgundy walls.

Nicholas dragged him down the long corridor. Murmurs and moans filled the cavernous walkway, hearing the excited voices and the groans of pleasure, sent blood racing to Anthony's stiff cock. Perhaps his body wanted this night more than his mind.

"Yes, Dickie. Oh, yes!"

Anthony could only imagine what Dickie was doing to that woman to elicit such a passionate response. Maybe learning a few things before marriage would help him and his future wife—whoever she might be.

"Come along, Anthony. You'll get yours soon enough." Nicholas stopped before the last room on the left and then opened the door.

Anthony followed him inside a small room painted a dark red and filled with all things feminine. A large four-poster bed with a white, Belgian lace coverlet took up most of the room. The table nearest the bed contained a variety of lotions and oils, which permeated the room with exotic scents of the Far East.

"Lady Whitely is assisting another patron but will be here in a few minutes to help you decide on your best choice of women," Nicholas said by the doorway. "Have fun and stop listening to your father's voice in your head. I'm quite certain even he has been known to visit a brothel."

Anthony almost laughed as Nicholas shut the door behind him. His father would never call on a strumpet. He was the one who always told Anthony to control his base urges and save himself for marriage. After all, Mother had been dead for eight years and his father had never remarried or kept a mistress, at least as far as Anthony knew.

He sat down on the edge of the bed and thought about what kind of woman he wanted for his first time. Closing his eyes, visions of his little orange blossom, as he liked to think of her, came to his head. Perhaps if he asked for a young woman with blond hair, blue eyes, and a smile like an angel, Lady Whitely could provide him with his fantasy. Opening his eyes, reality sank in. Even if she did find him a woman who looked like his orange blossom, she wouldn't smell fresh and clean with a hint of spicy orange to her.

A quick knock scraped across the door. This was it. Time to face Lady Whitely, choose a lady and become a man. He rose unsteadily and cleared his throat. "Come in."

The door opened and a woman in her mid-thirties walked into the room. Her dark blond hair had been lavishly swept back, except the few curls artfully left to frame her oval face. As she stared at him, her perfect smile seemed frozen in place.

And he stared back, wondering why she looked slightly familiar to him. Neither moved. They only gazed at each other as if trying to decide how they knew each other. A small clock on the nightstand ticked away the minutes.

"Anthony?" she finally whispered.

That voice! He knew that voice. He'd heard it so many times when he'd been scared at night or when she sang him to sleep.

No!

It could not be her. She was dead. It must be the brandy addling his mind tonight.

"Anthony, is that really you?" Slowly she approached him. She reached her hand out to cup his cheek.

He reeled away from her as if her light touch had

burned his skin. Turning back to face her, he said in the most damning tone he'd ever used, "Mother?"

She blinked away tears and pressed her lips tightly together. She acknowledged his condemnation by taking a step away from him.

"It is you, isn't it?" he asked.

"Of course."

He grabbed the post of the bed and hung on to it like a lifeline. Hundreds of questions bounced in his head but only one came out. "Why?"

"Why what?" She moved to the end of the bed, sat on the edge and looked up at him. "Why did I leave you and your sister? Why did I leave your father? Why did I come here and set up such a house?"

There was only one more important question. "Does Father know?"

A delicate shudder visibly rolled through her body. "Yes," she whispered.

Anthony clung tighter to the bedpost. It was one thing for one parent to lie and deceive her child, but quite another when both parents were in collusion to betray their children. But his father would never do such an underhanded thing. He must have only recently discovered the truth of her deception.

"How long has he known?"

"Almost from the day I left."

Anger broke through his drunken haze. "He's known you were alive and did nothing to save you from this life?"

His mother laughed softly. "I know you may find this difficult to believe, but my life has been far better away from your father than with him."

"How can you say that?" He finally released the bedpost, stood in front of her and hoped the world would stop spinning soon. "You make your living by . . . by . . ."

"By what, Anthony?"

"Lying with any man who would pay you."

She reached out to clasp his hand but he pulled it away. Her dainty shoulders drooped. "I only lie with the men I wish to be with."

"And that is supposed to make me feel better?"

She shrugged. "I suppose not." Slowly she stood before him, barely reaching his shoulders. He had not realized just how small she was . . . petite, with dark blue eyes that flashed in anger at him. "You have no idea what I've been through with your father. When the time is right, I shall be happy to tell you."

"Then tell me now," he growled.

"No. This is not the time. You're intoxicated, and you've had far too much of a shock. You need to go home and think about what you discovered tonight. And when you are ready, I shall explain everything to you."

"I'm supposed to just leave here and accept the fact that my dead mother is actually alive and well, living as a prostitute?"

Her face whitened. "I am not a—"

"Oh? You run this house. You already said that you lay with whomever you please. You are a strumpet."

Before she could try to deny her profession again, he strode to the door and down the stairs. He passed a footman on his way up the steps with a bottle of fine brandy on a silver salver. Anthony grabbed the bottle and ran from the house of horrors.

He raced down Maddox Street until he nearly collapsed at the side entrance to St. George's Church.

After sitting down on the brick step, he opened the bottle of brandy and gulped a large amount down.

How?

How had his mother kept herself from them all these years? Hadn't she cared about her children, if not her husband? She was alive. The past eight years had been a complete farce, which made him nothing but a fool for believing everything Father had ever told him.

A prostitute.

A common strumpet.

His mother was no better than a lightskirt. And even worse, his father had known all along. His father had lied to him . . . and his sister. Genna didn't even remember her mother. His sister had been only two when the whore had left. If it ever came out that their mother was a prostitute, his sister would be ruined.

Genna must never discover the truth.

A cold November rain dampened his breeches. He pulled his legs in under the archway of the stoop and took another long draught of the stolen brandy to chase the chill away. He couldn't go home drunk and furious. First, he had to determine exactly what he would say to his lying father when he confronted him.

He'd never felt so lost and alone in all his life. Not even when his mother had died. He shook his head. But she wasn't dead. She left them to go sell herself to anyone who would have her. He dropped his head to his knees.

How could she have left her children?

The rain turned to a steady downpour as he sat there drinking the brandy. His mind turned hazy as he watched the carriages drive by his spot. Suddenly something, or rather someone, stumbled over his feet in an effort to be out of the rain.

"Bloody hell," he mumbled. "You almost spilled my brandy."

Blinking, he tried to get his eyes to focus on the small body huddled in the opposite corner. The fresh scent of oranges washed over him. It was her. His orange blossom. The woman he'd truly wanted tonight.

"It doesn't appear to be much left in the bottle," she replied, holding it up.

"Help yourself."

"I intend to." She held the bottle up to her lips and drank some down.

Fascinated, Anthony stared at her slender neck as she tilted her head back and drank from the bottle. "Who are you?"

"No one." She handed the bottle back to him. "Thank you."

"Why are you here?"

She laughed softly. "The same reason as you, to get out of the rain." She shivered and her teeth chattered.

He pushed the bottle back toward her. "Drink."

She accepted it back greedily. "Th—thank you again. It's helpin' me get warmer." She sipped some more before asking, "What's yer name?"

He hesitated just a moment. "Tony." Although, only Genna called him that. "Why were you out selling oranges so late tonight?"

"I tried to sell all the oranges. Today wasn't a good day."

"No. Definitely not a good day," he agreed, staring at the basket half full of fruit.

"Did you lose too much gamblin' tonight?"

"How did you know I'd been gaming?" he asked.

She shrugged. "Isn't that what most young bucks do? It's either gamblin' or whorin'."

Maybe she wasn't the innocent she pretended to be, he thought. "Actually, I won a substantial sum tonight," he said, pride lacing his voice. "What do you do with your money?"

"You mean the measly amount I get by sellin' oranges?" She pressed her lips together. "I just try to get ahead."

He shifted and his shoulder collided with hers. A jingle of coins rang from the pocket in his coat. "What if I offered to buy the rest of your lot?"

"I don't take charity. I work for the extra money I need."

"Hmm, a woman with scruples." He inched closer to her warmth. "I like that."

"I should get home," she whispered.

"Don't."

She turned her head toward his. Mere inches separated them. The urge to move slightly until his lips touched hers was almost too much to resist. Would she taste sweet like the oranges she sold?

"Have another sip." He shifted away and handed her the bottle.

"I have to go." She scrambled to her feet and picked up her basket. "I—"

He stood up quickly. "I want to kiss you," he whispered, trapping her between the stone and his body.

"No," she whispered.

"I need a woman who isn't like her," he muttered.

Anthony brought his lips to hers. Pulling her to him, he slid his tongue across her lips until she opened for him. Drowning in a desire as he'd never felt before, he knew he had to have her. He needed her comfort, her softness. As he brought his hand to cup her breast, he heard her gasp.

"No," she cried softly. "Not like this."

Only Anthony was far too gone to understand her meaning.